TAKE

THIS

Regret

A.L. JACKSON

A.L. Jackson
www.aljacksonauthor.com
Cover Design by RBA Designs
Photo by Perrywinkle Photography.
Formatting by Mesquite Business Services

The characters and events in this book are fictitious. Names, characters,
places, and plots are a product of the author's imagination. Any
similarity to real persons, living or dead, is coincidental and not
intended by the author.

Print ISBN: 978-1-946420-17-6
eBook ISBN: 978-1-983404-04-7

TAKE

THIS

Regret

More From A.L. Jackson

prologue

CHRISTIAN

Elizabeth shook her head, appearing to struggle against her tears. She backed two steps away from me.

"I'm having this baby, Christian."

"Think about it, Elizabeth." My words came out harsher than I intended, and I suddenly realized just how angry I felt that she'd already made this decision without me.

As if the way I felt didn't count.

"How do you expect to go through law school and have a baby? Have you even thought about it? Have you even thought about how we would handle this? Make it through law school?"

She had to see just how impossible the situation was.

Elizabeth looked confused. As if she couldn't grasp what I was trying to say.

Her response was stuttered. "I . . . I don't know. We . . . we'll figure it out."

"No, Elizbeth, we won't."

When she started to cry, I squeezed my eyes shut and turned away from her.

I was doing my best to rein in my temper. To think about how she was feeling right then. Even though what I really wanted to do was yell at her and tell her just how stupid and irrational she was being.

This would ruin our lives—*my* life.

Somewhat unconsciously, I found myself thinking thoughts I'd worked so hard to overcome.

Thoughts of myself. What I needed. What I wanted.

Suddenly, I didn't see the hurting girl in front of me, the girl I loved, the girl I'd had every intention of spending the rest of my life with.

The only thing I could see was somebody standing in my way.

Quickly, I turned and leveled my eyes at her, face hard. Manipulative words fell from my mouth before I could really think through their meaning. "I'm not joking, Elizabeth. It's me or the baby.

You can't have us both."

She swallowed deeply and nodded her head.

Visibly, she accepted the ultimatum that I had laid out before her.

After all, I knew there was really never a decision to make.

"Goodbye, Christian."

For the second time that day, I had to work to make sense of what Elizabeth had said.

With her head dropped, she pushed passed me as if she didn't have another choice and reached out to turn the doorknob.

"Elizabeth."

When I called her name, she paused.

From behind, I observed the rise and fall of her uneven breaths. "Come back when you've changed your mind."

Part of me was shocked at the heartless words I spat at her back. But what other choice did I have?

She shook her head as she swung the door open and slammed it shut behind her.

I stared at the closed door, torn between running after her and waiting for her to return.

If I went after her now, that meant one of us was going to have to concede, and it wasn't going to be me.

Two hours later, I was sitting at my desk,

studying for my politics midterm.

All the while, I couldn't help but listen intently for the sound of footsteps outside my door.

I knew she would come back.

She had to.

I trained my attention on the heavy textbook in front of me, trying to ignore the growing anxiety I felt each time I picked up my cell phone to check if I'd missed any messages.

None came.

Anxiety had started to crawl through my veins.

An unease I couldn't shake.

Everything wrong.

It was well after midnight when I finally gave up and crawled into bed.

She just needed some time to realize I was right.

I had to be right. I wouldn't allow myself to think otherwise.

So, every time that wave of guilt came, I pushed it aside.

I envisioned her awake, just as I was, tossing uncomfortably in her small bed that rested in the far corner of her studio apartment and slowly coming to terms with what she needed to do.

Tomorrow she would have to her senses. I was sure of it.

But when I dragged my unrested body from my bed the next morning, my phone was still void of messages.

I had been cruel—I knew it. I could only hope I hadn't pushed her too far.

I just needed her to somehow understand the only thing I was just trying to do was protect our future.

I ate a bowl of cold cereal and then forced myself into the steam of my shower, desperate to find anything to chase away the fatigue.

My head was in a damned cloud, both from lack of sleep and from the scenarios running through my mind.

Honestly, they were terrifying.

Ones including a life without Elizabeth.

What if she never came back?

Could I really give her up?

As I rubbed the soapy washcloth over my body, I tried to picture an existence without her.

A life void of the perfect pitch of her voice, the way it rang out when she laughed. A life in which I didn't get to touch the softness of her skin or have the right to pull her body against mine.

A life without a child crying out from the next room as I tried unsuccessfully to study for the bar.

Groaning on the last, I shook my head to clear the fog and forced it all away.

It wouldn't come to that.

I was certain when I saw her in class today, she would take her normal seat beside me in the lecture hall, lean in, and whisper in my ear that I was right.

But when her seat remained vacant, my unease grew, gnawing at my stomach.

It was torture sitting there, and the moment the professor dismissed class, I raced from the room and to the café where Elizabeth and I studied every Monday, Wednesday, and Friday.

Frantically, I scanned the room, finding several mildly familiar faces but not the one I wanted to see.

By the time I reached her apartment complex, I was panting, both from exertion from the mile I had run and the constriction fear had placed on my heart.

I pounded on the door, giving her no time to answer before I yelled, "Elizabeth!"

There was no sound from the other side, no rustling of curtains or faint shuffling of feet.

Shit.

Fumbling with my keys, I found my spare and pushed it into the lock.

The door opened to the quietness, the small studio comfortably cluttered as always.

The only thing that seemed amiss was the blankets from her normally neat bed were strewn on the floor.

I crossed the space to the only separate room. The door to the bathroom rested ajar, that room as empty as the first.

Pressing my back against the wall, I took a deep breath.

I wasn't prepared for this. Never thought it would go this far.

Reluctantly, I forced myself out of the apartment, shutting and locking the door behind me before I left.

As I clamored down the vacancy of the stairwell, hating the voice inside my head that kept screaming this was for the best.

ELIZABETH

Reeling from the betrayal, I ran down the three flights of stairs and away from the man I had thought would always stand by my side.

I felt as if I'd been mortally wounded by his words. Christian knew that wasn't an option for me. How could he even have suggested it?

In the harshness of his words, I'd searched the depths of his blue eyes for the man I thought I knew but must have never really known.

The man I thought I knew would never have been so cruel.

When I'd told him goodbye, my voice had shaken with heartbreak, but my choice was unwavering.

There was nothing more important than the

child growing inside me.

When he'd called out to me just before I'd left, I'd prayed he had changed his mind.

Above all, I loved him and didn't want to live without him, but second to that, I was scared.

I didn't want to raise a child by myself.

But I'd realized I would have to do just that when I heard no softness in his voice, but more words to inflict pain.

Tears fell endlessly as I walked the half mile from Christian's apartment to my own. My stomach was in knots and protesting each step I took.

I refused to look behind me as I pressed forward, my feet heavy with heartbreak, the weight causing me to stumble.

Halfway home, the pain in my stomach intensified, and I vomited into some shrubs planted under the window of a storefront.

Stomach muscles aching. Retching and heaving.

It only caused me to cry harder and the cramps to worsen, which resulted in three more episodes before I made it to the single flight of stairs leading to my apartment door.

I clung to the railing, holding myself up as I vomited once more over the side.

Fear and heartbreak tumbled through me.

Uncontainable.

So much.

By then I was weeping, unable to control the shaking that had taken over my body. I made it to the landing of my apartment and, with trembling hands, let myself into the only place I came close to being able to afford.

I felt cold, my body convulsing as I pulled my clothes from my body and stepped into a shower that should have been hot enough to scald.

Even then, I found no warmth, and I curled in upon myself on the tiled shower floor, hoping for comfort.

I only quivered and shook more.

I felt as if I was frozen from the inside out. Nothing could thaw the chill that had settled deep in my bones.

Climbing from the shower, I wrapped myself in a towel and sank to my bathroom floor, heaving again into the toilet.

I was scared.

I'd never felt so terrible before.

I ached.

Ached in the worst way. From my skin to the depths of my soul.

The worst part was I couldn't discern the source of the pain—whether it was from something truly wrong with myself or from the trauma of having my life shattered around me.

Most of all, I worried about my baby.

I didn't know many things about pregnancy, but

nothing about this felt normal. So, when my stomach recoiled again and nothing came up, I was sure I needed help.

I pulled myself up to stand, steadied myself with a hand against the wall when I swayed with dizziness, and prayed I could make it to my phone.

I wanted Christian so badly, and my first instinct was to dial his number, but I forced myself to dial seven different digits than the ones I so desperately wanted.

Christian was no longer mine. No longer one I could rely on. There was only one other person in this city that I trusted.

His voice was scratchy and hoarse with sleep when he answered, "Hello?"

More time had passed than I had realized. It was nearing midnight.

MATTHEW

"Matthew," she rasped, my name barely audible. The desperation in her voice pulled me from my haze, and I shot straight up in bed.

"Elizabeth?" I became frantic. "What's wrong? Are you okay?"

At least three seconds passed before she wheezed out a shaky, "No."

I pulled on pants and stuffed my arms into the

first button up I could find while keeping the phone pressed between my ear and shoulder.

I tried unsuccessfully to sound calm. "Elizabeth, sweetheart, tell me what's wrong."

I was already out the door and starting my car before she could answer with a weak, "I'm sick. Really sick. I need your help."

I was at her apartment and up the short flight of stairs before five minutes had passed, where I found my friend curled up on her bed, shivering under a pile of blankets.

"Elizabeth?" I rushed to her side, pulling the covers back to expose just her head.

Her blonde hair was darkened to a near brown from the profuse sweat pouring down her forehead.

I reached out to push her hair away so I could see her face, shocked by the paleness of her skin and the swollen redness of her eyes.

I wanted to ask her a million questions, but she was passing in and out of consciousness.

No doubt, she needed more help than I could give.

I pushed her covers to the floor except for the one I wrapped her in before bringing her into my arms.

Her small body was heavier than I anticipated, completely limp, and I struggled to maneuver her down the stairway and to my car.

I contemplated dialing 911, but the hospital was so close, I was certain I would get her to the emergency room before an ambulance could arrive.

Within minutes, I was pulling around the circular drive under the bright red glow of the sign that read, "Emergency Room."

Carrying her, I entered through the automatic doors.

"Help!" I yelled, fear crawling through my veins.

With a flurry of activity, several orderlies pulled Elizabeth from my arms and placed her on a gurney.

The nurse led me to a small curtained area where Elizabeth lay unconscious. I felt overwhelmed as the nurse hammered me with questions I could not answer.

"Date of birth?"

"Is she on any medications?"

"Does she have any allergies?"

"When did the symptoms start?"

I shook my head that had begun to pound from the immense amount of stress. "I'm sorry, I don't know."

I slumped into a hard, plastic chair that was pushed against the far corner of the wall and watched as they began to poke and prod at my friend. I felt helpless, having no idea what I was supposed to do.

Should I call someone?

Christian?

Elizabeth's mother?

No. She had called me, and that in itself gave me a clue.

She needed me, and so I chose to be there for her, even if it meant waiting around and having no idea what was going on.

As I sat silently in the corner and watched the nurses and a doctor work over Elizabeth, I thought about how she'd come into my life.

I'd met her the year before at the small diner where we worked on the weekends. The two of us were a lot alike.

We both lived in a city neither of us could afford, attending a college we'd dreamed of most of our young lives, living off scholarships, grants, and mounting student loans we'd undoubtedly be paying for well into our thirties.

The tips we made on a Saturday shift barely covered food and necessities for the week.

But neither of us looked at those things as negatives. Instead, we embraced the opportunity and ran with it.

Because of it? We'd become fast friends.

I obviously knew how beautiful Elizabeth was. I wasn't blind, but I'd never viewed her that way and didn't harbor unrequited feelings. I loved her as a friend.

Truly.

That didn't mean I liked her boyfriend.

To me, Christian was nothing but a spoiled rich kid who was slumming it while he played at college.

Couldn't shake the instinct that Christian would break Elizabeth's heart.

When they inserted a long, thick needle into Elizabeth's forearm, I cringed, unable to look away as they attached an IV bag to the line.

For what seemed an eternity, I watched over her sleeping form while the color slowly came back to her face as the bag dripped its contents into her veins.

Really, little more than an hour had passed when the very young doctor who had examined her returned, chart in hand.

He extended my free hand across the small space. "Dr. Lopez."

I nodded and returned his handshake. "Matthew Stevens."

The doctor began to speak quickly. "All of her test results are back . . . severely dehydrated . . . anemic . . . pregnancy . . . too much stress . . ."

I tried to focus on all the details the doctor was giving, but really, I heard nothing more than *pregnancy*.

God.

Elizabeth was pregnant.

This was bad.

I felt lightheaded with the implications this would have for her, and they only got worse when everything clicked into place.

The late-night phone call made to me when it should have been made to someone else. The swollen, red eyes. The doctor's words about too much stress triggering shock.

I curled my fists, sickened that someone could treat my friend so poorly—anyone that poorly.

I had to beat down my first instinct, which was to go straight to Christian Davison's apartment and tear him apart.

Instead, I moved to sit on the edge of Elizabeth's bed and ran my hand through her matted hair.

Silently, I promised her I would always take care of her.

CHRISTIAN
SEVEN MONTHS LATER

I stood in front of the full-length mirror, studying myself in the long, black gown.

I saw nothing more than a pathetic, excuse for a man staring back at me.

I should have felt *proud*.

Receiving my bachelors at Columbia with top

honors should be a *proud* day.

My mother and father had just left my apartment to await me in the car, but not before my father, for the first time in my life, had proclaimed how *proud* I made him.

But I didn't feel *proud*.

The only thing I could process at that moment was shame.

I'd seen her about three weeks before in line at the store, though she hadn't seen me.

I had run in to grab a few things I needed—deodorant, shampoo, and toothpaste.

I'd been making my way back up to the registers, scanning for the shortest line, when I'd seen the wavy locks of blonde hair I knew so well.

The same honeyed color that I would never forget.

Immediately, I'd felt a pull, the need to go to her, but I had frozen when she turned to the side, exposing the large protuberance in her abdomen.

Like a coward, I'd hidden myself, watching her with an almost morbid curiosity from behind a row of shelves.

Nausea had hit me when I'd stood there like a total asshole, watching the woman I still loved, but had betrayed, strain to reach the items in the cart—diapers, blankets, and small things I didn't recognize.

She was preparing for her baby to be born.

Fear had pulled at my chest when I noticed that she now seemed thinner than I remembered, her skin sallow and chalky.

Gaunt.

As if the growing mass in her front had stolen all the life from the rest of her body.

Even then, she was still the most beautiful woman I had ever seen.

But, like I'd already known myself to be, I remained the coward and did nothing but watch as she paid for her things and walked out the door.

It was the only time I'd seen her since we'd fought at my apartment. She'd never returned to class, had never called or sought me out, had never changed her mind.

I had made no real effort of my own since that first day when I'd gone to her place, only calling once and hanging up when a man had answered her phone.

I could have tried harder—should have tried harder—but I'd taken the easy way out.

I'd convinced myself that I didn't ache for her. Pretended that my sleepless nights had nothing to do with my worry for her.

I'd tortured myself with the idea that she'd moved on, that she didn't need me, that she'd found her own way.

But even if she had? It still didn't absolve my responsibility for the child.

So as my guilt had grown, I'd done more and more to drown it out, spending long days in class and even longer nights with my head spinning from the amount of alcohol I'd consumed, then waking to unfamiliar women in unfamiliar beds.

No, today was not a *proud* day.

I grabbed my cap and trudged downstairs to join my parents in their waiting car.

The celebratory dinner was everything I had expected it to be.

The sound of forks and knives clattering against china filtering into the stuffy atmosphere of the Club, the waiters in tuxedos and far too willing to accommodate.

My father, Richard, lectured me that my schooling had only begun and that the next three years of law school were going to be the toughest of my life.

My mother had sat withdrawn as she listened to her husband giving me the instruction I obviously didn't need.

It was nothing I hadn't heard before.

Every conversation I'd ever had with my father had been the same. I'd hoped that for just one night, he would be satisfied.

That for once we could just relax and talk, but it was always about the next step, the next achievement.

Thankfully, my mother interrupted the berating. "So, your father and I will be going to Rome this summer. I can't wait to visit. It's one of my favorite cities in the world."

My father stared her down. "Claire, I'd appreciate it if you didn't interrupt me when I'm talking to my son."

For the first time ever, I noticed my mother roll her eyes at him.

She seemed irritated by him this evening, her smile tight and no real light coming from her blue eyes.

Normally, she remained mostly quiet during family conversations, sipping from a glass of wine and nodding agreement with whatever my father was cramming down my throat.

Tonight though, she seemed anxious, as if she would explode if my dad uttered one more word about my future.

Sitting there, I couldn't help but watch my mom from across the table, couldn't help but wonder about her happiness.

In all the years I had thought her perfectly content in her huge house and endless social gatherings, was she was ever really happy at all?

Because when I really looked hard, I saw no true joy in her face.

It was a shame that I couldn't even remember

the last real conversation I'd had with my mother. So, I smiled at the stories she told.

Getting lost in it.

In the little flickers of the memories of the way I'd once imagined her to be.

Caring and warm.

Her face took on a new vibrancy as she talked of me as a child, and I relaxed into my chair, no longer guarded.

That was until she asked a question I hadn't been prepared to answer. "Whatever happened with that girl you were dating? What was her name? Elizabeth?"

Shame slammed me, and instantly, my tension returned. But I found myself answering her because I needed to tell somebody. Needed to tell her.

Looking at my plate, I muttered, "We broke up."

"Oh?" she asked like a gentle prod, as if she expected further explanation.

One she would be shocked to hear.

Even more shocking was I wanted to tell her.

I lifted my eyes to hers and spoke, even though it was choppy and reeked of confession. "She's having a baby."

Almost simultaneously, my parents dropped their utensils to the table, staring as they waited for me to clarify.

Unease rippled through my being. But I refused to deny what I'd done.

"She told me in the fall. I told her I didn't want it, so she left. I haven't talked to her since."

I struggled to maintain eye contact with my mother as I said these things but had to look away when I saw the disappointment race across her face.

Her voice shook but was still the strongest I'd ever heard. "Christian," she demanded, "How could you treat someone—"

Richard's cut her off with a vicious rant. One about irresponsibility and money and tarnished reputations.

I was the only one who noticed when my mother stood and ran from the table.

The ride home from the restaurant was tense and silent.

When my mother had left the table, for the twenty minutes she was away, I was scolded by my father.

As if I needed the reminder of disgusting I was.

Of course, none of those things were what my father was worried about.

When my mother had returned, it was obvious she'd been crying, her makeup smudged and her eyes red. After she had taken her seat, no one had spoken a word nor had they since.

The driver pulled up in front of my building, and my father made no move, though my mother exited the car and hugged me in a way she hadn't for many, many years.

When she pulled away, her face was wet with tears again, and her hand trembled as she raised it to touch my cheek. "Make this right."

I hadn't expected this encouragement, and it left me confused as I watched her take her place in the backseat of the Town Car. I stared at their taillights as they drove away and disappeared into the night.

Hanging my head, I made my way to my apartment, knowing what my mom had said was true.

I could make this right, but I also knew I would probably never be brave enough to do it.

Once upstairs, I changed and then walked to the building next to my own to join the people I could barely consider friends, as they celebrated their graduation the best way they knew how.

The music was loud and the apartment cramped, the room almost alive with the movement of people who considered this one of the best days of their lives.

I had never felt worse.

With a platinum blonde on my lap, I sat on the couch, draining my sixth beer and wondering what the hell I was doing there.

The crowd had become rowdy and obnoxious, and I wanted nothing more than to escape from it all. I just had no idea where I wanted to go.

My eyes slammed shut, and I pretended I didn't hear the loud, drunken voice of Nathan, a guy I could hardly stand when I was sober, let alone after he'd consumed half his weight in alcohol.

But I couldn't ignore it when he slapped me on the back, his booming voice slurred with laughter as he shouted, "I hear congratulations are in order for the proud papa."

The blood drained from my face, leaving me lightheaded, barely able to force out, "What?"

Nathan cackled as if nothing had ever been more entertaining to him. "What? Didn't you hear, man? You became a daddy this morning."

Shock hammered me.

No.

Stumbling to standing, I pushed the giggling girl from my lap.

Never had I hated myself more than right then.

How could I have done this? I loved Elizabeth, didn't I? But people didn't do things like this to people they loved.

I barely made it outside the door before I vomited in the hallway—not from the alcohol I'd consumed.

My sickness was nothing but disgust.

I stumbled home and into bed, praying I would

fall asleep and awake with all of my regret gone.

But sleep never came, and I lay staring at the ceiling, unable to will my mind to stop long enough to find rest.

At four o'clock, I gave up and got out of bed, still wearing wrinkled jeans and a T-shirt that smelled like beer.

Pulling on a discarded Columbia sweatshirt from the floor, I just . . . walked.

Subconsciously, I knew where I was going, though I wouldn't allow myself to admit it.

I entered through the emergency room entrance because all the other doors had been locked for the night.

When I arrived on the maternity floor, a nurse stopped me. Visiting hours didn't start for another three hours, but when I explained I was a father and showed my ID, the woman allowed me through.

I gathered all my courage and pushed forward, preparing to admit to Elizabeth I was wrong. I would tell her that I was sorry, that I would take it all back if I could.

I was prepared to beg for the forgiveness I knew I didn't deserve.

I'd do anything to *make this right.*

But what I wasn't prepared for was finding Matthew with his back to me, sitting in a chair and gently caressing Elizabeth's face while she slept.

I froze when I realized I was too late. I'd done too much harm.

Silently, I stood and watched the man who was only supposed to be her friend sit in the spot where I should have been.

Watched Matthew adoring the girl who deserved every touch and embrace, the girl who deserved a man better than me.

She deserved a man like Matthew who had stepped up and filled the place I should never have stepped away from.

Pain welled up in my chest, fierce and permanent, and I felt something inside me crack as I said a silent goodbye to the girl I would always love.

Stepping back, I let the door drift closed between us.

Then I fled. As I escaped down the hall, I trained my attention on the floor, not allowing myself to look through the large glass window where I knew my child slept

If I saw?

I would never be able to walk away.

Elizabeth was taken care of and happy, and for once, I would do something that I wasn't doing for myself.

After all, it was for the best.

One

I stood in the middle of my office, taking in a deep breath as I looked out over San Diego Bay. What seemed like thousands of sailboats dotted the water, bobbing in the cool breeze.

It was beautiful, calming, and so different from the urban chaos I'd lived in during my first two years as an attorney serving as a public defender in New York City.

I'd never been to San Diego, though I'd heard so much about it.

Elizabeth was from San Diego, growing up here.

I'd spent countless hours listening to stories about her, her mother, and her two sisters. Every Saturday they'd take a trip to the beach no matter what the weather.

They hadn't had a lot of money, and it was an outing that cost nothing more than the small amount of gas it took to get them there.

Elizabeth would never say they had been poor, though clearly, they had been. She would assert so many were far worse off than her family. She would say her mother worked hard and she and her sisters never went without the things they needed.

I wondered about her often, even though it had been almost five years since I'd walked out of that hospital and carried on as if there weren't a completely different life I should be living.

I'd always expected to hear something, a subpoena for a child support hearing or a request that would be altogether unbearable—one asking that I relinquish my rights as father because somebody else wanted that title—but none had ever come.

I'd ensured I would always be easy to find, it taking nothing more than entering my name in a search engine, and Elizabeth could pick up the phone and call me directly. But she never did.

I was haunted by the choices I'd made, plagued by insomnia and anxiety with most nights spent wide-awake in regret. I knew nothing of my own child.

Countless times, I'd typed Elizabeth Ayers into my computer, but found I could never complete the search.

As much as I wanted to know, I didn't deserve to know. What gave me the right to delve into their personal lives, to know where they lived, if Elizabeth had married, my child's name?

No, I had no right, but that never kept my thoughts far from them.

I sighed heavily when the buzz from my phone pulled me from my thoughts. I dug into my pocket, sliding my finger across the faceplate to accept the call.

"This is Christian."

"Christian, how are things coming over there?" Without greeting, which was no surprise, my father got straight down to business.

"It's going just fine. The building is perfect, and the staff is more than I could have expected. Everything is going along better than planned."

My answers were always short and abrupt, keeping my conversations with him as short as I could.

Besides, how much could I really know.

I'd only arrived the day before and had gone directly to my condo, exhausted from the three-day drive.

I'd flown out the month before to meet with my realtor and purchased a new high-rise condo just a five-minute drive from the new office.

I'd always known one day I would work for my father's firm, I just had no idea my father would open a new branch on the other side of the country and ask me to head it. I wasn't sure how I felt about it.

As the years had progressed, my respect for my father had dissipated and my resentment had grown, leaving us little more than business partners. The night of my graduation dinner had been the last of the family I had known.

It was the night my mom had packed a suitcase and my father had watched the best thing in his life walk out the door and had done nothing about it. I hated him for it because it only made me see myself.

When I had glimpsed the discontent in my mother's eyes that night, I'd had no idea how deep it went.

It had been a new beginning for us as mother and son.

She had come to me, weeks later, distraught and in tears, confessing the many ways she believed she had failed me.

She told me that as a young woman, she had been blinded by wealth and society, and she had pushed me to do great things because she loved me and wanted the best for me but had somehow forgotten to teach me to be compassionate and kind along the way.

She had told me she'd grown to care nothing about those things, and when I'd sat there and told her about Elizabeth, it had broken her heart. She felt that she'd somehow failed me.

I had disagreed. My failure was all my own.

But most of all, her concern had been for Elizabeth—the girl who had given birth to a grandchild Mom would probably never be given the chance to know.

Mom had admitted then that she'd been so fond of Elizabeth, though regretfully she'd never shown it. She had said that Elizabeth had reminded her too much of the girl she used to be before she'd lost herself to a world that had been so appealing when she'd married into it.

Through it we'd become desperately close, relying on one another because we were the only person the other had.

She was my closest confidant—*my only confidant*—and it was clear to her that I held myself in reproach.

Honestly, she did too.

She wanted to know how I slept at night, knowing I had a child out there somewhere.

I told her I didn't.

She begged me to go find them, still

encouraging me to *make it right.*

She disagreed with my rationale. She told me that keeping distance would do nothing but cause more pain, not nullify it. Obviously, the distance *caused* me pain. Yes, she knew I was to blame, but she insisted that didn't mean I didn't deserve a second chance.

Since my mother had left him, my father had never once mentioned her name. Every conversation had centered on my schooling and, once I'd graduated, the firm.

Just like today.

I finished the short call with my father and hung up after promising him I would call him the next day with an update.

Looking around my office, I wondered where to begin.

A large mahogany desk sat facing the door, the dark wood gleaming with the sunlight shining in through the floor-to-ceiling windows.

On its surface sat only a phone and nameplate, belying the clutter of the rest of the room. Stacks of boxes leaned against one wall and volumes of books sat in front of the matching mahogany bookcases waiting to be organized.

Years of case studies needed to be filed, most of them sent from the main office in Virginia.

I exhaled a weighty breath through my nose, not yet ready for the task ahead of me.

Instead, I found myself on the waterfront. I wore a light coat, my hands stuffed in the pockets as I walked along the paved trail and kept to the side in order to stay out of the way of the runners and cyclists. The air was cool, but not unpleasant for an afternoon in early May.

Everything felt so foreign.

I'd been so accustomed to the rush of New York, the surge of the mass, the sense that there was not a moment to spare, but here it felt as if the second hand had been slowed.

I faced into the wind and closed my eyes. My hair whipped around my face while the sun warmed it, my senses filled with the sound of gulls and the scent of the sea.

In the calm and peace, I'd never felt so alone.

Pulling out my phone, I dialed. I needed to hear the familiar voice. She answered on the second ring.

"Christian, sweetheart."

"Hey, Mom."

"How was your trip?"

I laughed humorlessly. "Tiring."

"I can only imagine. You should have taken me up on my offer to help you drive out."

"I wish I would have."

"So, what do you think of San Diego?"

"I don't know. I haven't really had the chance to explore yet, but . . . it feels lonely."

I supposed I was always lonely but being somewhere so unfamiliar made it worse.

Claire sighed. "Christian, please . . ." I could hear the urgency in her tone. "Make the best of it, meet new people. It's a new place, a new start."

I ran my hand through my hair as I stared out over the water, wishing I could.

It wasn't like I hadn't tried.

I'd dated, once even somewhat seriously, but I'd only ended up hurting her. She'd wanted more than I could give, my heart and my hand, and I refused to marry someone I would never really love.

With that realization, the idea of dating had become pointless, and I refused to wake up in another stranger's bed, so for more than a year, I had slept alone in my own.

My pause told Mom more than any response I could give, and with the growing unease, I changed the subject.

"When are you coming out?"

"Soon. Possibly in the next couple of months."

"Good. I miss you already."

I could sense my mother's sad smile and it made me miss her even more. "I miss you too, sweetheart. Call me soon, okay."

"Okay, Mom. Love you."

"I love you too."

"Bye."

The small amount of comfort my mother's call brought passed quickly, leaving me once again questioning my decision to move to California.

I lingered by the water for more than an hour after my call with my mother, immersed in the solitary tranquility of the bay, before finally forcing myself back to my empty condo.

I figured since I had taken the day off, I should put it to good use and get some things done before I dove into the massive workload I had waiting for me at the office tomorrow.

Thankfully, I'd purchased a furnished unit, and the moving trucks had already delivered my belongings from my apartment back in New York, but my kitchen cupboards and refrigerator still stood barren.

Though I was a bachelor, it was rare to find an empty pizza box left haphazardly on my coffee table or frozen meals in my freezer. It wasn't that I especially liked to cook, but that I liked to eat well.

I had to admit there was some draw to San Diego as I climbed into the driver's seat of my gray Audi A8. I'd had little use for it while living in New York, and I was sure, as I pulled into the huge parking lot in front of the grocery store and parked in one of the many free spaces, it was something I could easily grow accustomed to.

Slowly I moved up and down each aisle, filling my basket with every item I would need to stock my kitchen. The store was not busy, as I presumed was probably common for a Thursday afternoon.

I took my time and was in no rush to get back to the emptiness of my condo. I took even more time as I walked through the produce section.

As I filled a bag with peaches—I felt it—eyes upon me. The fine hairs prickled on the back of my neck, not in dread, but with a sense of awareness.

Turning to glance over my shoulder, seeking the source, I froze when I was met with the origin.

She stared back at me, looking at me as curiously as I looked at her, neither of us able to turn away.

She was absolutely beautiful.

Her black hair was pulled into a ponytail. Her round face was framed by short bangs and a few strands of hair that had fallen out of the band. Her cheeks were pink against her pale skin, unblemished by the sun, but it was her eyes that stopped my heart in my chest.

Their intense blue watched me in fascination, wide and intrigued and so *familiar*.

I tried to shake myself out of it and turn away. I was sure my mind was only playing tricks on me, punishing me a little more by teasing me with the idea that I knew this girl.

But then her mouth turned up in an earth-shattering grin, exposing a row of perfect square teeth, so small there were little gaps between them.

The staggering amount of emotion that hit me nearly brought me to my knees as I fell in love with the tiny person in front of me.

The small child continued to grin up at me from where she clung to the leg of a woman standing with her back to me.

I couldn't help but smile back at her. It caused her to giggle and made me smile even wider.

The woman glanced down at the girl to see why she was laughing. She followed the child's attention to where I still stood, grinning wildly at her.

I reluctantly looked up at the woman, loathe to pull myself away from the moment the child and I had just shared, but immediately felt self-conscious when met with the disturbed expression on the woman's face.

She was young, maybe in her early twenties, and barely over five feet tall. Her blonde hair was cut short above her shoulders, and her body was curvy and clad in a hooded college sweatshirt, shorts, and flip-flops.

The casual attire was something I was quickly coming to appreciate as very common in this new town.

I studied the woman's brown eyes, searching for recognition, any proof to confirm the connection my heart had already made. I found nothing.

I was certain I had never seen this woman before.

But the child . . .

With longing, I turned my gaze back to her, sure she was no stranger.

The woman set a protective hand on the girl's shoulder and gave me a fierce stare, a warning that caused me to look back at her face.

I wanted to say something to explain, but before I could form the words, the woman took the girl's hand and hurried her away, her voice stern and gentle at the same time as she reminded the child to never talk to strangers.

Grimacing, I attempted to turn back to my fruit selection, but my intrigue was too great.

Trying to keep a distance, I trailed behind them, pretending to shop for items that were already in my cart as I followed them down the same aisles I'd already visited. I knew I shouldn't, but I couldn't stop myself.

I was every bit as drawn to that little girl as she seemed to be to me.

In vain, I attempted to appear nonchalant as I essentially stalked the pair, counting to one hundred in my head before I followed them into the next aisle.

This time when they came into view, the child was no longer walking but sat in the seat in the front of the cart.

God, I felt like a creep. I was making the woman nervous, and I could only imagine what she was thinking. Fear was palpable as it radiated from her.

She began to move faster, literally throwing things in her cart.

But what could I do? Call out to her that I wasn't some sort of sick pervert? Assert that I thought I knew the child—that I believed she was mine?

Even to me those words sounded crazy.

They would only frighten the woman more.

When they finally got to the checkout, I slipped into a line a couple of rows down from them, absentmindedly loading my groceries on the conveyor belt while I tried to watch them out of the corner of my eye.

She was precious—perfect. I was completely mesmerized.

From where she sat two rows down, I could really see her, her plump arms with the small gold bracelet that she wore on one of her wrists, the pink bow that held her hair in the messy ponytail, and the little cleft in her chin that matched my own.

"Sir?"

I jumped when I realized someone had been speaking to me. My attention was so wrapped up in the girl I'd forgotten where I was. I looked at the cashier, having no idea what she'd said.

She rolled her eyes at me before repeating, "One-hundred and seventy-two dollars and ninety-three cents."

Digging out my wallet, I made my purchase while still keeping an eye on the girl. Every time we made eye contact, she smiled again.

When they headed for the exit, I felt as if I were in a race for time, as if this were the one chance I'd been given, and I felt desperate to catch one last glimpse of the girl before she was gone from my life forever.

Pushing my cart through the sliding doors, I scanned the lot and easily spotted the blonde woman awkwardly throwing her plastic grocery bags in the trunk of a small white sedan while she kept one hand across the belly of the child who still sat in the cart.

I felt bad for causing the woman so much distress, but I was powerless to the call the child had on me.

I pushed my cart up the opposite side of the same row they were parked in, stopping a mere fifty feet from them. I stood, staring unabashedly, allowing myself a sad smile in return to the brilliant one the girl gave me.

The woman gasped when she looked up, finding me so close to them. She slammed the trunk shut and yanked the girl up in her arms, catching the child's shoe on the basket.

It tumbled to the ground.

She looked at the shoe and then at me, her eyes wide with fear, before she turned and abandoned it on the ground.

From over the woman's shoulder, the child watched me, her little hand reaching out to me.

I lifted my own in a silent goodbye, filled with an immense sense of loss as I watched the small car jerk into reverse out of the spot, then speed quickly away.

Sighing, I shook my head, suddenly wondering if I had completely lost my mind. I had just terrified a complete stranger because I was inexplicably drawn to a little girl, and I couldn't help but feel more than a little ashamed for it.

But it had been a nagging pull, one that could not be ignored.

Walking slowly to where the woman's cart had been abandoned in the middle of the parking lot, I picked up the tiny pink canvas shoe and held it to my chest, wondering what in the hell I was supposed to do now.

I tossed uneasily in my bed, unable to force my eyes closed. I was more than accustomed to sleepless nights, but this was something entirely different. My whole body protested against lying idle, singing out that I had something to do.

I realized now that subconsciously this was what I'd hoped for and probably was the real reason I'd ever agreed to come to San Diego, believing there was a possibility Elizabeth had moved here, hoping one day, though I knew the chances were slim, I would run into her or one of her family.

Just the idea had been enough to make me accept my father's offer.

Sitting up on the side of my bed, I clutched my head in my hands as my elbows dug into my thighs. I took deep breaths and tried to calm my racing heart. I looked at the tiny pink shoe resting on my nightstand and knew there was nothing else I could do.

It was no different now than it had been all those years ago.

If I saw the child, I would never be able to walk away.

Just this afternoon I'd questioned my choice to come here, but now I knew there had been a reason.

I stood and crossed the room to the desk where my laptop sat. The screen lit as I raised the lid, illuminating the otherwise darkened room.

I took a deep breath as I entered the name—something I'd done so many times before—but this time it was different.

This time I completed the search.

two

ELIZABETH

I sat in silence, my mind a thousand miles away from the congested road I traveled. My thoughts were on a man I both wished I could forget and clung desperately to all at the same time.

Why I did this to myself, I didn't know. But every morning, it was the same.

After dropping my daughter off at preschool, *he* would invade, the recessed memories clawing their way out and into the forefront of my mind.

Why couldn't I just forget him? My daughter was almost five years old, but it felt like it had just been yesterday since Christian had callously forced us out of his life.

And it still hurt.

I was so angry because of the bitterness that remained, my incapacity to move on—my inability to love again.

Shaking my head, I fought against the tears.

A car horn blared, making me jump and pulling me from my daze. The lane sat open in front of me where the cars ahead had already passed through the intersection. I grimaced as I glanced in my rear-view mirror at the frustrated driver behind me, threw my hand up in an apology I wasn't entirely sure he would see, and accelerated to free the buildup of traffic.

I wasn't always like this. Really, the pain only surfaced in the quiet times. I had so much love in my life. I would never discount it or take it for granted. When I was alone, though, it was impossible to ignore the heaviness in my chest—the ache.

I hated him for leaving it there.

No one should ever have that much control on someone else's heart, and I would never allow myself to become so vulnerable again.

Arriving at the bank five minutes before nine, I drove around to the back and parked in the same spot I did every day.

My aspirations of becoming an attorney had long since been forgotten. Finishing my bachelor's degree had been nearly impossible, it taking me more than two years of night school to finish my last year. Three grueling years of law school were not something I could entertain.

I wasn't willing to sacrifice the time with my baby girl.

Lizzie was my world.

My pregnancy had been incredibly difficult. The blow Christian had inflicted had affected me both emotionally and physically.

That first night had been one of the most terrifying of my life.

Every coherent thought I could form as I came in and out of consciousness focused on the possibility that I might lose my baby. It was a possibility I was sure I would not survive.

My heart had been left in tatters—mangled.

The love I had for the child was the last string holding me together. I could feel my body trying to reject the pregnancy while my heart and mind warred to keep it.

I'd remained hospitalized for three days before my body finally conceded to the growing child within me, but at that time, I had no idea of the fight ahead of me.

I'd been ill the entire time, my body never fully giving in to the normal phases of pregnancy.

While my doctor told me morning sickness tended to last through the first twelve weeks, I'd vomited every morning until the day Lizzie came. I'd had to withdraw from classes and put my academic career on hold while I sat at home and nursed myself through those nine miserable months.

But I couldn't complain. I had accepted it was a small price to pay to keep my child.

I'd been in love with my baby since the moment I'd learned I was pregnant, but that love couldn't prepare me for what I felt the first time I held Lizzie in my arms.

There were no words to describe the love and the devotion that flooded me as my baby girl was placed against my stomach, her shrill cries rattling through the delivery room.

As I had reached out and ran my fingers through the shock of black hair on my daughter's head, Lizzie had immediately calmed.

With that caress, I'd found the purpose for my life.

Releasing a heavy breath, I leaned my forehead on the steering wheel, trying to clear my mind of the conflicting emotions swirling through me.

The contrast of love I had for my daughter and disdain for Christian made my head spin, knowing without Christian there would be no Lizzie.

I couldn't even begin to regret a relationship that had brought my child into the world. I could only regret the way it had ended.

I ran my hand through the front of my hair and pushed my long, blond bangs from my face before reluctantly stepping from my car. I stood on the pavement and straightened my white blouse and black slacks, bolstering myself for another day of insignificance.

It wasn't that I particularly disliked my job. I was thankful for it. It was just hard to spend the long days of unfulfilling monotony away from my daughter.

Clicking the button on my key, my red four-door Honda Civic chirped, assuring it was secure for the day.

After being hired at the bank a little more than a year before, I'd bought the car and my house, both used and a little worn, but mine nonetheless.

It was something I had worked so hard for, a house in a safe neighborhood with a backyard for my daughter to play in, and it was an accomplishment of which I couldn't help but feel proud.

I walked through the doors, immediately greeted by Selina, one of the other tellers. "Morning, Elizabeth," she said, ever cheerful.

"Good morning." I smiled back at the young woman who was barely more than a girl, her dark brown hair pulled back in a stylish ponytail and her makeup done to perfection around her dark chocolate eyes.

Selina had an aura about her, an unmistakable zest that drew me in. I supposed it was a subconscious connection to the girl I used to be.

I took my spot two windows from her and plastered an over-friendly smile on my face.

I spent the day fielding the constant influx of customers, focusing only on the simple tasks in front of me and the ticking clock, counting the hours until I was back with my Lizzie.

As soon as the clock hit five, I was on my feet and heading out the door, anxious to make it home before Lizzie and my cousin Natalie.

Flipping open my phone, I read a text from her.

Natalie: Going to the grocery story. Will be home by five-thirty.

I freed a long sigh of appreciation as I buckled myself into the seat of my car.

Natalie was a lifesaver.

I honestly didn't know what I would do without her and Matthew.

Next to Lizzie, they were the two most important people in my life.

Matthew had been the one person I could rely on while I was ill with my pregnancy. From the moment I woke up in the hospital to the moment I gave birth, he had been there.

I almost felt embarrassed to remember that we'd

once been lovers, though it was a relationship that was never meant to be.

It wasn't that either of us found the other unattractive. It was just that Matthew had felt no spark in our touch, and my heart still belonged to the one who had destroyed it.

When we'd moved to San Diego when Lizzie was five months old to be close to my mom and the rest of my family, I'd known the precarious relationship Matthew and I shared couldn't last.

I'd just had no idea it would end so soon.

It was here he met Natalie.

When they'd eloped to Las Vegas seven months later, my family, especially my mother, had been so angry with them and couldn't understand why I *wasn't*.

What they *didn't* understand was how much Matthew had already sacrificed for me, for Lizzie, and there was no chance I'd stand in the way of his happiness.

At the time, Natalie had just turned eighteen, but it didn't take long for me to see the real connection they had.

Natalie may have been young and naïve, but it didn't minimize the love she felt for Matthew.

And Matthew—he adored her.

The four of us had become a sort of pseudo-family, but a family nonetheless.

The couple lived less than five minutes from

Lizzie and me, partaking in the daily care of the little girl as if she were their own. I knew Matthew and Natalie loved the role they served in our lives, though I couldn't help but feel indebted to them.

Who wouldn't?

It was selflessness in its purest form.

Just before five thirty, I pulled into the garage of my small two-story house, the white paint fresh and lawn trimmed from the countless hours of effort Matthew had put into its care.

The moment we'd pulled up in front with the realtor, I'd known that this cozy house would become our home. I'd immediately fallen in love with the flowering myrtle trees flanking each side and the two citrus trees out back.

I gathered my things, and just as I stepped from the car, Natalie pulled up in her small white sedan and parked on the street.

My face lit up in a smile. It was here I found my joy.

It was a joy that erased every painful memory of the day.

Here I couldn't remember the ache in my heart or the sadness that washed over me in the quiet of my car. Here I was happy.

I smiled and waved as I walked down the driveway.

Before I could reach them, the back-passenger door flew open and Lizzie shot out, throwing her arms up in the air. The child's face glowed happiness as she ran barefoot up the drive, her blue eyes flashing excitement.

"Mommy!"

I scooped her up. "Hi, baby girl."

I clung to her, kissing the soft apple of her cheek, finding relief in the weight of my daughter in my arms.

Being away from her for so long during the day was nearly unbearable.

Lizzie snuggled in closer, her tiny fingers gripping the back of my neck through my hair. Drawing her nearer, I breathed her in.

I was certain no one had ever loved a child as much as I loved mine.

I pulled back to see my daughter's perfect face, my voice soft as I spoke. "How was your day, sweetheart?"

"Oh, Momma, I had so much fun." Lizzie leaned away, pulling her arms from my neck so she could express her story with her hands. "It was *B* day at school today, and then we sang a bee song 'cause it starts with the letter *B* and . . ."

I grinned at my daughter, my face bursting with the force of my smile. The sound of her voice made my heart soar, my chest filled with affection as Lizzie relayed a play-by-play of her day.

I was in awe of how smart my daughter was, how intuitive, how perceptive she was of the things around her.

"Then we colored pictures, and I made one for you and Auntie Natalie and Uncle Maffew," Lizzie prattled on with excitement and distinct preschooler pride.

"That sounds like so much fun. I can't wait to see the pictures you colored," I cooed at my child. "So, were you a good girl for Auntie Natalie after she picked you up today?"

As if I really needed to ask—I couldn't remember a time when my daughter had misbehaved.

"Mommy"—Lizzie's voice turned very grown up, and I had to bite my lip to keep from laughing— "I'm always a good girl."

"Yes, you are, aren't you?" I sang as I nuzzled my nose into Lizzie's neck, causing her to squeal with laughter.

"Stop, Mommy! No tickles!"

Laughing, I leaned over to place my daughter on the ground, but not before Lizzie looked up to me, her face in near wonder. "And I saw a nice man today, Momma."

Confused, I looked to Natalie for clarification, wondering what on earth my daughter was talking about.

Natalie grimaced with Lizzie's words, but mouthed *later*, obviously wishing not to discuss it in front of her.

It left me feeling uneasy, but I shrugged it off, assuming it couldn't have been anything major since I hadn't received a call from Natalie.

Natalie and I unloaded the groceries from the car with Lizzie in tow.

I followed them into the living room of my modest house, a feeling of satisfaction coming over me.

I still was unable to believe I finally had my own place.

The comfortable brown suede couch sat in the middle of the room, facing the television, the beige carpet in between littered with toys and pillows.

This was by far my favorite room.

It was a rare day Lizzie and I weren't on the floor, playing toys or sitting on the couch reading a book.

Lizzie skipped along in front of us on the pathway between the back of the couch and the stairs on the way to the kitchen, humming the song she'd learned earlier in the day.

As we piled grocery bags atop the faux-granite countertops, I couldn't help but notice the way my cousin's hands trembled, her jaw held rigid. It was completely out of character for someone so laid-back.

Digging blindly into a bag, I started putting away groceries while I observed Natalie, finally becoming too impatient to wait for her to offer an explanation.

"What's going on with you today?" I demanded, my tone low and concerned.

Natalie glanced over at Lizzie, who sat at the kitchen table coloring, before she looked back at me.

"There was just this guy who freaked me out at the grocery store." She tried to play it off with a shrug, but the grimace on her face revealed her alarm; her voice was little more than a whisper as she attempted to hide our conversation from Lizzie.

With my brow creased and head tilted to the side, I tried to read on her face. "What do you mean?"

"He just . . ."

Natalie squeezed her eyes shut and shook her head as if it were painful for her to recall the event.

"He just kept staring at Lizzie." She opened her eyes to meet mine. "The most disturbing part of it was Lizzie seemed to be just as interested in him as he was with her. It was just . . . so . . . *weird.*"

Natalie hesitated before she settled on the word as if she were unable to find another way to describe the interaction.

My daughter's words from earlier came to me, the ones about seeing a nice man.

I was going to need to have another talk with her later about the dangers of talking to strangers.

Right then, though, I was after details, unsure if this was really something I needed to be concerned about.

While Natalie's intentions were always good, she had the tendency to exaggerate.

"What did he do that made you so uncomfortable?"

"Well . . ." Natalie breathed heavily through her nose, turned back to the groceries, and resumed the task as she spoke, "I was picking out apples, and when I turned around, they were just staring at each other."

Okay, so that did sound *weird*.

Chewing on my lip, I tried to keep the panic welling up in me at bay, focusing on listening to Natalie while I set two boxes of Lizzie's favorite cereal into the cupboard.

"Then it was like every aisle I went down, he was there, and I was sure he already had things from those aisles in his cart. It *really* felt like he was following us. The scary thing was, Lizzie kept asking me to slow down so she could talk to him. When I asked her if she knew him, she said she thought so, but when I asked from where, she said she didn't know."

Goosebumps prickled my skin and chills ran down my spine.

I looked over my shoulder, just needing to confirm that my daughter was there.

Lizzie was still coloring and quietly humming to herself—safe.

I said a silent prayer of thanks, before turning back to the bags in front of me.

"What a creep," I muttered under my breath.

It was a comment Natalie must have heard because she continued, "Oh, it gets worse. I was loading the groceries into the trunk of the car, and when I turned around, he was *right* there, just standing there and staring at her. I don't think I've ever been so scared in my life. I grabbed Lizzie, threw her in the car, and took off."

She cringed, adding regretfully, "I lost one of Lizzie's favorite shoes, but I wasn't about to take the time to stop and get it."

A breath of relief left my lips. "Don't worry about the shoe. We'll replace it," I said, just grateful my cousin had been so cautious with Lizzie.

Honestly, the whole thing had probably been harmless, but when it came to my daughter, safe was always better than sorry.

I would much rather Natalie overreact than be complacent. It was one of the reasons I trusted her with Lizzie's care.

I went back to putting away groceries, glancing between what I was doing and Natalie. I could see she was still shaken and questioning herself.

"You did the right thing, Natalie. We'll just keep

an eye out, and if we notice anything else strange, we'll report it, okay?"

Hoping to calm her down, I reached out and hugged her.

Natalie nodded against my shoulder as her tension visibly dissipated. "Okay."

When she pulled away, I squeezed her hand in a show of support before I turned and grabbed a couple of boxes from a bag. "So, can you describe him?"

A little more collected, Natalie leaned her back against the counter. "Well, yeah, I don't think I could forget him. He definitely wasn't someone who would typically make me nervous. I mean, he was wearing a business suit . . . a nice business suit . . . like you could tell he had money."

I frowned, rearranging the image I'd had in my head, because a man in a business suit definitely wasn't what I'd pictured.

"He was tall and pretty thin, but I don't know, muscular at the same time?" Natalie used her hands to demonstrate about how big she thought the man had been. "He was probably about your age, and really, really good looking."

The more Natalie described him, the more I began to think she had exaggerated the whole thing.

Her depiction sounded more like most women's vision of their dream guy than some creepy stalker.

"He had black hair . . . and his eyes . . . he had the most striking eyes . . . they were an intense blue."

I gasped, dropping the boxes I was holding as I clapped my hands over my mouth to absorb the cry that broke loose.

Oh God, please no.

Natalie jumped back, looking shocked by my sudden change in demeanor, her eyes following mine that locked on Lizzie.

The little girl looked up and smiled widely when she noticed the two of us staring at her, her sparkling blue eyes filled with mirth, totally unaware of anything amiss.

"Oh my God," Natalie murmured quietly when it all snapped into place.

I tossed uncomfortably in bed, unable to escape the fear that had followed me into a night of restless sleep.

I dreamt of him again and again, sometimes finding myself wrapped in the tenderness of his arms and other times met with the harshness of the last words he had spoken to me.

I didn't know which was worse.

When I couldn't bear to see his blue eyes in my dreams any longer, I rose and crept down the hall to Lizzie's room.

Her door sat partially open, just enough for the dim hall light to stream in, basking her room in a soft glow.

I leaned against the doorjamb, gazing at my daughter and wondering how any creature could be so beautiful.

She faced me, one cheek pressed into the pillow as she slept on her side, her hair strewn out behind her. She clung to her favorite blanket, the plain pink one with satin trim. It was pulled against her chest, her tiny hand fisted in the material.

Never had I felt so helpless. I would do anything to protect my daughter, but really, I didn't know if there was anything to protect her from.

Even if the man *had* been Christian, what made me think that he would try to take Lizzie from me now? He'd made it clear he wanted nothing to do with the child, and I was sure a chance meeting was not going to change that.

Still, I couldn't help but feel threatened by the thought of him being here, in my city.

Standing silently in my daughter's doorway, I promised myself that no matter what happened, I would never allow him to destroy my family, whether he came today or in ten years.

Never would I allow Christian the chance to hurt Lizzie the way he'd hurt me.

By the time I made it to work the next morning, the rational side of me had discredited the possibility that the man at the store had been Christian.

Even though somehow, in my heart, I knew it was.

I told myself he wasn't the only black-haired, blue-eyed man in the world, and that Christian was probably over two thousand miles away, by now a big-shot lawyer in his father's firm.

I forged through work, thankful it was Friday and that I had the entire weekend with Lizzie. I'd planned a trip to the beach, something that had become somewhat of a tradition for us.

I'd loved it when I was a child.

Some of my best memories came from the endless days I'd spent playing in the sand with my sisters, and I wanted to provide my daughter those same experiences.

The house was empty when I got home. Matthew had the day off, so he and Natalie had taken Lizzie to the zoo and said they wouldn't be home until around six.

It gave me a chance to pick up around the house, tossing the toys from the floor into the toy box against the wall and straightening the kitchen, chores that always seemed to get neglected during the week.

Just as I turned the dial to start the dishwasher,

the doorbell rang five times in a row.

Grinning, I headed to the front door, knowing there was only one person who could be so impatient. I swung it open.

"Lizzie!" I sang, leaning down to my daughter's level so I could hug her, peppering her face with noisy kisses.

"Hi, Momma. Look what Uncle Maffew got me." Lizzie proudly held up a small stuffed giraffe.

"Oh, how cute. That was so nice of him."

Matthew ambled up the sidewalk, and I smiled widely at him as I rose, giving my unvoiced appreciation.

He never failed to make my daughter feel special.

"Hey, Liz." Matthew leaned in to peck me on the cheek as he walked through the door, followed by Natalie who stopped for a hug.

"Hey, guys. Thanks for taking Lizzie. It looks like she had a blast."

I glanced between the couple and Lizzie who was on her knees on the floor digging out the toys I had just put away, muttering about her matching stuffed elephant.

Matthew took the baseball cap off his head and ruffled his hand through his short brown hair. "No problem. We had a great time, didn't we, Lizzie?"

"Yep!" she agreed from her spot on the floor.

"You guys feel like staying for dinner? I'm

making lasagna."

Matthew glanced at Natalie and then shook his head apologetically. "Sorry, Liz, but we planned a date night."

I tried unsuccessfully to hide the disappointment that flushed my face. "Oh, okay."

Matthew imparted a sad smile. It was one I knew well, one that told me it was okay to move on and that I didn't have to be alone.

While I appreciated the sentiment, it was something I would give no consideration.

The only relationship after Matthew I'd attempted had ended in near disaster, and I'd accepted that I would never love again.

That knowledge rendered dating senseless.

I'd only be wasting precious time that could be spent with my daughter.

Pretending not to notice the silent conversation Matthew attempted to have with me, I called to Lizzie to come and tell them goodbye.

We followed Matthew and Natalie out to their car, Lizzie giving hugs and kisses for the weekend away.

I hugged them both, whispering, "Thank you so much for everything you do for us."

"We should be thanking you," Natalie told me. "We love her so much. Just like we love you."

Standing at the edge of the road in the driveway, Lizzie and I waved and watched them drive away.

I glanced down at Lizzie who was hugging my leg and grinning up at me.

She was just so precious.

Lovingly, I ran my hand through my daughter's hair, my toothy smile matching hers. "Are you hungry, princess?"

Lizzie nodded against my hand when I moved it to cup her cheek, her smile evident where it was pressed against my palm.

Breathing deeply, I savored the emotion that traveled between us, only to go rigid when I heard a voice I could never forget calling out my name.

"Elizabeth?"

three

Seven point three miles.

I stared unblinking at the screen as I turned the number over in my head.

Elizabeth Ayers lived seven point three miles away.

My finger shook as I traced the line on the map, the fantasy of my child living near becoming a firm reality. My chest filled with the same emotions of adoration I'd felt earlier when I'd first seen the child.

I allowed my mind to wander with possibilities, possibilities of knowing her, of loving her—of being her father.

I wanted desperately to fill that position.

And I knew she wanted me too.

At the same time, I was terrified of seeing Elizabeth again.

The thought of her in another man's arms was almost unbearable, made worse by knowing I had forced her there. But greater than all of that would be standing in front of her with the shame I bore.

I knew I deserved nothing of them, deserved to play no part in their lives, but whether I deserved it or not, I could not turn away.

The child's face was burned in my mind.

Work passed much too slowly. I spent the day trying to focus on the things I had to finish, but my mind continually strayed to a little girl with black hair and blue eyes.

The moment my last meeting of the day adjourned, I was on my feet and heading out the door, dodging the inevitable interference of employees with need for direction.

On any other day, I wouldn't have minded, but today was different.

I quickly excused myself from each conversation with little more than a word and hurried to the elevators to the parking garage below.

Entering the address I had memorized the night

before into my GPS, I set out to find my daughter.

Each beat of my heart pounded harder the closer I got.

By the time I turned onto the narrow street lined with small houses, I could hardly breathe.

The ability left me altogether when I came upon the address.

Standing in the driveway was *my daughter* in Matthew's arms, the same child I had fallen in love with the day before.

She was hugging him fiercely.

I was overcome with jealousy and loss as I watched the scene in front of me.

I beat back those emotions, reminding myself that this was my fault.

Quickly, though, my jealousy morphed into confusion as I watched Matthew set the child down and pull Elizabeth into a hug before placing an unassuming kiss against her cheek.

That confusion only grew when Matthew turned to the same woman from yesterday, took her hand, and led her to his car.

Quickly, I pulled to the curb across the street, making sure the two cars parked on the road obstructed the view of my car.

I sat perplexed as I witnessed Matthew lean across the console of his car and kiss the girl after she sat down in the passenger seat.

The kiss was not obscene, but clearly one shared

between lovers. Then the two drove away and left me struggling to make sense of what I had just seen.

My heart sank as shock shifted to realization. I shook my head, biting the inside of my mouth and drawing blood.

"No." I squeezed my eyes shut, willing myself to just breathe before I passed out.

Matthew was not with Elizabeth. I slammed my fist down against my leg, my head filled with accusations as I silently cursed myself for being so incredibly stupid.

He was supposed to be *with* her, *loving* her, *caring* for her.

I literally felt sick with the hatred that coursed through me, that judgment directed only at myself.

Opening my eyes, I looked back toward the driveway. A lump formed in my throat when I gazed at Elizabeth.

She was so beautiful—too beautiful.

My body burned for the one woman I had ever loved.

Why had I ever been so stupid, so selfish? As if anything could have been more important than she was.

Elizabeth stroked her hand through our daughter's hair, the love apparent in the gentle expression her face as she touched the child's cheek.

TAKE THIS *Regret*

I could wait no longer.

I stepped from my car and called to her from across the street.

four

"Elizabeth."

A chill ran down my spine as his voice penetrated my ears, seeping through my body.

The sound came like warmth rushing through my veins, leaving a shock of cold as it passed.

My head snapped up, meeting his face, his blue eyes intense, emotion pouring from them as he looked from Lizzie to me.

It was all I could do to keep from falling to the ground as I felt the world I had built come crashing down around me.

Lizzie's words were barely distinguishable as she tugged on my arm, attempting to get my attention. "Momma, it's the nice man."

All I could think about was that Christian had returned, here to squash the last piece of my heart.

With one hand, I clutched my stomach that twisted in knots, the other pressed over my mouth to cover the cry rattling around in my throat.

I found myself unable to look away as I stared at Christian through hot, angry tears.

Surely, he could see it on my face and in my eyes, the love for him I still held there like some foolish girl awaiting the return of her long-lost lover.

It enraged me that he still had that kind of control over me.

But this was not about my broken heart. This was about the little girl pulling on my arm, trying once again to get my attention.

I had to protect her. "Lizzie, go inside."

When I spoke, Christian turned his attention from me and gazed down at Lizzie with adoration.

Why was he looking at her like that? Like she meant *everything*.

With eyes alight, Lizzie stared up at him, grinning as if any second she would run across the street and into his arms.

I could not let this happen.

"Lizzie . . . go inside, now."

"But, Momma—"

"Now!" I cringed, hating the way I sounded, especially because it was directed at my daughter.

The look on Lizzie's face tore me apart, the confusion at being yelled at when she had done nothing wrong.

Tears fell down her chubby cheeks, and she hesitated a moment longer, looking one more time at Christian, before running into the house.

Undoubtedly, I had broken a part of my daughter's heart by sending her inside, but what I was protecting her from was so much greater than that.

Her innocent mind could not begin to fathom the hurt this man would ultimately bring her.

Slowly, I turned back to Christian, struggling to appear strong, to be forceful, and to make him understand he was not welcome here.

My knees were shaking almost as much as my bottom lip and I was certain he knew I was anything but.

Every emotion I'd ever experienced boiled just under the surface—the love, the hate, the fear, the loss, and most of all, the betrayal—the turmoil within causing my body to tremble with rage.

He looked at me, his expression remorseful, earnest.

Hopeful even.

It made me furious.

Standing in front of me was the man who had left me to raise a child on my own, certainly never giving us a second thought.

Now he stood just feet from me, expectant, as if Lizzie and I owed him something?

Unbelievable.

"How dare you." The words were not what I expected to flood from my mouth, but they were fitting.

How dare he show up here at my house after what he'd done.

Quickly, I wiped my tears, trying to erase them from my face. He didn't even deserve them. He deserved nothing.

"Elizabeth." His eyes filled with emotion that I had once believed to be genuine, a softness that spoke of love and loyalty, but I knew now it was nothing more than a tool of manipulation. I refused to fall victim to it again.

"How dare you come here." I stood up taller in an attempt to stand my ground.

What I said did nothing to sway Christian from whatever purpose had brought him here, and he took another step into the street.

I began to panic, my mind grasping for anything that would make him comprehend just how serious I was.

"If you take one more step, I'll call the cops."

Christian halted in the middle of the street,

looking shocked and a little bit frustrated as he roughed his hand through his black hair.

He shook his head, the pain in his voice catching me off guard.

"Elizabeth, I'm not going to hurt you." His words brought me firmly back to reality.

A barking, contemptuous laugh escaped my lips. "You're not going to *hurt* me?"

I looked him in the eye, making sure he understood. "Nobody has ever hurt me as much as you hurt me, Christian. *No one.*"

Yes, I sounded like a lover scorned, but that was exactly what I was.

"Now I want you to leave."

"Elizabeth, I'm so sorry. It was my fault. I know. Please don't do this."

I watched as he stumbled over himself, tried to apologize as if any excuse he could give would gain him access into our lives. I refused to believe his lies.

Once I would have trusted him with my life, but now I knew better. I'd never allow my daughter or myself to be put in the position for Christian to freely dispose of us again.

"Leave."

"Please, Elizabeth. I need to see my daughter."

His daughter? All these years I had known Christian to be a selfish man, but I could never have imagined the depths it went to.

I swallowed hard, shaking my head at his impudence, unable to believe what he had just said.

"She's not your daughter. She's *my* daughter."

He could apologize all he wanted, but it would never change what he did. He had discarded us and he had no right in our lives.

I turned and left him standing there. I couldn't bear to be in his presence a moment longer.

Lizzie was at the window, appearing wounded and frightened by events she couldn't understand. In just five minutes, Christian had managed to throw my family into complete turmoil, and I had no idea how to repair the damage he had already done.

All I knew was that my daughter was hurting. I rushed inside and pried her away from the window. At first, she resisted, struggling in my arms to get back to him, before she buried her face in my neck.

I could feel her confusion, the way she needed me to comfort her all the while being drawn to the man outside. Her tears ran down my neck and onto my shirt.

I shushed her as I rocked her, holding her with one arm while my free hand ran from the top of her head and down her back over the silky strands of her hair.

"It's okay, sweetheart," I murmured against her head. "It's going to be okay."

She pulled back, her perfect face tearstained and

broken, and asked me the one question I felt incapable of answering. "Mommy, who is that man?"

How could I tell her that the man I had just sent away was her father or deal the questions that were sure to follow?

Instead, I pressed my lips to her forehead and whispered, "Mommy loves you so much, Lizzie."

She nodded against them as if her four-year-old mind understood that I was asking her for time, that my heart was not yet ready to break hers any further.

She clung to my neck desperately as I hugged her before I reluctantly set her on the floor.

"Can you be a big girl for Mommy and go upstairs and play in your room until dinner is ready?" I caressed her cheek as I implored with my eyes. She gazed up at me, never looking more like Christian than in that moment. I smiled sadly at her, wishing that it didn't hurt so much.

She cast one last glance toward the window before looking back at me. "Okay, Mommy."

Once she was safely upstairs, I cautiously peered through the curtains, praying that Christian was gone, though intuitively knowing he was not.

He sat in his car, his gaze meeting mine, his eyes pleading for forgiveness while mine silently begged him to just leave us alone.

Dinner was quiet. Lizzie said very little the entire evening other than, "Thank you, Momma," when I set her small plate of lasagna down in front of her.

Neither of us ate much, and I knew her mind was focused just as much on what had happened this afternoon as mine was.

I owed her an answer to her question, but I still hadn't found the right way to tell her.

We went through our normal evening routine, albeit halfheartedly. Her nightly bath lacked the normal giggles and splashes, and for the first time in her life, she didn't want a bedtime story.

She climbed into her bed, and I pulled the covers up over her chest and kissed her softly on the head. I hoped she would snuggle into her pillow and yawn the way she usually did, but instead she looked up at me, waiting.

I sank onto my knees beside her bed, knowing I could put this off no longer. I opened my mouth, searching for the right way to tell her, but she spoke first.

"Was that my Daddy?"

All the air left me as her timid, soft words came like a whisper into her dim room. They were filled with such hope, and now I could do nothing other than crush that hope just as soon as it had been born.

A single tear slid down my face as I nodded.

Swallowing, I looked around the room as I tried to gather enough courage to speak.

Finally, I turned back to her. "Yes, baby, it was."

Lizzie knew little of Christian.

She had asked once, right after she had started preschool. She had wanted to know why she didn't have a daddy like the rest of the kids.

I had only told her that her father lived far away. I knew that one day I would have to explain the choice he had made. I just didn't think it would come so soon.

"Where had he been?"

Breathing deeply, I reached out and brushed her hair from her eyes, playing with the long strands while I began to speak. "Your father chose a different life. One without us in it."

Sadness washed over her face as I described him abandoning us as gently as I could. I prayed she wouldn't understand what that really meant.

Of course, I should have known better.

My ever-insightful child looked me directly in the face and asked, "You mean my daddy didn't want me?"

How was I supposed to answer that? I found that I couldn't.

Wouldn't.

No child should ever feel rejected the way she had been.

Instead, I climbed into bed next to her and

pulled her to me. I kissed her forehead. "Did you know I wanted you from the moment I knew you were to be born? You are my greatest joy, Lizzie."

Christian may not have wanted her, but I had never wanted anything more in my life.

"I know, Mommy."

We stayed like that for what seemed like hours, me gaining solace from my daughter while I tried to provide her the same, her breath finally beginning to even out as she drifted to sleep.

I allowed myself to relish in the quiet comfort of my child.

Nearing sleep myself, Lizzie snuggled deeper and pressed her face into my chest, mumbling from somewhere in her subconscious, "But my daddy wants me now."

My stomach twisted as my cell phone rang. I picked it up from the center console of my car, glancing at the screen as I drove—not that I needed to.

I knew exactly who it was.

He'd been calling continuously since last Friday when he'd shown up at my house. I'd spent that night in Lizzie's room, unwilling to leave the warmth of her presence.

Saturday morning, I was awakened by a playful kiss on my cheek. I had opened my eyes to find

Lizzie grinning over me. It had seemed the perfect start to the day.

That feeling hadn't lasted long, disappearing when I discovered the four missed calls, two voice messages, and three text messages—all of them from Christian.

They were all alike, filled with apologies and pleas to make atonement.

Initially, I'd been shocked.

I had no idea how he'd even gotten my cell phone number.

Over the following week, the number of calls had increased in direct relation to the fervency in his voice.

I pushed end to silence the ring, and in my frustration, I threw the phone against the passenger seat.

I was scared.

He was so *desperate* as if his life depended on whether or not he saw Lizzie again.

My paranoid mind had begun to conjure terrifying scenarios, most of them centered on a call from Lizzie's school saying she had suddenly disappeared, last seen with a man that bore an uncanny resemblance to her.

If I approached the situation realistically, though, I knew there was little chance he would ever do something so criminal.

That was my worst fear, though, what was legal,

what rights he might have.

Each night this week after I'd tucked Lizzie into bed, I'd researched.

It seemed it all came down to what the court would believe would be in the child's best interest.

The problem was, I *knew* what was best for my child and that was to keep her away from the man who would ultimately end up hurting her, but would they see it that way?

It left me feeling completely out of control, unsure of our future. Vulnerable.

I cringed as my phoned chimed again, indicating a new voice message. I prayed that if I ignored him long enough, he would finally give up.

Work passed in a fog. Faces were a blur, and I hoped that the daze that surrounded me wasn't affecting my job. It turned out I had hoped in vain.

Scott, one of our two loan officers, tugged on my forearm and pulled me aside, his expression concerned.

He was a thirty-two-year-old divorcee, and second to Christian, probably the most attractive man I'd ever seen.

He didn't drop his hold as his green eyes searched my face, his thumb running circles over my skin.

"What's going on with you this week, Liz? I'm worried about you." His voice was soft, tender, dripping with the affection I'd told him time and time again I could never return.

He'd settled on being my friend, though I was certain he believed one day I would have a change of heart.

Pushing my bangs from my face, I sighed heavily.

"I'm fine," I whispered under my breath. "It's just been a bad week."

What an understatement.

It had been one of the worst weeks of my life.

"You want to talk about it?"

I shook my head, hoping my small, forced smile would project my appreciation. "No, I'm fine. Thanks. I just have a lot on my mind right now."

He nodded, squeezing my arm. "Okay, Liz, but I'm here for you." He dipped his head, meeting my eyes. "You know that, right?"

"Yeah, I know."

"Try to focus out there, okay," he added reluctantly, plainly uncomfortable bringing up my deficiencies over the past week. "I'm not the only one who's noticed you've been off your game this week."

He gestured with his head in the direction of our branch manager, Anita, who was watching us from her desk across the lobby.

I cringed, feeling guilty and embarrassed for allowing my personal issues to affect my job.

"Thanks for the warning."

"You're welcome. Now get back to work," he said as his tone turned teasing.

I grinned at him, shaking my head as I walked back to my window.

I took a deep breath as I got back to my drawer, giving myself a mental pep talk about leaving my personal issues at home.

Even if the smile I flashed at my next customer was fake, it was at least a smile and not a grimace. She completed her transaction and wished me a good evening, and I bid her the same.

I called next as I glanced at my computer screen, clearing it to prepare for the next customer.

"Elizabeth, I need to talk to you." His low voice hit me just as hard as if he'd slammed me against a wall.

Christian stood at my window, his hands gripping the counter as he leaned in toward me. I tried to look away from his penetrating eyes, to escape the intensity behind them.

The passion swimming in them was probably the single most frightening thing I'd ever seen. It was then I realized he wouldn't give up.

Overwhelmed, I burst into tears.

"Please, leave us alone," I begged, imploring with him to just once not think of himself.

"I'm sorry, Elizabeth, I can't. I have to see Lizzie." His face lit as he said her name.

It made me sick.

I shook my head. "No." I wasn't giving in. I would not allow him to hurt my baby.

"Please, don't do this, Elizabeth. You can't keep her from me," he stated as if he had a claim on her.

As far as I was concerned, he had given up that claim the moment he had sent me out his door.

I was going to tell him that very thing, until the words, "I love her," passed through his lips.

He loved her? I could feel my face redden as anger surged through my veins.

"You what?" I seethed, unable to contain the fury boiling over. "You don't love her."

Five years with no contact and now he loves her?

I could feel myself begin to shake, and this time I wouldn't hold back.

He needed to know just how misguided he was.

"You're too selfish to know what love is, and I will not stand by and watch you break Lizzie's heart when you've had your fill of her, just the way you did me."

Christian paled at my words, almost as if he hadn't known he'd broken my heart, and if he hadn't realized that, then he was truly a fool.

I had loved him—so much. I'd told him every day, and I'd meant it. He'd promised to marry to me, to spend his life with me, to love me forever.

Apparently, I'd been the fool to believe it.

"Elizabeth." His voice was raspy as he pleaded, "I'm not that person anymore. Please, give me a chance. I promise I'm not going anywhere."

I wanted to laugh in his face. "I haven't forgotten the last time you made that promise, Christian."

How many times had he told me he'd never leave?

I took advantage of his pause, his loss for words, and hardened my voice. "Stay out of our lives, Christian."

He needed to know that no amount of repentance would earn him forgiveness. What he'd done was unforgivable.

Christian gripped his head in his hands, and when he looked back up at me, his face was contorted in an anguish I didn't understand.

"Please, Elizabeth . . . don't . . . don't make me take this to court."

My knees went weak as he vocalized my greatest fear, and I was certain my heart would falter in my chest.

He was really going to try to take away my child.

I took a shaky step back as the room began to spin. There were so many emotions swirling, consuming, but one thought overrode them all. I opened my mouth, and even though the sound barely came, I was certain he heard.

"I *hate* you."

I covered my mouth as I rushed to the break room, hoping to hide myself away before I completely broke down.

The moment I was safely behind the door, I lost it.

Loud cries echoed through the small room, my body convulsing, gripped with fear. I tried to steady myself against the table but fell to my knees, my legs unable to support the weight of what had just occurred. I felt as if I were drowning.

Sounds came in muddled waves against my ears, and I sensed movement and knew I was not alone, though I was unable to focus on anything but the feeling of dread that coursed through my body.

The pressure in my chest left me gasping, searching for air I couldn't seem to find.

Somebody shook me, an alarmed voice repeating, "Elizabeth."

I struggled to see the face, to hear the voice, and finally opened my eyes to find Scott kneeling in front of me. The look of concern he'd had earlier had been replaced by one of panic. His hands trembled as he held my shoulders.

A soft hand rubbed my back as Selina's soothing voice coaxed, "Calm down, Liz. Take a deep breath. Just relax."

With her words, my anxiety attack gave way to a flood of tears, and I collapsed into Scott's arms, sobbing into his shirt.

Selina stood and returned seconds later with a cup of water and a cool, wet cloth, pressing one against my forehead and the other to my lips.

Scott helped me into a chair and I accepted the water, allowing the coolness to soothe my burning throat, though it could do nothing to soothe my soul.

All I could think was that I had failed my daughter.

Selina drove me home and Scott followed in my car. It was apparent I was in no condition to finish out my day of work. Selina offered to come inside, but I refused. I just needed to be alone.

I plodded upstairs, each step sucking me deeper into despair. By the time I entered my bedroom, I was back on my knees, weeping into the carpet.

I had no idea how much time had passed when I heard the front doorbell ring, then ring again. Finally, the sound of a key in the lock and the squeaking of the front door came.

"Elizabeth?" Natalie's voice carried from downstairs.

This was followed by Lizzie's joyful voice singing, "Where are you, Mommy?"

I cried harder into the floor, thinking of how one day soon Christian would steal that joy away.

Footsteps pounded against the stairs, and I could feel Natalie pause in the doorway to my room.

Lizzie's footsteps trailed close behind.

Raising my head, I met Natalie's face as she

took in the scene, her eyes wide as she apprised the crying mess I was.

"Please, don't let Lizzie see me this way," I managed to force out, my voice hoarse.

She hesitated, clearly wishing to come to my side before nodding and stepping away.

She stopped Lizzie just before she got to the door. "Lizzie, honey, your mommy isn't feeling very well right now. Why don't we go downstairs and start dinner?"

"Is she sick?" Lizzie's voice dropped to a whisper. I could sense her trying to peer into the room, and Natalie moved to block her view.

"Yes, sweetheart, but she'll be okay, don't worry."

The bedroom door closed between us, and I was left with only the echo of their retreat downstairs and the anxiety that had me nailed to the floor.

I wanted to get up, dry my eyes, and go to my daughter, but I knew I would be unable to stand in front of Lizzie and pretend that the life we knew had not just come to an end.

It seemed like hours had passed as I swam in my misery, but the sky had barely dimmed with evening's approach when my door opened and I was wrapped in the comfort of Matthew's arms.

He sat on the floor against my bed and pulled me onto his lap. He rocked me and shushed me as if I were his child, his hand running through my hair as he placed soft kisses against my head.

⸻

I leaned heavily against the table, staring into the lukewarm cup of coffee that sat untouched in front of me. Matthew and Natalie walked quietly into the kitchen.

"She's asleep," Matthew said just above a whisper. He released a heavy breath and ran his hand over his face.

Glancing up, I mouthed a watery, "Thank you."

Natalie and Matthew took a seat at the table, eyeing me cautiously. "Are you doing okay, Liz?" Matthew asked sympathetically, though with an undercurrent of fury I knew he was trying to hide from me.

Sniffling, I shook my head. I wasn't doing okay. Never had I been more afraid. I'd worked so hard to build this life, to provide a safe, stable home for Lizzie, one filled with encouragement and love. I'd established a family that she could count on; people who would never choose to leave her but who would always choose to stay.

And in one moment, Christian threatened to take it all away.

"What am I going to do?" I choked out, more tears pouring down my face as I voiced my fears. "I can't let him hurt her."

I knew I had to protect my daughter from him. I just didn't know how.

"Maybe he won't, Liz. Maybe he really just wants to see her," Natalie offered, her tone hopeful, her words causing a loud cry to erupt from me.

Matthew widened his eyes at Natalie, and he tilted his head to the side as if to say *you're not helping things.*

Natalie shrugged defensively. "What? I'm just saying what I saw. Now that I know who he is, I can understand the look on his face. It was as if he *wanted* to know her."

Her remark only made me cry harder.

Natalie grabbed my hand, squeezing it. "I'm sorry, Liz. I didn't mean to upset you, but what if he did change?"

I accepted the tissue Matthew offered and blew my nose while shaking my head. I wasn't upset with Natalie. She didn't know Christian like I did.

I was sure Natalie was right on some account, that Christian did want to know Lizzie now.

It was the day he became bored with her that concerned me.

Matthew reached across the table and covered Natalie's and my hands in his.

"Elizabeth, I think you should let him see her." His expression was compassionate, and although I knew he would never mean me any harm, it felt like he'd slapped me across the face.

"What?" I jerked my hand away and shook my head, unable to comprehend how Matthew could even suggest something so unreasonable. I would do whatever it took to keep my daughter away from Christian.

Matthew reached for me again, appearing tortured. "Look at me, Elizabeth."

His expression was intense, sincere as he looked across the table at me. He was hurting, every bit as much as I was. "I love Lizzie like my own, and I would do anything to protect her. You know that, right?"

Of course, I did. I nodded.

"Then this may be the best way. Think about it. You don't want that asshole to take you to court."

"I can't believe they'd give him custody," I said, wishing to sound confident.

Instead, it came out more a question. After what he'd done, how could they possibly grant him parental rights? Could they? More tears came.

"Liz . . ." Matthew paused, before looking at me with something akin to pity. "He's an attorney, and you're a bank teller . . ." he trailed off.

I knew he wasn't criticizing me. He was stating a simple fact; Christian had resources, access to the best family attorneys, and knew every aspect of the law.

I had a couple hundred dollars and some change

in my checking account.

"How can I stand by and watch my daughter get her heart broken by her own father when he leaves? I just . . . can't let that happen."

The thought was just too much. If I let Christian have his way, I'd be throwing Lizzie to the wolves. Every part of me screamed to protect my daughter from the harm Christian would surely bring, though realistically I knew what Matthew was saying was right.

It would be much worse if Christian had legal rights.

I couldn't imagine him having any legal say in the upbringing of my daughter.

A soothing hand rested lightly on my back as Natalie said in a soft voice, "It's going to be okay, Liz. We'll get through this."

Matthew leaned farther across the table and smoothed the matted hair from my face. "She's right, honey. We'll get through this, I promise. Whatever happens, we'll be here for Lizzie. She'll never be alone," Matthew promised.

Through bleary eyes, I looked up at Matthew and Natalie. I took a tissue from the box and dabbed at my eyes, nodding as I sat up and took a deep breath to try to ease the dread I felt.

I took some comfort in knowing that in the end, Matthew and Natalie would be there just as they always had been.

What I found no comfort in was the knowledge of what I needed to do next.

I rose and Matthew and Natalie followed. Sadness hung in the air with the decision that we had made. I hugged them, first Natalie and then Matthew. Pulling away, I held onto Matthew's hand and smiled somberly.

"Thank you."

He returned the embrace, pursing his lips as he nodded once, his expression stressing his reassurance. "We're here, Liz. Always."

"You guys better go home. It's getting late." It was well after midnight, and it had been a long, emotionally exhausting day.

"You sure?" Matthew asked. "We can stay if you need us."

I shook my head. "No, I'll be fine."

Matthew hesitated, glancing at Natalie, before he agreed. "Okay. We'll see you tomorrow."

Following them to the entryway, I hugged them each again, wishing them goodnight. Slowly, I shut the door behind them and locked it.

The moment it was closed, I was gripped with emotions I wasn't sure I had enough strength to deal with. It had all been too much. I turned and slid down the backside of the door.

Grasping my head in my hands, I buried it between my knees, crying out into the stillness. The pain coming from my mouth echoed through the house.

How could I just hand my daughter over to him? I knew exactly what he'd do, what game he played.

He would make Lizzie fall in love with him, just as he had done to me, make her believe she meant everything to him.

Then he would leave my child and take her heart with him. How could any mother make a decision to put her child in harm's way?

But I'd been left without a choice.

I pushed to my feet and marched upstairs. Once in my room, I dug through my purse on the floor and retrieved my cell phone.

Taking a deep, steadying breath, I dialed the same number that had caused me a near anxiety attack every time it had rang over the last week.

It was late, and I prayed it would go straight to voice mail.

I lost my voice and nearly my nerve when Christian answered.

Warmth spread through my body with the sound of his voice. I squeezed my eyes shut and shook the foolish reaction away.

I hated him, I reminded myself, and he was *dangerous.*

No matter what feelings I still harbored for him, I could not forget those two crucial truths.

five

CHRISTIAN

Lying on my bed, I stared at the ceiling, clueless as

to where to go from here. I knew I should give up, stand down, but found myself unable to entertain the thought of not seeing Lizzie again.

I rolled over and buried my face in my pillow, hoping to find answers there. None came. I lifted my head to my nightstand, looking at the clock that read twelve thirty-seven.

It was late in San Diego and much later in Virginia, but there was no one else who would understand.

Making a quick decision, I sat up on the side of

my bed, picked up my phone, and dialed.

She answered on the first ring. "Christian, what's wrong?"

Mom's voice was raspy from sleep, but her mind was clear enough to know I would not have called her in the middle of the night if something weren't wrong.

I uttered the first words that came to mind. "Mom, they're here."

Silence hovered thick in the air. The miles between us were filled with an unspoken language, soundless joy and overwhelming regret.

Finally, Mom spoke when the shock wore off, and I could tell she was crying. "Tell me about my grandchild."

I cleared my throat of some of the emotion, just enough to speak. "Her name is Lizzie."

Mom whimpered, causing my chest to constrict further. The gathering of moisture in my eyes brought me as close to crying as I had since I'd been a small boy.

My voice was full of adoration as I described to my mother our first encounter, how I'd known I was connected to the child the first time I saw her, how I'd fallen in love with her in the same moment.

My tone became alarmed as I told her of going to their house and about Elizabeth sending me away. My distress increased to near hysteria when I got to the part about going to her work.

"Mom, Elizabeth hates me." Her assertion that afternoon had devastated me. To have injured this beautiful creature to the extent that she hated me—I couldn't bear to think of the pain I'd caused her.

"She's angry with you, Christian, and she has every right to be, but I can't believe that she hates you."

I shook my head against the phone. Mom hadn't seen Elizabeth's face. I knew what she had said was true.

Mom sighed. "Christian, I'm not going to lie to you to make you feel better. What you did to her was terrible. Hurtful. And you're going to have to realize you can't undo almost six years of wrong in a day. You're going to have to be patient."

I fidgeted uncomfortably. I didn't want to be patient.

I wanted my daughter.

"Think about it. She hasn't heard from you since the day you essentially kicked her out, and then out of the blue you show up at her house. She has to be shocked, and honestly, probably a little scared of the way you've been acting. She doesn't know your intentions. If I were her, I'd probably react the same way."

Resigned, I lay back against my bed, rubbing my eye with the heel of my hand.

Mom was right.

Elizabeth was probably freaking out. I'd been acting like a lunatic, showing up at her house unannounced, calling incessantly, and going to her work. I shook my head at my stupidity.

I took a deep breath and released it slowly. I could almost feel Mom relax through the phone as she realized she was getting through to me.

"I know, Mom. I just want to fix this so bad. What if she won't give me the chance?"

Mom's voice was soft, comforting. "I know you do. But you need to take a step back. Give her some space to breathe. She will have built her own life, one without you in it, and it's going to take some time for her to find a place where you do fit in it."

She paused, giving me time to absorb what she was saying. When she spoke again, her voice was still sympathetic but firm. "You owe her that time, Christian."

This was exactly why I'd called my mother. She always had a way of putting things into perspective when I couldn't see it. "You're right. I promise I'll give her some time."

My mother's satisfaction traveled through the phone. "You'll make this right. You'll see."

I couldn't help but grin. How many times had she encouraged me to make it right?

I just hoped one day Elizabeth would actually let

me.

I sighed. "Thanks, Mom."

"You're welcome, honey. Now hang in there a bit, okay?"

"Okay," I promised. "Sorry I called so late."

I could hear my mother shaking her head. "Don't apologize. I'm here for you. Always."

"I love you Mom." It meant so much to me to be able to say those words to my mother, free and without hesitation.

"I love you, so much, Christian." It meant even more for her to say them back to me. "I can't wait to meet my grandchild. Goodnight, sweetheart."

"Night."

Pacified, I placed my phone on the nightstand and curled into my pillow. I could rest with having a plan, with having some insight, some guidance. I would give Elizabeth some time to deal with my resurgence in her life, and then I would slowly try to make contact with her. Like my mom said, I owed her this.

Drifting toward sleep, I jerked, startled by a vibration on the nightstand.

I grinned when I realized where the offending noise was coming from and answered the phone, eager to hear whatever advice Mom had forgotten to tell me.

"Hello?" I mumbled through my sleepy smile.

Where I anticipated hearing my mother's voice,

there was silence.

"Hello?" I asked again, my stomach suddenly uneasy.

I pulled the phone from my ear, checking the number I'd paid no attention to when I'd answered.

My heart almost stopped.

"Elizabeth?" I pled, more terrified than excited to hear her voice, having no idea why she would suddenly be calling me well after midnight.

After what seemed like a forever, she finally spoke, her words teeming with disdain. "If you really want to see Lizzie, meet me at the McDonald's on Fairmount and University at five thirty on Saturday."

Relief flooded me, and I released an audible force of air from my lungs, preparing myself to thank her, but the line went dead before I was given the chance.

Gripping the steering wheel, I peered up through my windshield at the yellow arches and fought to bring my breathing under control. To merely say I was nervous would be an injustice. The anxiety was suffocating. I knew today would be the defining moment in my life.

Today I would meet my daughter.

I wanted nothing more, but truthfully, I was

terrified. I had no idea what to expect, how to act, or how to be a father. I didn't even know if Lizzie knew I *was* her father.

Worse than all of those fears was the worry that this would be the one chance I would have, the one encounter with a daughter that I knew nothing of but loved with all my soul.

I had no idea what had made Elizabeth change her mind, what caused her to call me in the middle of the night, but I had to hold onto the hope that she saw my sincerity, that she understood I only wanted to make things right.

I rubbed my damp palms against my jeans before stepping from the car. Elizabeth's little red car sat empty across the lot from where I'd parked.

My heart pounded, and I tried unsuccessfully to keep my hands from trembling as I moved to the entrance.

Pausing at the door, I drew a breath deep into my lungs in an attempt to calm myself before stepping inside.

There were people everywhere, but my eyes were drawn across the restaurant to where Elizabeth and Lizzie stood, waiting hand-in-hand.

Lizzie's face was graced with the most amazing smile the moment she saw me. My racing nerves were soothed by her warmth and an uncontained smile spread across my face. She started bouncing in place as I made my way across the room and, if it was possible, her smile only grew.

The only thing that kept me from running and sweeping Lizzie into my arms was Elizabeth.

Her face was nearly expressionless, though I could see everything behind her eyes, could feel it radiating off her body.

Hate.

Elizabeth hated me.

My face fell along with the hope I had had that perhaps she was softening toward me.

I held her malignant gaze for a split second before tearing my attention from her and placing it on the reason I was there. I knelt on one knee in front of my daughter.

Lizzie's blue eyes gleamed with delight, her smile unending.

My eyes wandered over her, and for the first time, I was able to fully take in my daughter.

Her black hair was pulled into pigtails on each side of her head, accentuating the roundness of her face. She wore denim shorts and a pink T-shirt with flowers and butterflies embroidered across the front. I couldn't help but grin when I saw her small feet clad in bright pink flip-flops—her tiny toes painted pink.

My baby girl liked pink.

The soft skin of her arms and legs was pale and smooth.

Desperately wishing to hold her, I wanted

nothing more than to have her wrap her arms around my neck.

Smiling softly when I looked back at her face, I spoke for the first time to my daughter. "Hi, Lizzie."

She giggled. "Hi."

The sound of her laugh took my breath away.

"I'm . . ." Suddenly, I became very uneasy, unsure of how to introduce myself.

Wary, I glanced up at Elizabeth, hoping for direction, an indication of how she would want me to proceed.

She glared at me, almost as if she were daring me to say it.

Swallowing heavily, I opened my mouth once more, trying to force out the words, "I'm your—"

Lizzie laughed again. "I know who you are, silly. You're my daddy."

Daddy.

I was struck with the magnitude of what that meant, the responsibility of being a father.

Waves of devotion swept through me as I silently promised her I would always be there for her, would always love her, would be the best father I could possibly be.

Nodding slowly, I reached a shaky hand out to her face, running the back of my hand along the softness of her cheek. "Yes, I'm your daddy."

A wounded cry escaped Elizabeth, and she

jerked, her body shrinking away from us while she still held onto Lizzie's hand as if she were trying to remove herself from the situation without leaving her daughter's side.

She turned her face as far from us as possible, but not far enough to hide the stream of tears that flowed down her cheeks.

Guilt that would have brought me to my knees brought me to my feet. Stepping to her side, I tried to meet her face.

"Elizabeth." It came out strangled and small, filled with desperation.

She put up her hand to block the obvious apology that was coming. "Just . . . don't."

Dropping her hand and shifting her focus from me, she looked down at Lizzie, and her hardened face melted into sudden tenderness. "Let's get something to eat, sweetheart."

Lizzie nodded with excitement and followed her mother, Elizabeth's hold still firm on our daughter's hand. I trailed by a few steps, getting in line directly behind them.

While a gentleman would have volunteered to pay, I was wise enough to know the firestorm that particular offer would bring. I watched in adoration as Lizzie swayed beside her mother, glancing over her shoulder at me every few seconds and flashing me the sweetest smile I'd ever seen.

I loved her—so much so it hurt, and with each second that passed, it only grew.

After ordering, Elizabeth moved aside, and I stepped to the register.

Honestly, the last thing I felt like doing was eating, but I asked for first thing I saw when I glanced at the menu. I allowed Elizabeth to lead, following her and my child to fill our drinks before setting my tray on the opposite side of the table from them.

It was probably the most awkward situation I'd ever been in as I slid into the booth. I watched as Elizabeth hovered over the table. She took their food from the tray and put it on the table, jamming straws into their drinks and refusing to meet my face.

The worst part was I couldn't take my eyes off her.

Very unsuccessfully, I tried not to ogle her as she leaned in, tried to ignore how the gray tank top she wore exposed just a hint of the swell of her breasts, tried to pretend her tight black jeans didn't remind me of the perfection of her body and how it had felt against mine.

Damn it, Christian. Get yourself together.

This was not why I was here.

That reason suddenly climbed into the spot beside me, shocking me by choosing to sit next to me.

I grinned at her and scooted down a little to make room for her.

She sat on her knees so she could reach the table, and then inched even closer so we were touching. Instinctively, I wrapped my arm around her back and pulled her closer, nestling her against my side. It felt amazing.

Then she *kissed* my cheek.

I froze, overcome with the staggering warmth created with that one simple gesture. I stared at her, unwilling to look away from the love swimming in Lizzie eyes.

"Lizzie, please eat your dinner," Elizabeth said as she sat down across from us.

Affectionately, I patted my daughter's side, gesturing with my head toward her food.

As much as I didn't want break the connection we'd just shared, the bond we were building, I hoped to keep from upsetting Elizabeth any more than I already had.

Eating in front of Elizabeth felt odd. We'd shared what seemed like a million meals before, but now I felt extremely self-conscious as I took small bites of my burger, feeling on edge as silence loomed over the table.

Elizabeth appeared even more uncomfortable, probably because of the glances I kept sneaking at her every chance I got.

I had missed her so badly, never imagining I'd

see her again. My eyes wandered over her face, taking in the changes and all that remained the same.

She was thinner now, her cheekbones more prominent, but not to the point of appearing unhealthy as she did when I had seen her just weeks before she had given birth to Lizzie.

Her hair was mostly the same, still dark blond and woven with natural highlights just a shade lighter than the rest, though she now wore long bangs that continually seemed to fall over her eyes.

When she'd push them aside, I would glimpse a foreign scar that ran just above her left eye.

My gut wrenched with the possibilities of where it had come from.

Lizzie ate her nuggets and apples quietly, almost reserved, as if she could sense the tension in the air. Hugging her body closer, I tried to pull her attention away from the sad place her mind seemed to have gone and whispered against her head, "I'm so happy to be here with you."

She turned to me, her expression hopeful. "Really?"

I wanted to ask her why she would think I wouldn't be, but I already knew the answer. Instead, I reassured her with a resolute nod of my head. "Really."

With that, her insecurities seemed to fade away, and she launched into what seemed to be an impromptu game of twenty questions.

She would ask me something, and after I answered, I would ask her a variation of the same question in return. It made me terribly sad that I was asking my daughter these things for the first time when she was almost five years old, but the fact remained that I didn't know what she did on a daily basis, her favorite foods, her favorite places.

I didn't know what made her scared or made her cry. I learned today that it was seeing her mommy cry.

I wanted to tell her it made me sad, too, but couldn't find the courage to say it aloud.

Elizabeth squirmed through our conversation, never offering an opinion and only answering when Lizzie specifically asked something of her.

Many times, she looked away, holding her jaw rigid, though it still shook as she seemed to struggle through every minute of the conversation Lizzie and I shared.

The only time she added anything was when Lizzie asked me where I lived, and I told her down near the water on Harbor.

Elizabeth huffed and visibly rolled her eyes as she mouthed a sarcastic, "Nice."

I'd winced, expecting her anger but not her spite.

Lizzie, on the other hand, was thrilled to hear I lived by the water. She bounced in her seat as she squealed, "You live at the beach?"

Lizzie kept up an almost constant chatter as we ate—not that I minded.

She had the sweetest voice I'd ever heard. She drifted closer the longer we talked, so close she was nearly sitting in my lap by the time she finished off her last nugget.

She continually smiled and constantly reached out to touch my face and hug my neck.

I felt so unworthy of the affection she gave. She loved so freely, trusted so easily.

Would she feel the same when the innocence of her mind faded away, when she understood the meaning of betrayal?

"All done," she sang as she swallowed her last bite. "Can I play now, Momma?"

Elizabeth nodded tightly. It was apparent she would prefer not to be left alone with me. I, on the other hand, had been praying I'd have a chance to talk to her in private.

Lizzie started to scramble down, but she paused and looked at me. "Daddy, is it okay if I play now?"

Trying to be discrete, I glanced over to Elizabeth, sure the simple sentence would cause her great distress, before uttering softly, "Of course, sweetheart."

I understood what that sentence meant. She had accepted me, not only as her daddy, but also as her parent. Clearly, Elizabeth understood it too. Her face flashed red, burning resentment.

I watched my daughter until she disappeared into a red tube, before I slowly turned to face Elizabeth. She leaned heavily on the table, staring at a fry she absentmindedly swirled in ketchup.

"Elizabeth," I said tentatively, hoping for once to have a civil discussion with her. She lifted her head, leveling her eyes at me.

I sighed, averting my gaze as I ran my hand over the back of my neck, trying to chase away some of the tension before I gathered enough courage to look directly at her.

"Thank you."

I needed her to know how grateful I was that she was giving me a chance, even if it didn't seem like she really wanted to give it.

"You didn't leave me much of a choice now, did you, Christian?" she said, her voice low and full of hostility.

I shook my head. "What are you talking about?"

"Are you joking?" she asked incredulously. "You're really going to sit there and act like you didn't threaten to take me to court if I didn't allow you to see her?"

Shit.

I should have known. The idle threat I'd made was the only reason I'd been allowed to see my daughter.

Elizabeth hadn't *chosen* to let me see Lizzie. She felt she'd been *forced* to.

What an ignorant asshole I continually proved to be. For one brief, self-indulgent moment, I considered not making the correction.

But while I wanted nothing more than to see Lizzie, to have a relationship with her, and to be a part of her life, there was no way I could go on with Elizabeth living in fear that one day I would try to take Lizzie away from her.

If I were ever going to earn her trust back, I would have to start by being honest.

"No, Elizabeth." I leaned into the table, speaking barely above a whisper, "I won't do that. I was upset that you weren't returning my calls, and . . . I . . . I just got caught up in the moment and it came out. I won't put you through that . . . I won't."

I made the promise as I searched her face, praying she'd believe what I said, and praying even harder she wouldn't be angered further by the realization that she'd essentially been tricked into this meeting.

When I'd threatened to bring the courts into it while I was at her work, I'd immediately wished I could take the words back.

Law was what I knew, what came naturally, and it had dropped from my mouth before I could stop it. I would never want to put Elizabeth through something as harrowing as a child custody battle. I was certain we could work this out between us.

She sat up straight as she shook her head in disbelief. Oozing cynicism, she said, "You always manage to get your way, don't you, Christian? I always knew you'd make the best lawyer. What was it you used to say? 'Twist it until it fits?' "

"Elizabeth . . . " I pleaded. Manipulating her had never been my goal, but somehow I'd managed to do it without even realizing it. I should have made it clear then, when I'd seen the look on her face, but I'd been too injured by her parting words that it had never dawned on me what had spurred them. "I'm sorry."

"You say that a lot."

I shifted uncomfortably, muttering as I stumbled over my remorse, "I have a lot to be sorry for."

The hardness on her face faltered, her eyes washed in sadness, before the walls were back in place.

But in that fleeting moment of vulnerability, I saw it, the light that had been Elizabeth, and it gave me hope.

Elizabeth jerked as she heard *Mommy* called from somewhere above.

Daddy followed quickly after.

I looked up to find Lizzie waving wildly from a clear plastic orb that nearly touched the high ceiling. Irrational fear gripped me when I saw her.

Logically, I knew these playgrounds were made for children, designed for their safety, but I couldn't help the chill that shot down my spine.

My eyes darted to Elizabeth who waved with just as much excitement at Lizzie. I turned back, waving too, though clearly without the enthusiasm the two of them shared.

"Isn't she a little small to be up there by herself? It seems a little . . . high."

Elizabeth continued to wave as she spoke through her obviously forced smile, "It's terrifying being a parent, isn't it?"

For the first time, her voice lacked its biting edge, and it felt like her assertion was more for herself than for me.

Gazing up at Lizzie, I could do nothing but agree. "Terrifying."

In silence, Elizabeth and I continued to watch Lizzie, each of us turned to sit sideways at the end of the booth. The question had been burning in my mouth the entire time we'd been here, and I finally found myself bold enough to ask it before I no longer had the chance.

"So, you and Matthew aren't . . ." The pregnant pause supplied the rest.

Elizabeth jerked her head toward me, clearly shocked by my question. "What? No." Her nose wrinkled in the way it always had when she seemed genuinely confused by something. "What . . . how did you?"

Her brow creased as she looked at me, puzzled.

"I just—"

She stopped me when the shock seemed to wear off. "You know what? What I do with my personal life is none of your business."

Shaking her head, she pushed her bangs aggressively from her face before turning her attention back to Lizzie.

Right.

None of my business.

Frustrated, I leaned on my elbows, digging them into my knees, and raked my hands over the back of my head while I stared at my shoes.

A now-familiar warmth spread through me, and I looked up, coming face-to-face with a very excited little girl.

"Did you see me up there, Daddy?" She pointed proudly at the clear ball. "I was so high!"

"Yes, sweetheart, I did see you. You're such a big girl."

I left out the part where she had nearly given me a heart attack.

Elizabeth began to clear the trash from the table, piling their empty cartons and wraps on a tray, and I knew the most important day of my life was coming to an end.

God, I didn't want it to end.

With great reluctance, I stood and began to clean up my area.

Was this it? The last I would be allowed to see of my baby girl?

I choked on the pain elicited by that thought, my head pounding and stomach turning as every cell of my body protested.

"Come on, Daddy." Lizzie tugged on my hand that was suddenly in hers.

Shaken into motion, I numbly followed, hating each step that brought me closer to the end. Elizabeth walked with purpose ahead of us as if she had finally found her escape.

Faster than my mind could process, we were standing beside their car, my hand firmly gripping Lizzie's.

I was terrified to let it go.

Lizzie, don't let me go.

"Daddy, are you coming to my birthday party next Saturday?" I was pulled from my inner discourse by her shocking question, it formed as if she had heard my thoughts.

I cast a sidelong glance at Elizabeth, trying to gauge her reaction.

She tensed before she finally spoke, the words controlled as she tried to hide the obvious tenor of irritation in her voice. "I'm sure he already has plans, Lizzie."

I shook my head rapidly. "No plans."

Unless she wanted to consider me sitting on the couch, flipping mindlessly through television channels, *plans.*

Elizabeth huffed and turned away as she seemed to war with something within herself.

Finally, she turned back to us and raised her chin as she said, "Three o'clock. My house."

They were not just words. They were a warning that I heard loud and clear.

Don't mess this up.

Swept in relief, I released the heavy breath I'd been holding and promised, "I'll be there."

The look Elizabeth gave me told me, *You'd better be.*

Lizzie squealed beside me. "Yay!" Then she threw herself into my arms, catching me off guard. I lifted her almost awkwardly, never before having held a child, and then hugged her to me, holding her tight enough to feel her heart beating wildly against mine.

She squeezed her arms around my neck and buried her face in my chest. I breathed in the moment, memorizing everything.

Then against my ear, she whispered, "I love you, Daddy."

I gasped and hugged her even closer as, "I love you," poured from my mouth.

My eyes burned with emotion, so much so fast, overwhelming. Tears slipped away before I understood what was happening.

For the first time since I was a child, I was crying.

Opening my eyes to find Elizabeth staring at me, I mouthed a soundless, "Thank you."

Whether she understood it or not, she had just given me back my heart. She held my gaze for an instant before dropping her face to the ground.

My heart ached as I set Lizzie back on the ground, wishing to hold her forever, but pacified in knowing I would see her soon.

She climbed into the booster seat and strapped herself in.

Leaning in, I pressed a soft kiss to her forehead.

"Goodbye, precious girl."

She grinned up at me, scrunching her nose in the cutest way. "Bye, Daddy."

Shutting the door was probably the hardest thing I'd ever done.

Elizabeth shuffled her feet in discomfort, her arms wrapped protectively around herself.

I wanted to say so much, to explain, but figured today I'd pushed my luck about as far as it would go.

"Goodbye, Elizabeth," I said softly.

Her face contorted, twisted in agony as she chewed on her trembling lower lip.

I hated that I made her feel this way.

Rushed with the urge to comfort her, I reached

out, sooner than I had the chance to think better of it.

Wide-eyed with shock, she reeled back.

My eyes grew as wide as hers did when I realized what I'd done.

Then she jumped in her car and sped away.

Six

ELIZABETH

Out of breath, I tied off what felt like the thousandth balloon I'd blown up today. Not surprising, they were pink.

All of them.

Strong hands came to rest on my shoulders while soothing fingers massaged in an attempt to chase away the tightness in my muscles. "Are you doing okay, Liz?"

I shrugged against his hands, glancing over my shoulder at Matthew. What was I going to say? That I was okay? Because I wasn't.

Nothing seemed worse than Christian invading

the safety of my home. Sympathetic eyes promised he understood.

Really, I didn't know how I was going to make it through today.

Watching Christian interact with Lizzie last Saturday had been nothing less than excruciating. I'd prayed that he just wouldn't show up, ending the whole thing quickly, instead of dragging the inevitable out.

Of course, he came.

Hearing Lizzie call him *Daddy* had broken my heart all over again and hearing him agree had made me want to spit in his face.

I couldn't watch as Lizzie snuggled up to him, how he wrapped his arm around her, how he looked at her. I'd spent most of the time studying greasy fingerprints on the wall, fighting against the urge to grab my daughter and run out the door, and reminding myself that this was the lesser of two evils.

Then the bastard *thanked* me as if I'd given him a gift and denied that he would have taken me to court.

So typical, he'd played the good guy after he'd gotten what he wanted. I'd decided right there that I was going to end this.

I wouldn't allow him to play games with me or with my daughter.

That plan was squelched when Lizzie had

invited him to her birthday party.

What was I supposed to do? Refuse my daughter?

Her face had held more hope than I'd ever seen. I'd searched for an excuse, a reason for him not to come, certain he wouldn't sacrifice two Saturday afternoons in a row for a child that he didn't even know, a child that I refused to believe he cared anything about.

And since nothing ever goes my way, he'd countered, saying he had no plans. Lizzie was thrilled and had jumped straight into his arms.

The moment that followed had nearly ruined me, almost unable to bear what was taking place. I'd wanted to turn away but couldn't as Lizzie buried herself in his arms, her words muffled though clear. She'd told him she loved him and he'd returned the affection.

His tears almost made me question my resolve, the sincerity of his whispered, "Thank you."

Then when he'd stood before me, I'd almost broken down, the questions that had swirled in my head the entire time fighting release from my mouth.

How could you?

Did you think of me? Did you think of our child?

Why didn't you love me enough?

Did you even love me at all?

Why now, after so many years?

And in that second, I wanted to know why he was looking at me as if he wanted me.

His move to touch me had shocked me back into my reality.

Dangerous.

I had been there before, and I knew that if I allowed him to speak, to explain, I would so easily fall prey to his deceit.

I would *believe*, and believing in Christian Davison again would be the most foolish move I could ever make.

"Hey, Liz, where do you want this?" Mom stood in the doorway between the living room and kitchen, holding up the heart-shaped piñata she had filled with candy and little goodies for the kids.

"Um . . . I think Matthew has a rope set up for it outside." I glanced at him and he nodded, already walking her way.

"I'll take care of that, Linda."

"Thanks." She handed it to him, and Matthew disappeared through the sliding glass door to the backyard. Mom lingered, watching me as I gathered the last bunch of balloons to take outside to finish off the decorations.

"You okay?" Mom's voice was deep with concern, her face etched with the kind of worry only a mother could feel.

I smiled sadly at her. Mom and I were very close and shared most almost everything. She knew how deeply Christian had wounded me, and there was no one who understood it as well as she did.

My own father had left her for another woman, leaving her alone to raise three little girls. He'd just disappeared in the middle of the night from our lives forever.

"I'll be okay, Mom."

She searched my face, not believing my answer. It was as if she could sense every fear I had.

"You'd better go upstairs and finish getting Lizzie ready. It's nearly two-thirty. I'll help them finish up outside." She tilted her head toward the ceiling, breaking the intense moment we'd shared.

I nodded and started up the stairs. Lizzie's laugh floating down to me lightened my mood. Her cousins were obviously very successful in entertaining her while the rest of us prepared for her party.

My family was so supportive and I couldn't be more grateful. Happily giving up an entire Saturday for us, everyone had shown up first thing this morning to set up.

All three children were on Lizzie's bedroom floor. Lizzie and her cousin, Angie, who was just a year older, were listening intently as Angie's older brother, Brandon, read them a story. It was so adorable.

I watched them for a couple of minutes before interrupting. "Hey, Lizzie. It's time to get dressed.

Your guests will be coming soon."

She jumped up, squealing and running around in circles in her room. "Yay!"

She was wound up tight, but I could only grin because of her excitement. I pulled her princess dress from her closet and she squealed again when she saw it, clapping her hands wildly.

"Oh, Mommy, I'm gonna be so pretty!"

Maggie and Brandon left the room, and I helped Lizzie into the pink, frilly dress, which was really a dress-up costume, one she'd seen at the toy store and had fallen in love with.

It was a bit out of my price range, but I'd set aside a little over the last month and surprised her with it after I'd gotten home from work last night.

"You are the prettiest princess I've ever seen," I said with a smile, kissing her nose. She giggled and twirled in front of the full-length mirror on the back of her door. I pinned the plastic tiara in her hair, and she stepped into the little satin slippers.

My princess.

"Thank you, Momma." Her voice was soft and filled with appreciation and love as she looked at me. She was the most amazing child.

I hugged her tightly before sitting back and holding her small hands in mine. "You are so welcome, sweetheart. Happy birthday."

I wasn't surprised to find tears in my eyes. I was feeling very emotional, both saddened and joyed that my baby girl was turning five, not to mention the intense strain Christian had brought to my life.

Lizzie reached out, catching a tear with her finger.

"Don't be sad, Mommy."

I shook my head, vehement. "No, baby. These are happy tears."

She'd seen me cry so much lately, and I refused to allow another emotional breakdown to affect her day.

"Come on. Let's go see your surprise." I stood, holding my hand out to her. She took it, my assurance enough to erase the concern I had caused in her. Her feet were anxious as she dragged me down the stairs.

Lizzie froze the moment she stepped outside, her face alight in awe.

"Oh, Momma," she whispered as she slowly took in our small backyard that had been transformed into her kingdom for the day.

Matthew had rented a huge white tent that covered the entire yard from the end of the patio to the wall, the kind normally reserved for weddings.

Hundreds of pink balloons hung from it, covering the entire underside. Silver streamers curled out from them, glinting and shining in the afternoon sun.

Natalie and my little sister, Carrie, had painted a

mural they'd attached along the back wall with a scene depicting a white castle surrounded by rolling green hills scattered with white unicorns.

A few tables sat under the patio, covered in pink tablecloths, each centered with a different fairy tale princess surrounded by fresh-cut flowers.

My older sister, Sarah, had volunteered to make a cake, and the huge 3-D princess cake sat proudly on a table that was pushed up against the wall.

Her face glowed. "Thank you, Mommy." She looked up at me from where she stood at my side, her hand still firmly in mine.

I gestured with my head to the rest of our family who had gathered in front of us, each of them eagerly awaiting her reaction. "It wasn't just me, Lizzie. They did this for you."

Never would I have been able to do this without them. They were so good to my daughter, so good to me, and I loved them more than the world.

Lizzie shot forward, hugging and kissing each of them, giggling and blushing as everyone claimed that she was the most beautiful princess they'd ever seen. I gazed upon my family, silently thanking them for everything they'd done.

Their eyes swam with affection, holding the promise that they wanted it no other way.

They'd never viewed us a burden, even though sometimes I felt that way.

Lizzie's eyes grew wide in excitement with the

sound of the doorbell, while mine grew wide with alarm.

"It's party time!" Natalie sang, swooping in to take Lizzie into her arms and spinning her in an exaggerated dance as they disappeared into the house to answer the door.

Nervously, I ran my hand over my face and through my hair in a vain attempt to calm myself.

Sarah appeared at my side, nudging my shoulder. "Relax."

I suppressed a snort.

How could I relax when I had to welcome Christian into my home, the one who had wounded me deeper than anyone, the one who haunted my days and held me in my dreams?

Impossible.

The worst part of it all was, somewhere deep inside me, I knew that allowing him here today was officially inviting him into our lives.

seven

*A*nticipation stirred, pushing me forward.

Yeah, I was nervous and unable to imagine how an afternoon spent with Elizabeth's family could turn out pleasant, but I didn't care. Seeing my daughter again, sharing her birthday with her, was the only thing that mattered.

Last Saturday had been the most important day of my life—wonderful, perfect, and entirely horrifying—but the most important. Standing in the middle of the McDonald's parking lot and watching the taillights of Elizabeth's car disappear, I'd been hit with so many emotions that I couldn't discern them all.

For the first time, I really understood what I'd missed. I hadn't been there when my child was born, had no idea what she looked like as a baby, hadn't witnessed her first steps, her first words.

I'd missed birthdays and holidays, years of love, and certainly plenty of heartache.

I *missed* Elizabeth.

God, I missed Elizabeth.

Sleep eluded me that night as I dealt with the anger, all of it directed at me. Lizzie had undone me that day, and once she'd loosed the regret that I'd kept bottled inside for years, I could not hold it back any longer.

My soul mourned for what it had lost, for every day I had lived without them, for every moment wasted, for time that could not be reclaimed.

I'd buried my face in my pillow as I thought of Elizabeth and the pain I had caused her and what she must have felt.

Shame.

I'd felt it before, but that night it devoured me. By the time the sun broke through the night, I'd accepted that I could never do anything to erase those mistakes.

They had marred our lives, sending them on a course they never should have gone.

The only power I had was in today, and I was determined to live every day for Lizzie and

Elizabeth.

Even if Elizabeth never forgave me, I would live for her.

That didn't mean I'd forgotten what my mother had told me. Elizabeth needed time to deal with my return, time to figure out where I would fit into their lives.

I started by asking for *seven fifteen*.

When I called at seven fifteen on Sunday evening, Elizabeth had answered, sounding irritated, icy.

But at least she'd answered. I'd take what I could get.

I'd only offered a quick, unreturned, "Hi," and asked if I could speak with Lizzie to ask her what she wanted for her birthday.

As strong as the urge was to apologize again and to try to talk to Elizabeth, I'd realized my words were never going to mean anything to her until I showed her I really meant them.

Of course, I wanted to know what Lizzie wanted for her birthday, but it was really just an excuse to call.

The disquiet I'd felt the entire day in her absence was put to ease with the sound of her voice, giggling as she sang, "Hi, Daddy," into the phone, her words a warm embrace.

When I'd called the next day at the same time, Elizabeth had seemed just as irritated but maybe less surprised. By the third night, Lizzie answered, squealing, "Daddy," into the phone.

The amount of love that surged through me each time I heard her voice was shocking, more than I'd ever imagined possible.

I spent those calls listening to her, learning her, knowing her. Through them, I also gleaned information about Elizabeth, small tidbits that answered some of my questions and others that only gave rise to more. I never asked, but whatever Lizzie offered, I was all too happy to accept.

Seven fifteen Lizzie could count on, whether I was alone on the balcony of my condo, staring out at the bay, or if it drew me from a board meeting—it was our time.

My breath caught in my throat when I turned onto their street and saw the number of cars lining it. Pink balloons tied to a mailbox flapped in the breeze, confirmation for partygoers that they had come to the right place.

A shaky feeling swept through me when I stepped from my car and heard the sounds of children playing and adult conversations coming from Elizabeth's backyard. I pulled the four presents from the trunk of my car and attempted to balance them with one hand while I swept the other hand through my hair in another futile attempt to calm my nerves.

Ringing the doorbell, I felt my chest tighten with

excitement and dread.

I shifted uncomfortably while I waited unsure of who I would face first. When the door swung open, I looked around the stack of presents I had balanced in front of me.

The smile on the woman's face melted into a hardened scowl. I recognized her as Sarah, Elizabeth's older sister, though I'd only seen her in pictures.

The two bore a remarkable resemblance. The only difference was the five years and probable twenty pounds Sarah had over Elizabeth, though neither of those things made her any less attractive.

I offered a feeble smile.

She narrowed her eyes and stepped back against the wall. She crossed her arms over her chest and allowed me inside without a welcome.

I grimaced and dropped my eyes to the floor as I stepped over the threshold.

This was going to be uncomfortable.

"Everyone's out back," she mumbled.

I offered a meek, "Thank you," that remained unreturned.

Shifting the packages in my arms, I took in my surroundings and grinned.

Elizabeth.

The place screamed it. It was warm and cluttered and messy.

In the middle of the room sat a cozy brown

couch with fuzzy blankets draped over the back and large pillows thrown randomly against it.

A toy box overflowed, spilling toys out onto the carpet.

Framed pictures sat on every shelf and table, mingled with the books on the large bookshelf in the corner, and covered the walls that led upstairs.

I wanted to study each one to discover Lizzie at every age.

Instead, I forced myself to follow the noise from the backyard. I walked through the small living room and the archway that led into the kitchen.

A sliding glass door sat wide open to the party happening just outside.

I took a deep breath, tried to convince myself I could do this, and stepped through the doorway.

"Daddy!" Lizzie screamed over the roaring volume of voices.

Silence washed over the gathering. Guests trailed off mid-sentence as they turned to look, or rather, glare at me—everyone except the precious child who threw herself around my leg, hugging me. I smiled at her, dropping to my knee to pull her into a one-armed hug as I continued to balance the packages in the other.

I nearly melted when I saw what she wore.

"Hi, sweetheart." I kissed her dark, silken hair, careful to avoid the adorable tiara she wore.

"Happy birthday."

"I'm so happy you came, Daddy."

For a moment, I forgot she was a five-year-old child. There was so much emotion in her words and maturity in her tone as if my presence was a validation of trust and she understood my heart.

I could only pray she did.

"Me too," I said to reassure her, hugging her to me again. "Me too."

I patted her back before releasing her. She grinned and then raced to rejoin the group of children running and playing on the grass.

Me too.

Even if it meant enduring the quiet hostility that had settled over the small group of adults in Elizabeth's backyard, it was worth it.

They stood straighter, backs rigid, taking a protective stance. I didn't even want to begin to imagine what these people thought about me, though I couldn't blame them.

If our positions had been reversed, I was sure I would feel exactly the same way.

Averting my gaze, I busied myself by searching for the gift table. I placed the packages on it, stalling a moment before I turned back to face the awkwardness of the situation.

Everyone had returned to their conversations, though they now spoke in hushed whispers that I could only assume had much to do with me.

Palpable tension clung to the air, the festivity dampened by my presence.

I warred against the need to justify myself to these people, to explain my intentions, and to apologize. Words meant nothing, I reminded myself.

I had to earn that forgiveness, and that forgiveness could really only come through one person—Elizabeth.

She'd ignored my arrival. Her back was turned to me as she spoke quietly to a couple I didn't recognize, and she acted as if she hadn't noticed the shift in the mood—pretended it meant nothing—that I meant nothing.

I found reprieve in a plastic chair at the far corner of the yard where I sank out of view and watched Lizzie play. She ran in and out of the house, the children playing a game of chase, all of them squealing and laughing as they moved in a pack.

I leaned my elbows on my knees, straining to get a better look as they wove through tables, chairs, and in between the adults where they stood talking.

Lizzie's face glowed, happiness pouring from her as she raced around the yard.

So beautiful.

My child.

Never had I imagined that loving someone could hurt so much.

I did my best to keep from staring at Elizabeth, but there were times I couldn't help but search for her, to watch as she chatted with her family and friends, her hands animated and her laugh free, pure honey, thick and warm—sweet.

When she'd feel the intensity of my eyes upon her, she would immediately tense, but she still never turned to meet my gaze.

So wrapped up in the woman in front of me, I jumped when the chair beside me shifted.

Shit.

Matthew.

He sat back, and from a distance, he would have appeared calm, though I knew he was anything but. His jaw twitched from muscles held taut in restraint.

What felt like an hour passed as we sat in silence, neither acknowledging the other while tension ricocheted between us.

When at last he spoke, his voice was low, indignant. His nostrils flared as he forced heavy, controlled breaths through his nose. "You've got a lot of fuckin' nerve, man."

Stiffening, I fought off the instinct to become defensive.

The group of children came barreling back outside, all of them chasing Lizzie who laughed harder than I'd ever seen.

I watched her, allowing her to remind me of

why I was her, relaxing as that knowledge soothed me, calmed me.

Matthew laughed, cynical and sarcastic, when he caught me staring at Lizzie. "Did you know you almost got your way?" Matthew gestured to her with his head as she ran by.

His statement tore my attention from Lizzie. "What?"

"You have no idea what Elizabeth went through while you went on living your cushy little life, do you?" He pressed his clenched fists into his thighs, his anger barely constrained. "How she struggled every day, how she sacrificed . . . how she almost lost that child because of what you did."

All the blood drained from my face. I felt lightheaded, faint with visions of Elizabeth suffering, the idea of Lizzie not being a part of this world a sick delusion.

And I had wanted it, *demanded* it.

I gripped the back of my neck, struck by searing guilt.

"And now she finally has her life together, and you waltz back into it like it's your God-given right," Matthew said with a tone that held a hint of a growl, each word delivering a blow directly to my gut.

But I took it, deserved it—needed it. I needed to know what I'd done.

Elizabeth's laughter carried in our direction. I

looked at her, pained and sickened with the realization that I'd wronged her so severely. I was sure the surface of that wrong hadn't even been scratched. It seemed that at every turn, I learned I'd only cut her deeper than I could have imagined.

So much for unfounded nobility, so much for the fairy tale I'd painted in my mind, one I now realized I'd conjured only to make myself feel better.

Matthew's lip trembled as he swallowed and dug his fists deeper into his legs. "I don't know what your game is, but you need to know I will do whatever it takes to protect them. Do you understand what I'm telling you?"

"What do you want me to say, Matthew?" My voice came out raspy, regret laced with frustration. "That I'm sorry? Because I will if it makes you feel better, but that's not going to change anything that I did in the past."

He snapped, turning to me in what seemed to be disbelief. "You think I want an apology?" He shook his head, looking incredulous. "What I want is for you to stay out of their lives."

"Well, that's not going to happen," I shot back harder and faster than I'd anticipated.

Matthew needed to understand that I was not playing some game and there was no way in hell he would keep me from Lizzie.

He narrowed his eyes. "If you really care about

them, you'll stay out of their lives."

I wanted to laugh because he was feeding me the same bullshit line I'd fed myself for the last five years—to the day.

"I'm not going anywhere, Matthew." I kept my voice low and determined, but free of contempt.

Matthew might hate me, but he had been there when I hadn't, and my daughter adored him.

Without fail, Lizzie had mentioned him in every call we'd shared this week. The bottom line was I respected him, and my actions had given him no reason to return the favor.

I accepted that.

He hesitated, dubious, before his expression hardened and he stood to hover over me. "Hurt them and I swear to God I'll make you pay for it."

I saw his threat for what it was—a desperate attempt to protect two people he loved, a threat no sane man would ever make good on. I could have easily thrown it back in his face.

Instead, I nodded in submissive understanding, knowing I'd never give him a reason to consider it.

He bobbed his head, curt and with what seemed to be a sense of satisfaction, before he turned and joined the very young woman who I now knew to be his wife.

How Matthew had ended up with Elizabeth's cousin remained a mystery.

When Lizzie had gone on about her Uncle

Maffew and Auntie Natalie, I'd burned with curiosity, wishing I could come right out and ask about it. Somehow, I knew Matthew and Elizabeth had been together, but for one reason or another had ended up only as friends—or whatever they were.

Seeing Matthew and Elizabeth interact was like watching an overprotective brother worrying over a little sister.

I sank further into the chair and forced myself to relax while observing the people who were here because they loved my daughter.

The yard was small enough to overhear names. Some names I recognized from stories Elizabeth had told me and I recognized some faces from pictures.

There were also the unknown, small children and friends who had become a part of Elizabeth's life after I'd left.

It had probably been close to seven years since I'd seen Linda, Elizabeth's mother.

Her face and hands were worn from years of hard work, but her eyes were gentle as she watched her family from where she sat on the patio under the awning.

She'd always struck me as cautious, slow to trust, but having loved with everything she had when she did.

To Elizabeth she'd been a hero, a rock.

Elizabeth's older sister, Sarah, worked ceaselessly, flitting in and out of the kitchen with bowls of food while her husband, Greg, manned the barbecue.

Their little sister, Carrie, stayed at Natalie's side, the two in constant conversation, laughing and giggling with their elbows hooked as if they were the best of friends.

And then there was Elizabeth. It was useless to try to keep from watching her. I sensed her every move, so I finally gave up and gave in.

My eyes trailed her as she mingled with her guests, her smile wide and gracious as she welcomed each one, thankful for their presence.

I knew she could feel me, conscious of watchful eyes.

Being near her stirred me—my love and guilt and desire—emotions that left my heart heavy and my legs weak.

It hurt.

I had to remind myself that anything I felt now could only pale in comparison to what I had put Elizabeth through.

Self-pity would only serve to discount my own actions.

Knowing that wasn't enough to stop the surge of jealousy I felt toward *him*—Scott.

He was the same man who had told me to leave the bank that day I'd shown up at Elizabeth's work, the one who I heard her call out to as he stepped through her door, the one who continually reached for her.

They were light touches, small caresses from hands that clearly wanted more.

I found myself thanking God when she returned none of them but put space between them in an almost indiscernible way, in a way likely only noticed by Scott and me.

It filled me with relief, which I realized only made me all the more pathetic, taking comfort in the hope that Elizabeth was alone.

I wondered if I could ever stop being a selfish asshole.

"Burgers are ready!" Greg made the announcement, and the small group of people broke apart, falling into line with their smiles wide as they filled their plates.

The thought of a burger straight off a backyard grill made my mouth water, but I had no intention of eating. It would be far too uncomfortable to expect food when I wasn't even welcome, though I shouldn't have been surprised when Lizzie stood before me, her small hands clutching a plate extended in offering.

"Are you hungry, Daddy?" Kind blue eyes looked up at me, perceptive and aware.

I gulped down the awe and nodded. "Thank you, sweetheart."

She graced me in that same consuming smile when I accepted her gift, tiny teeth exposed, dimples drawn, leaving my heart in my throat as I watched her dance away and take her place at the small children's table.

I ate my meal in my sheltered corner, though not alone as I felt Lizzie's spirit linger at my side. It was almost too much to be showered in her undeserved love.

Once the food had been eaten and plates set aside, Elizabeth, Natalie, and Carrie brought Lizzie's gifts over and placed them around her on the grass.

Lizzie bounced with excitement.

In admiration, I watched as my five-year-old daughter took time to have her mother read each card to her. She opened her gifts carefully and thanked whoever she'd received it from.

Her surprise was genuine as she unwrapped each one, never expecting anything, but gracious to have received it.

Elizabeth had raised the most incredible child, so humble, so appreciative.

Lizzie's eyes went wide when she opened the largest box I'd given her.

A doll.

She'd asked for a doll, which had turned out to be a more difficult request than I'd imagined.

There were hundreds of them at the store, and

I'd been thankful when the young employee had helped me select one.

The doll was lifelike, handmade, and had long black hair and blue eyes. As soon as the woman had shown it to me, I'd known it was perfect, even though I'd had to pry my jaw off the floor when I'd found out how much it cost.

The look on Lizzie's face told me it was well worth it.

She unwrapped the other gifts from me, each a different accessory for the doll, each a piece the saleswoman insisted she would love.

When the other boxes had been opened, Lizzie rose and raced across the lawn and into my lap, throwing her small arms around my neck. "Thank you, Daddy! I love her!"

I held her to me, murmuring against her head, "You're welcome, sweetheart. Happy birthday."

She sat back, her smile so wide it stretched over her entire face.

My heart felt as if it would burst against my chest.

I would do anything to see that smile.

I reached out and pushed back a lock of hair that had fallen into her eyes, my smile soft. "I love you, precious girl."

"I love you too, Daddy."

She hugged me again, hard, and then scooted off my lap and ran to finish opening the rest of her gifts.

I lifted my head and caught everyone staring at me.

All of them were quick to avert their attention back to Lizzie who started to open the last of her presents—all except for Elizabeth's mother.

Her expression was unreadable but intense and probing. I shifted in discomfort. If there was one person here besides Elizabeth and Lizzie who I'd let down, it was Linda.

I would never forget the last time I'd seen her, when she'd pulled me aside and made me promise her that I'd never break her daughter's heart.

In a heartbeat, I'd sworn that I never would.

When Lizzie had thanked everyone a final time for her gifts, Elizabeth announced it was time for cake. Everyone gathered around the table, including myself.

Unable to resist, I pulled out my phone and recorded Lizzie as she grinned ear to ear, her eyes darting around to the people who loved her as they sang "Happy Birthday."

She sucked in a deep breath before blowing out all five candles in one fell swoop while everyone clapped and called out, "Make a wish."

Elizabeth's face was indescribable as she celebrated with her daughter, full of life and so much love.

I saw joy and no evidence of the pain I had

caused her. I stared a beat too long, and Elizabeth caught my eye.

Her happiness drained, despondency taking its place.

Shame urged me to look away, but I held fast.

For a moment we were caught in each other, verging on something familiar, longing obscured by years of separation.

She blinked rapidly, breaking our connection, her hand shaking as she took a knife to slice into Lizzie's cake.

I coerced myself back to my corner while thick, pink pieces of cake were passed out on even pinker plates.

Natalie stopped in front of me, arm extended. "Cake?"

I raised a brow, caught off guard before shrugging and accepting the small plate. "Thanks." I offered a very cautious smile.

Her smile was wide as she plopped into the chair her husband had occupied earlier.

My smile faded as I prepared for attack.

"So, how are you holding up?"

I frowned. Was she really asking me how I was doing?

"Uhhh?" was about all I could manage, confused.

She chuckled, the sound warm in her throat. "That bad, huh?"

I shook my head and laughed under my breath at the unexpected exchange. "Nah. I'm just thankful to be here."

She took a bite of cake and murmured, "Hmm."

I turned and tried to read her, to search for her intent. Her face was soft, free of displeasure as warm, brown eyes smiled back at me.

In an instant, I was taken back six years to the tender sweetness of Elizabeth.

Kindness.

Natalie radiated it.

For a moment, I looked away and gathered my courage before turning back to her.

"Listen, I'm really sorry about what happened at the store a couple of weeks ago." I winced at the memory, the blatant terror in her eyes when I'd faced her in the parking lot.

I swallowed, needing to explain myself. "I just saw her . . . and . . . *I knew.*" I shook my head with regret. "I didn't mean to scare you."

She grimaced but shrugged one shoulder. "Yeah, you scared the hell out of me. I love that little girl so much. I'd do anything to protect her."

She glanced at Lizzie and then back to me, her expression serious. "But now that I know who you are, I . . ."

She pressed her lips together as if she were debating what to say. "I get it."

Did she really understand?

She must have seen the desperation in my face, because sympathy fell across her own. "I believe you."

"You believe . . . what?" I asked.

"That you love her . . . love them." She motioned to where Lizzie and Elizabeth sat on the grass, sharing a piece of cake. She looked back at me, searching my face. "You do, don't you?"

"Yeah," I whispered. "I do."

She gave me a curt nod. "Good. Then don't mess this up."

I ran my hand through my hair, trying to make sense of this conversation.

Two hours ago, her husband had all but threatened to kill me and she seemed to be encouraging me.

She grinned at my confusion, scooped her last piece of cake into her mouth, and hopped up. "See you around?" she prodded, her brow raised.

I nodded and repeated what I'd told her husband earlier. "I'm not going anywhere."

Satisfaction spread across her face, and she extended her hand. Tentative, I reached out and shook it. "Well then, it's nice to finally meet you, Christian Davison."

She breezed across the lawn, leaving me shaking my head, baffled to find such an unlikely ally, but thankful nonetheless.

The party wound down and friends filtered out,

saying their goodbyes and thank yous.

I lingered.

I didn't want to say goodbye.

When the last of Lizzie's guests had left and only Matthew and Natalie remained, I reluctantly stood and made my way across the lawn. Lizzie sat in the grass playing with the doll I had given her.

I crouched down to run my hand through her soft hair. "I have to go now, sweetheart."

Lizzie saddened. "Already?"

Apparently, she didn't want me to say goodbye either.

Smiling, I settled down in the grass next to her, pulling her onto my lap and into my arms. I hugged her to me. "Yes, my angel, I have to go."

She hugged me tighter, and from her mouth came a whispered plea. "Will you come back?"

I choked on her fear.

I pulled back, looking her in the eye. "Yes, Lizzie, I'll be back. I promise."

Glancing up, I caught Elizabeth watching us from inside the kitchen window, her wounds prominent in the lines across her forehead.

"I promise," I said again as I buried my face against the side of Lizzie's head.

I had to force myself to stand, to turn my back, and to leave my little girl sitting in the middle of her yard. My feet were heavy as they entered the kitchen of the small house.

My steps faltered when I came upon Elizabeth.

She stood with her back to me. Her hands were flat against the kitchen counter and her breathing was audible as she stared out at Lizzie through the window.

"Thank you, Elizabeth," I whispered.

She whimpered, her voice a quiet rasp. "Please, don't hurt her."

All the air left me.

"I won't." *Never.*

Her body trembled as a quiet sob escaped. "What do you want, Christian?"

What did I want?

To make her smile, to wipe away her tears, to hold her.

To be a father, a real father, not one in title, but one who'd earned that right.

I wanted to stay.

"I want my family," I forced through the lump in my throat.

Elizabeth went rigid, her hands digging into the counter for support, her words sharp. "Get out of my house."

I swallowed down my pain, the fear that I might never receive forgiveness, and nodded.

"Okay," I said quietly as I turned to leave.

I hesitated in the archway, looking back over my shoulder. "But I'm coming back."

eight

*F*riday had always been a day I looked forward to, filled with anticipation for the weekend ahead and excitement for time spent with my daughter.

Now it was a day of dread.

I glanced at the digital clock on the microwave.

Only fifteen more minutes.

Plunging my hands into the soapy water, I tried to focus on the task in front of me instead of how much I hated this, but a mindless job like washing dishes wasn't enough to cover up the ache in my heart.

Sharing my daughter was torture.

The day after Lizzie's birthday, Christian had called at seven fifteen just as he had every night the week before and every day since.

He'd asked to speak to me after telling Lizzie goodbye. He wanted to know when he could see her next, and more specifically, he wanted a day of his own.

The man had the audacity to ask me for Saturdays.

Saturdays were *mine*, a day without interruption for my daughter and me, just the two of us.

There was no way I'd concede to that.

Instead, I'd given him Friday evenings.

So for the last two months, Christian had shown up at my doorstep every Friday at six to pick Lizzie up and had dropped her off at the same place at eight.

He had two hours.

To me, even that was too much.

He deserved no time at all.

The worst part of it was how much Lizzie always looked forward to those nights with Christian, how excited she would become as she watched the clock near six.

She never questioned whether he would show or not; she expected him to, trusted him to.

And I was left waiting on the sidelines to pick up the pieces *when* he didn't.

It sucked.

I loaded the dishwasher and wiped down the counters, preparing myself to face Christian. Just those few minutes at my stoop exchanging "our" daughter were excruciating.

Two minutes later, the doorbell rang.

Taking a deep breath, I dried my hands and tossed the hand towel aside, wending my way to the front door.

Glancing through the peephole, I unlocked the door and swung it wide to Lizzie and Christian standing on the stoop.

"Hi, Mommy." Lizzie grinned up at me, her hair in pigtails and her eyes alive. She clutched her doll to her side, that outrageous toy that must have cost a fortune, the one she never went anywhere without.

"Hi, sweetheart." I smiled down at her, refusing to begrudge the joy my daughter found in her father. "Did you have a good time?"

She glanced back at Christian and smiled wide before looking back at me and nodding. "Yep. Daddy took me to the park and we had a picnic."

I covered my grimace and forced out, "That sounds like fun, honey."

My eyes flitted to Christian.

His hands were stuffed deep in the pockets of his slacks, his tie discarded, the first two buttons of his white dress shirt undone.

His hair that had been styled when he'd shown

up at my house earlier was now in disarray, locks of hair obscuring the vibrant blue of one of his eyes.

He was gorgeous. And I hated him for it.

I turned my attention back to Lizzie, gesturing to her father with my head. "It's time to tell your dad goodnight, Lizzie."

Her face fell along with my heart. It was agonizing, watching her tell Christian goodbye, how she clung to him, their whispered words of love and promises of how they would miss each other until they saw each other again.

Christian kissed her on the head once more before releasing his hold on her and nudging her toward the door. "Goodnight, my princess."

"Night, Daddy."

I closed my eyes, wishing I didn't have to witness this. "Lizzie, go on upstairs. I'll be there in a minute to get your bath started."

"Okay, Momma." Lizzie mounted the stairs as Christian and I watched her go, and then I slowly turned back to him.

This part always felt so awkward, especially in light of the declaration he'd made on Lizzie's birthday.

I'd known what he meant, his intention.

He wanted me back.

I had spent a fleeting moment fantasizing about being in his arms again before my rational side had screamed at me for being a fool, and I had demanded that he leave my house.

He'd never stepped inside since.

"Goodnight, Christian." In his case, I'd given myself over to feigned pleasantries.

He stared at his feet before looking back at me as he ran a hand through his hair, a nervous habit of his I hadn't forgotten. "Listen, Elizabeth . . ."

I braced myself. This was it.

My mind raced with what I would tell my daughter, how I would comfort her.

He scratched the back of his head, shuffling his feet, before he grimaced and said in a rushed voice, "I need a favor."

I scowled, sitting back on my heels and crossing my arms. He wasn't leaving. He was asking for more.

Damn him.

"What?"

He released a heavy breath from his nose, his expression hopeful. "My mother is coming into town next weekend, and I was hoping we could take Lizzie to Sea World on Saturday?"

I shook my head. "You know Saturday is my day with Lizzie, Christian. Why can't you take her during the week?"

As if I would make concessions for his mother, that shallow, pretentious woman who'd done no more than look down her nose at me.

And God knew Christian could afford to take the day off.

"Because my mom isn't getting in until late Friday night, and she has to leave Sunday to get back to work. It's the only day we can go," he explained as if it made complete sense where it made none.

That woman had never worked a day in her life. I didn't realize I was frowning in confusion until Christian spoke.

"Yes, Elizabeth, my mother works," he said, sounding mildly irritated. "She and my father divorced five years ago."

"Really?" I asked, surprised.

The question had escaped me before I could reel it in.

I don't care about him or what his family does, I reminded myself.

But really, I was a little curious.

Claire Davison working? The woman who put on airs, who walked around as if her social life were the most important thing in the world?

The thought was comical.

Christian chuckled, his eyes glinting amusement. "Shocking, isn't it?"

"Yeah." Why I answered, I didn't know.

His voice softened. "She's not who you think she is, Elizabeth."

I shook my head, wishing to divert the line of

conversation that drew me into his personal life, getting back to what mattered—the precious time I had to spend with my daughter.

"Saturdays are mine, Christian." The words were soft, but firm.

He sighed and for a moment looked away before his eyes darted back at me, determined. "Come with us."

What? I couldn't imagine anything as tortuous as spending an entire day with him and his mother.

He took a step forward, dipping his head to capture my gaze. "Please, Elizabeth."

My heart sped with his nearness, the warmth of his presence washing over my face and through my chest to where it settled somewhere in the pit of my stomach.

Dangerous.

"Um . . . I . . ." I fumbled over the words, searching for an excuse.

"Please, Elizabeth. Just one day." His voice dropped lower as he begged, "Please . . . come."

The intensity of his eyes shattered my resolve. "Fine."

Gratitude filled his face, his mouth quirking into a small, satisfied smile. "Thank you." His face was so beautiful and appeared so sincere.

I wished I could believe it.

In an attempt to resurrect the wall between us, I stepped back and away from the claws that I felt him slowly, steadily sinking into my skin.

I whispered, "Just this once."

His smile didn't falter. "Okay then, I'll pick you two up at nine next Saturday."

Pursing my lips, I nodded once before I shut the door and shut him out.

I turned to find Lizzie's face pressed through two bars of railing at the top of the stairs, her smile unending.

Closing my eyes, I shook my head, wondering what I had just done.

Lizzie sat on her knees in a pink t-shirt and denim shorts, her feet in white sandals, watching out the front window.

Her small backpack was secured over her shoulders, her doll secured in the crook of her arm.

She had been there for almost a half an hour, and it wasn't even eight thirty yet.

She'd woken me before dawn by jumping on my bed, yelling in excitement for me to get up. I'd buried my face deeper in my pillow, loathe to face the day.

Christian had picked her up yesterday evening at six just the same as always, only this time Lizzie accompanied him to the airport so she could meet her *Grammy*.

That's what Lizzie had called her.

She went on about the woman for more than an hour after Christian had dropped her off at my door well after nine thirty last night.

Grammy.

The woman who had never shown any interest in Lizzie, had never called, had never once tried to contact us.

Grammy.

It was enough to make me see red.

Dressed in shorts and a t-shirt, I stepped into a pair of flip-flops and pulled my hair into a messy ponytail, then stuffed a towel, sunscreen, and sweatshirts into my backpack.

Lizzie loved Sea World, and we'd been enough times to know she'd get wet and cold.

"All ready, Mommy?" Lizzie looked back at me from where she was perched on the floor, her small body buzzing with anticipation.

I forced myself to smile back. "Yes, baby. I'm all ready."

As much as I dreaded this day, I would never let Lizzie know it.

I flitted around the house, straightening up in an attempt to thwart the panic setting in.

How will I get through a day with Christian and his mother?

She'd always disliked me. The few times we'd met, she'd never said much, offering no more than a cool hello, though her calculating eyes had watched.

I could only assume the horrible things she thought about me, things Christian's father had never hesitated to say aloud.

Gold Digger, Richard had called me, and she'd never disagreed.

It had hurt.

The only thing I'd ever wanted from Christian was his love, his commitment, but never his money.

Jumping up, Lizzie squealed, "Daddy's here!"

She struggled to reach the lock, unlatching it just as the doorbell rang. She threw herself into Christian's open arms, and he scooped her up.

"Good morning, baby girl." He looked over her shoulder at me as he hugged her close. "Good morning, Elizabeth."

"Good morning," I mumbled as I grabbed my backpack and purse and headed toward the door.

Christian put Lizzie back on her feet and took her hand.

I swallowed hard, feeling my face heat with my thoughts.

I swore he was doing it on purpose, the way he wore his black t-shirt taut over the obvious definition of his chest and stomach, his dark jeans slung low on his hips.

Forcing my eyes closed, I fought to remember what I felt when I'd left his apartment that final time, what he had said, opening them to remember why I hated this man.

I squared my shoulders and strode toward the door with my resolve firmly set in place.

As Christian and Lizzie walked hand-in-hand down the sidewalk, I locked the door, bracing myself for the anger I knew would come when I came face-to-face with Christian's mother.

I took the ten steps down the sidewalk and froze when I rounded the corner to the driveway.

Claire stood in front of Christian's car with Lizzie in her arms, her face buried in Lizzie's neck. Claire looked up, tears glistening in her eyes, a mixture of joy and pain on her face.

Instantly, a lump formed in my throat.

How could she hold my daughter like that after she'd rejected her all these years? I didn't understand this, any of it—Christian, his mother, how *I* felt, the sympathy that surged through me when I saw Claire's face. I didn't want to care.

With what seemed like great reluctance, Claire set Lizzie down. I stiffened as she approached me.

Her hair had grayed but shimmered in the tight ponytail she wore it in, her face virtually unmarred from wrinkles; the few around her eyes and mouth were subtle and soft.

Her eyes were just as blue as Christian's, just as intense, just as warm.

She was beautiful, incredibly so, but in an

entirely different way than I remembered. The conceit was gone, in its place a gentleness that I'd never associated with this woman.

She stopped two feet away from me, seeming unsure. Her bottom lip trembled when she said, "Thank you, Elizabeth." She stepped forward, grabbing my limp hand and squeezing it. "Thank you."

I shook my head in misunderstanding and took a small step back. I was not sure whether I was willing to accept her thanks.

Her mouth fell into a small, sad smile, and she squeezed my hand again before she dropped it and turned away.

Christian was buckling Lizzie into a booster seat in the backseat on the driver's side of his car, the two of them raving about how excited they were.

Christian had never been to Sea World and he deemed Lizzie his tour guide, tickling her as he made her promise to show him all of her favorite things.

Claire laughed and joined in on their banter as she climbed into the front passenger seat.

Sucking in a deep breath, I forced myself to walk around to the opposite side of the car to take my place next to Lizzie.

I slunk down into the black leather seats, feeling the most uncomfortable I'd ever felt in my life.

I didn't belong here.

Lizzie didn't belong here.

We'd been thrown aside, and now here we were, giving ourselves over to Christian's mercy. It was so wrong.

How I wished I could take back the decision I'd made to allow him to see Lizzie in the first place. He would have given up by now, and Lizzie and I would be living the quiet life I'd built for us, not waiting for the bottom to drop out of it.

In silence, I listened as Christian, Claire, and Lizzie chattered nonstop.

Claire asked Lizzie countless questions about her life, what she liked, what she didn't like. Claire sat sideways in her seat, her attention focused on my child and her son.

The hardest to hear were the stories she told Lizzie of Christian when he was a child.

Adoration radiated from her as she described a curious little boy, how inquisitive he had been and the trouble it had continually gotten him in.

Claire would reach out and caress Christian's shoulder or his forearm and sometimes even held his hand.

I stared at them, unable to comprehend what was happening in front of me. It was as if she wasn't even the same woman.

The woman I *had* known, Christian had been little more than indifferent to and I'd all but despised her, believing in my heart that she didn't even love her own child.

But now—

I shook my head, embarrassed when I caught Christian's eye in the rearview mirror when I did so, even though I couldn't look away.

He smiled softly, as if he were reiterating that she wasn't who I thought she was, that she was wonderful and lovely and that I shouldn't try to stop the fondness for her building up within me.

I tore my attention away, forcing it out the window to the world happening outside this car because it was impossible to bear what was happening inside.

I wiped the tears that began to run down my face, tears of frustration for being thrown into the midst of this reunion, tears of anger that it was happening now, five years late, and worst of all, tears of relief shed for the knowledge that Christian's mother loved him.

Those tears scared me most.

Twenty minutes later, we pulled into the vast parking lot of Sea World, already overflowing with cars.

The three of them scrambled out. I stalled, taking my time to adjust my backpack while I tried to get myself together.

The cool morning mist had begun to dissipate, and bright rays of sunlight broke through, warming my skin.

If we were here under any other circumstances, I would have thought this was the perfect day to spend here.

"Mommy, are you coming?" Lizzie yelled over her shoulder, looking back at me from where Claire and Christian had her flanked, a hand in each of theirs and standing about fifty feet away.

Nodding, I slung my backpack over my shoulders. "Right behind you."

Christian grinned in what could only be construed as pure excitement, while Claire gazed back somewhat sympathetically as if she knew how hard this was on me, though I was sure no one else could understand the kind of torture this would be.

I stayed at least ten steps behind them, careful to keep a distance. Lizzie squealed with delight as they traveled across the parking lot.

Christian and Claire swung her into the air every few steps. Their laughter rang out, high and low, melodious—joyous—a stark contrast to the resentment I felt inside.

I couldn't believe Christian was carrying on as if this were *normal*, as if I belonged here with them, as if he hadn't bulldozed me into suffering through this day.

We fell in line at the ticket booth, the three of them still hand-in-hand while I kept a small amount of space between us.

Christian stepped forward, next in line, passing a

credit card through the window. "Three adults and one child."

"Christian, no," I said, snaking around him to give my debit card to the woman.

"Elizabeth." His voice managed to hiss and plead at the same time. "Just let me pay. Please."

I shook my head in stubborn petulance. "I don't want your money, Christian."

Darkness clouded his expression, and he lowered his voice, inclining his head toward me. "I know, Elizabeth, you never have. You never even asked for what was yours."

Disarmed by the sadness I saw in his eyes, I found myself too shocked to resist any longer. I stepped back and self-consciously tucked my card back into my shorts pocket, terrified at how easily he'd just persuaded me.

Christian handed each of us a ticket. I accepted mine somewhat reluctantly, my attention directed to the ground as I muttered, "Thanks," under my breath, wishing not to owe him my gratitude.

I glanced up to find him staring, his lips pursed, pensive. He opened his mouth as if to speak but closed it and jerked his attention away.

"You ready, sweetheart?" Christian reached for Lizzie, the fervor back in his voice, though it sounded somewhat forced.

"Yep!" Lizzie accepted his hand, skipping beside him as they bounded toward the gates.

Disinclination weighed down my feet, and I trudged along behind them, grunting at the man who accepted my ticket and wished me a good day.

That would be impossible.

I spent the morning as an intruder in their trinity, in the outskirts of their pleasure. Christian met each exhibit with unadulterated wonder, as a child in awe.

I kept up my reluctant pursuit as they wandered through habitats, observed them as they marveled at sharks and dolphins and whales with sheer fascination. But their captivation with their surroundings paled in comparison to the enchantment they seemed to find with my little girl.

If it were possible, Christian had not once lost contact with Lizzie. Her hand was continually in his, and when her feet grew tired, he didn't hesitate to swing her onto his back.

Lizzie kept an eye on me to assure that I was never far behind, her precious face urging me near.

Christian cast glances my way, mindful, though he rarely lingered; his attention was focused on my daughter.

"Daddy, this is my very favorite!" Lizzie gushed as we approached the pools, and she rushed forward to stand on her tiptoes to dip her fingers into the water.

Bat rays circled, and Lizzie stroked their backs

as they floated by.

Christian leaned over the pool, his first touch tentative as he reached out, just grazing his fingertips along the edge of a small ray's wing.

He looked at Lizzie and then at me, unable to contain the thrill spilling from his smile.

"This is incredible." He shook his head just as mesmerized as Lizzie was as he sunk his hand into the water, this time running the palm of his hand down the center of the ray's back.

"Aren't they pretty, Daddy?" Lizzie asked, trailing her fingers lightly over the creatures soaring through the water.

Christian ran the back of his hand down her cheek and under her chin, his expression tender.

"Beautiful," he said, clearly speaking only of Lizzie.

I had to turn away, away from what I saw but refused to believe—away from what I'd seen every time he'd been with her.

He couldn't love her.

He just *couldn't*.

She was just a distraction, that's all. This, whatever it was, was unsustainable, fleeting. I had to hold fast to that belief.

Anything else would render us weak, vulnerable, and I couldn't afford to leave myself without adequate defenses.

In my discomfort, the morning passed slowly.

Each minute dragged in measure with my feet.

The four of us ate lunch at a table that was much too small. Extreme effort was spent focusing on my food and not the constant jokes Christian made, Lizzie's laughter infectious as she giggled over the silliness exuded by her father.

He was playful, unabashedly so, making no excuses for the ridiculous faces he made, his only concern to garner a reaction from Lizzie.

He looked so much like the man I once thought him to be.

A smile tugged at the corner of my mouth, one I refused to release. I bit my lip, cursing Christian's ability to wear me down, asking myself, more importantly, why I was allowing him to do it.

Relief swept over me when he finally stood to gather our garbage, piled it on a tray, and walked across the eatery to dispose of it. I was thankful for the moment's respite from his presence.

Christian returned seconds later, brushing off his hands as he asked, "Where to next, Lizzie?"

Lizzie clambered down from her chair, bouncing. "Can we go play in the water now?"

Five minutes later, we approached the play area. Christian and Lizzie had run up ahead, while Claire and I trailed behind in silence.

Lizzie glanced back, her impatient grin urging us to catch up.

"You wanna play, Momma?" she sang out once

we were in earshot.

Never once had I passed up an opportunity to play with my daughter, but in this setting, I couldn't imagine myself romping around alongside Christian.

It was just too *intimate*.

"Um, I think I'm just going to watch you this time, Lizzie. You go on ahead."

Disappointment flashed across her face, and I dropped to a knee in front of her, running an affectionate hand down her arm. "I'll be sitting right there, watching you the whole time. Okay, sweetheart?"

I pointed at a bench under the shade of a tree and forced myself to smile.

She glanced behind her, nodding when she turned back to me. "Okay, Momma."

I breathed a sigh of relief when she agreed. As much as I didn't want to let my daughter down, I was desperate for a few moments to myself to clear my head. I kissed her on the forehead before retreating to the welcomed seclusion of the empty bench.

The solitude didn't last long.

"She's a wonderful child," Claire said as she sat down beside me. "You've done such an amazing job with her."

I cast a sidelong glance. She looked ahead, watching Christian and Lizzie frolicking in the short bursts of water shooting up from the ground.

I nodded, unsure of how to respond or if I even wanted to respond.

Six hours ago, I'd thought Claire Davison to be coldhearted and void of emotion, but now, I could only see her as kind and gentle. I still wasn't sure how to handle that.

Lizzie shrieked, tearing my attention from Claire. Lizzie giggled as she dodged a burst of water. "Catch me, Daddy!"

Christian chased her, his laugh loud and surprised as a stream of water struck him against the side of his face, then again on his chest, soaking his shirt.

Lizzie squealed and danced. "You got all wet, Daddy!"

Christian darted for her, sweeping her from her feet and into his arms. He chuckled and teased, "And now I'm gonna get *you* all wet."

Lizzie kicked her feet, howling with laughter and screaming, "No, Daddy, no," though it was clear she relished every second of it.

My depression grew just watching them. Lizzie had fallen in love with her father, the thing I'd feared most. I had no idea how she would survive once he was gone.

Claire interrupted my torment by uttering softly, "He's a good man, Elizabeth."

I closed my eyes against her words, angry tears

breaking free and running hot down my face.

I had spent the entire day holding in my pain, pretending it didn't hurt to look at him, and I couldn't contain it any longer.

I was so scared, scared of the muddled mess of emotions swirling inside of me, scared of the part of me that wanted to believe he was a *good* man.

"I'm scared." The words slipped from my mouth before I could stop them.

She emitted a sad, slow sigh, her brow bowed in sympathy. "What he did to you was terribly wrong, Elizabeth, and I don't blame you for feeling the way you do. But I think you should know he's regretted every day he's spent without you, every day without his daughter."

I shook my head, my voice sharpened with bitterness and laced with agony. "If he'd really loved me, he would have come back."

She grimaced and nodded, though she wasn't agreeing. "He should have."

"Then why didn't he?" Desperation oozed from me.

She glanced to where Christian and Lizzie played and back at me. "That's something you're going to have to ask him."

She looked back at her son and granddaughter playing, shaking her head.

"I've never understood it myself." Her voice was low, and I was unsure whether she'd meant for me to hear the last part.

"I'm not asking you to forget what he did, Elizabeth, but I *am* asking you to give him a chance to prove himself."

She wasn't saying that she condoned what he'd done, nor did she condemn. She simply supported the son she loved.

Consumed with uncertainty, I watched the man who had crushed me and who still had control of my heart. I wanted to believe what Claire was telling me.

Believe that he'd really loved me, believe that he loved me now—most importantly, that he'd never hurt me again.

I just didn't know if I ever could.

As if she had read my thoughts, Claire patted my hand, understanding thick in her words. "Sometimes forgiveness takes time."

Heaviness settled in my chest, and I found it difficult to speak. "I don't know if I can."

"But you still love him," she said.

I sighed and turned my face away.

Loving Christian was something I'd never admit aloud, something I barely acknowledged in my own head.

Sure, Matthew and Natalie knew, though it remained unspoken between us.

"I see it in the way you look at him," she pressed on in conviction.

My silence could only affirm what she already knew.

Quiet settled over us as we watched Christian and Lizzie play. So much had changed in our years of separation, so much I didn't understand.

Somehow, her heart had softened and expanded while mine had grown hard and cynical. That prominent part of me screamed at how careless I was by exposing my feelings to Christian's mother.

But for a few peaceful moments, I chose to ignore that voice and just absorb the solace lent in her words.

"Thank you," I whispered. I was thanking her for so many things, for the advice I wasn't sure how to handle, for her compassion, for her understanding, for loving my daughter, for loving Christian—maybe even for loving me.

No doubt she'd already bound herself to my heart. Most of all, I was thanking her for showing me people had the ability to change.

Claire's hand tightened over mine, and she shook her head slowly. "No, Elizabeth, thank you."

The arena was packed for the last show of the day, the sky darkened, the air chilled.

We squeezed into a middle row near the top.

We were all worn out, Lizzie especially.

Christian had carried her in his arms for the better part of an hour, and even though we all knew better, Lizzie had insisted she wasn't tired at all and wanted to stay to see the nighttime Shamu show and fireworks.

Obviously, I wasn't the only one she had wrapped around her finger.

Christian settled next to Claire with Lizzie on his lap, and I had no choice but to take the small space beside him.

The afternoon had passed quickly this time as I'd paid purposeful attention to the way Christian interacted with my daughter.

I'd forced myself to not to watch them through betrayed eyes but with an open mind, to see the clear adoration in his face as he watched everything she did, the way his eyes lit up when she spoke, the gentle way in which he held her, just as he did now.

She was curled up on his lap, her eyes drooping in lazy contentment as we waited for the show to begin. She was asleep before the loudspeaker announced the start.

Christian stared down at her, his expression worshipful as he swept her bangs from her eyes, a tender hand ran down the side of her face.

I swallowed the lump in my throat, struggling to accept what my scarred heart warred against.

He loved her.

He tilted his face to mine, his eyes raging, so

many emotions swimming in their depths. "I love her so much, Elizabeth."

So many times, I'd heard him claim it as he told her goodbye, but this was the first time I believed it. He shifted her, cuddling her closer against his chest, turning away to press a kiss on her head.

"So much," he whispered, though this time the words were not intended for me.

I was sure the show was spellbinding, a magical finale that would have filled the wide-eyed crowd with awe, though I wouldn't have known.

Staring unseeing ahead, I was unable to focus on anything but the ardor emanating from the man who sat beside me, cradling my child. As the show ended and gave way to fireworks brightening the sky, I lifted my face to the cool night air, closed my eyes, and for one minute let it all go.

I was so tired of being angry and of living a guarded life.

In that moment, I convinced myself that this constant worry couldn't stop what was happening beside me, and for now, I would let Christian try to be a father.

He might fail, and he might walk away, but I just couldn't fight this any longer.

I would give him that chance to prove himself.

Though I knew Claire had intended more when she'd made that request, I doubted a wound that deep could ever be healed, that I could ever trust enough to risk my heart in that way again.

But as my body was washed in the warmth of his nearness, a part of me wished I could.

———

The ride home was spent in easy silence, and for the first time in nearly three months, I felt something resembling relaxation.

Lizzie had done little more than stir when Christian had transferred her from the cocoon of his arms into her booster seat.

Now I watched as moonlight filtered in through the window and across her face, her fair skin glowing.

A dull thrum of anxiety still echoed in my chest, a reminder of the responsibility that rested on me to keep her safe, and I was sure this uncertainty was something I would never truly be free of.

Christian pulled into my driveway just before eleven.

The neighborhood was quiet as I stepped from his car, both my body and my mind weary. Stretching, I was unable to stifle the yawn that came as I rounded the driver's side of the car.

Christian beat me to it and waited beside Lizzie's opened door.

"May I?" He inclined his head toward Lizzie.

Out of instinct, I almost said no, but instead I stepped back. "Sure."

Taken by surprise, he studied me for a moment before smiling sleepily and ducking his head into the back of his car.

Once again, his movements were gentle, mindful of the sleeping child as he unbuckled her and gathered her into his arms, fumbling as he tried to grab her doll and backpack.

"Here, let me get that." I nudged him aside, reached in, and collected Lizzie's things before I slowly led Christian and Claire up the sidewalk to my front door.

Taking a calming breath, I inserted the key, turned the lock, and pushed the door wide open.

For the first time since Lizzie's birthday, Christian stepped through the threshold and into my home, a fulfillment of the promise he'd made to return.

He stood in the foyer, holding my daughter and appearing, once again, to ask for permission.

With a small amount of reticence, I motioned with my hand toward the staircase. "Her bedroom is the first door on the right."

Christian quickly ascended the stairs, his footsteps light as he disappeared at the landing.

Claire reached out and cupped my face, her touch a grateful whisper.

I nodded against it, allowing a single, frightened tear to slip down my face.

She wiped it away and then hurried to join her

son upstairs.

Muted, soft words floated downstairs. I had no idea how many minutes I stood alone before Christian and Claire finally left Lizzie's room, their leaden steps revealing their reluctance to leave her.

I fidgeted, unsure of what to do with myself in my own home, thrown off kilter by their presence.

Christian moved toward the door, pausing when he stood in front of me, his expression solemn.

"Thank you, Elizabeth." He glanced toward the stairs and then back at me. "This was the best day of my life."

I looked down at my feet, unable to respond.

The day had been too much, and the sorrow that came with his statement nearly brought me to my knees.

He shuffled out the front door, and in his absence, Claire wrapped me in her arms. "Thank you, Elizabeth," she whispered against my ear. "You are an amazing, wonderful girl, and I'm so happy you allowed me to share this day with you."

In confusion and heartbreak, I clutched her to me, weeping quietly against her shoulder.

She shushed me and murmured, "It'll all work out. Just wait, you'll see." She pulled back and took my face in her hands. "You'll see."

She hugged me once more before stepping away and walking out the door.

Sniffling, I wiped my eyes with the back of my

hand, chuckling somewhat nonsensically at the doll I still held. I took it upstairs and tucked it in beside my sleeping daughter.

I kissed Lizzie's cheek and prayed that her grandmother was right.

nine

Something had changed. There had been a shift sometime during that day, the day that had been the most amazing of my life.

It had been a glimpse of what life would have been like had I not thrown it all away.

If *we* had been a family.

Of course, I'd sensed Elizabeth's discomfort, how she'd guarded herself in an attempt to protect herself from me.

But as the day had progressed, I'd felt her soften—thaw.

Relaxing in the damp comfort of the San Diego

evening, watching the beauty exploding in the night sky, surrounded by the three people I loved most, had been surreal, a fantasy I'd had a million times come true.

The warmth of Elizabeth's body beside me had been hypnotizing, and I could focus on nothing other than the perfect weight of my daughter in my arms and the heat radiating from Elizabeth's skin.

It was then that I'd felt the shift as the tension seemed to drain from her, a calm taking its place. I'd chanced a quick glance in her direction.

My breath had caught in my throat. My love for her felt as if it would burst through my chest.

I don't think I could ever forget the expression on her face.

She was so beautiful, and seeing her like that, so peaceful as if she had been freed of a suffocating weight, had brought me such relief.

That relief became overwhelming when she'd welcomed me into her home. Every part of me had wanted to wrap her in my arms, to thank her endlessly for the gift she had given me, trusting me enough to allow me into another part of Lizzie's world—her world.

It meant everything to me.

Obviously, something had transpired between Elizabeth and my mother, even though Mom refused to share it.

She insisted anything Elizabeth may have

confided in her was between the two of them, and with a gentle hand on my arm, she'd encouraged me, once again, to be patient.

And I would.

I'd wait forever for Elizabeth.

Bit by bit she opened up. Last night when I'd picked Lizzie up for our Friday night visit, Elizabeth hadn't vocalized the invitation, but stood aside when she opened the door in silent permission that I'd accepted.

As much as I wanted to, though, I didn't push it. At the end of the night, Lizzie and I said our goodbyes at the door.

I had no idea what to ask of Elizabeth or how far her forgiveness would go. But for now I rested satisfied in knowing I was doing *something* right on the way to gaining back her trust.

Every second she gave was precious.

I just wished the minutes away weren't so lonely.

Hugging the small, square pillow to my chest, I sank deeper into the black leather of my couch.

Restlessness nipped at my nerves as I flipped through channel after channel on the flat screen against the wall, the isolation reminding me again that I was living the wrong life.

It was Saturday night.

I should be with my family.

Sighing, I pointed the remote at the television and clicked it off, deciding to give up on the failed attempt to entertain myself.

I tossed the pillow aside, stood, and stretched my arms overhead, yawning as I made my way to my bedroom.

I shrugged out of my shirt, figuring a hot shower was my best shot at a soothing distraction.

From the other room my phone rumbled against the glass coffee table, buzzing before giving way to its shrill ring. I glanced at the clock on the nightstand.

Eight twenty-three.

I rushed back out to the main room, expecting it to be Mom calling to wish me a goodnight, although part of me hoped that it was Lizzie thinking of me.

I pictured her sweet face pressed to her mother's phone as she called just to say she loved me one more time before her mother tucked her into bed.

I grinned when I saw the caller ID.

Elizabeth's name and number flashed on the screen as the phone vibrated and rang out again.

I grabbed it, sliding my finger across the faceplate just before it went to voicemail.

"Hey, sweetheart." I could feel the force of my smile, thankful for the welcomed surprise.

"Christian . . ."

Sickness gripped me when I heard Elizabeth's voice, panicked and afraid.

"Elizabeth?" Immediately the panic in my voice matched hers. "What's wrong?"

When she spoke, her voice trembled, and I could tell she was crying. "Lizzie fell down the stairs."

Fear clawed up my spine, and I fought against the nausea rushing up my throat with the sick image that flashed through my mind.

I was back in my room and dragging my shirt over my head before I had time to respond. "Is she okay?"

I tried to remain calm and clearheaded, but I knew I was about five seconds from a breakdown. The thought of something happening to Lizzie—I'd never survive.

Elizabeth spoke in quiet distress, whispering, "I think she broke her arm and she has a cut above her eye . . . it won't stop bleeding." She stumbled over the last, choking on her worry, although her news instantly eased my racing nerves.

Lizzie's injuries definitely didn't sound as serious I'd first imagined them to be. I shoved my feet in my shoes and grabbed my keys from my desk.

I had started for the door when Elizabeth began fumbling over earnest words. "I tried to call Matthew, but he didn't answer, and Lizzie won't stop crying, and she keeps asking for you."

Her voice dropped as her unease increased. "Can you come? I don't want to take her to the hospital by myself."

A brief moment of silence fell between us at her request. Her discomfort in asking for my help was clear, but the need of our daughter was so much greater than that.

My condo door slammed closed behind me as I hit the hall and rushed for the elevator.

"I'm already on my way."

Traffic was heavier than I'd hoped, but I still made the short trip to Elizabeth's house faster than I ever had.

The neighborhood was already quiet when I turned onto their street.

Children no longer played on the grassy lawns of their front yards or on the sidewalks. Instead windows glowed as families had taken their activities inside.

I jumped from my car, not bothering to pause to knock when I reached the door.

I threw it open to find Lizzie on Elizabeth's lap where they were huddled on the couch.

Lizzie clutched her left arm protectively to her chest and whimpered while Elizabeth held a damp towel to her head.

"Lizzie," I said as both worry and relief rushed out of me from where I stood in the doorway, still clutching the door handle. My heart ached to see her this way but was thankful it had not been so much worse.

"Daddy." She sniffled but still managed to welcome me with a small smile.

I crossed the room, dropped to my knees in front of her, and brushed back the matted hair stuck to her face. "Oh, sweetheart, are you okay?"

My gaze swept over her, ultimately landing on the towel slowly saturating with blood that Elizabeth had pressed to Lizzie's forehead.

"My arm hurts." She grimaced and hugged her arm closer, her bright eyes wet with tears. The sharp stabbing in my chest made me wonder if it were physically possible to feel someone else's pain.

"I know, baby girl, I know." I smiled sadly and then shifted so I could pick her up. "Come on, let's get you fixed up."

Lizzie's eyes grew wide and she pulled away. For a moment, my heart fell with rejection before she shook her head stubbornly. "No, Daddy, I don't like doctors."

Oh.

I glanced at Elizabeth, her eyes pleading.

Say something.

I scooted closer. I tried to ignore the fact that as I did so, I hovered over Elizabeth, her knees brushing against my chest with every unsteady breath I took.

Instead, I focused on what was important—reassuring my daughter.

"Did you know I used to be scared of the doctor when I was a little boy?" I asked, keeping my tone light in an effort to comfort Lizzie.

She looked surprised. "You were?"

"Yup," I answered, nodding. "And do you know what I learned?"

She shook her head.

"That doctors want to help us feel better," I said, hoping I sounded convincing enough.

"But doctors give shots," Lizzie said, pressing her lips together in defiance.

I suppressed a chuckle. Even in her distress, she was still the cutest thing I'd ever seen.

I felt Elizabeth's smile, and imagined she was thinking the same thing.

Reaching out, I cupped Lizzie's face, running my thumb over her cheek. "Sometimes they do, but it's only to help you feel better."

Lizzie's bottom lip trembled. "But I *hate* shots, Daddy."

My expression softened in sympathy.

This was the first time I'd really seen my daughter frightened, and while I wanted to take away all her fear, to be her hero and to promise her I'd never let anyone or anything hurt her, I couldn't do that. I had to be honest with her.

"I know, Lizzie." I leaned in further. "But if you

have to get a shot, Mommy and I will be right there with you the whole time, okay?"

"Promise?" Lizzie whispered, still fearful, though I could feel her resistance fading.

"Promise." That was a promise I could make.

"Okay, Daddy."

Carefully, I took Lizzie into my arms and murmured how proud I was of her.

Elizabeth looked up at me as she handed Lizzie over and mouthed, "Thank you."

Her lips moved slowly, cautiously. I knew it was hard for her to put this much trust in me, to place our injured daughter in my waiting arms.

I nodded once as I met her eyes, wordlessly promising to never give her reason to regret it.

I carried Lizzie to the car where I strapped her into her booster seat, mindful of her injured arm. Elizabeth climbed into the backseat beside her, rattling off directions to the nearest ER.

Within minutes, we walked through the doors and had Lizzie signed in.

We tucked ourselves in the farthest corner of the waiting room. I cradled Lizzie on my lap and Elizabeth sat down in the chair next to me, closer to me than she was probably comfortable with.

Warily, we eyed the room overflowing with people sporting about every illness and injury we could imagine.

I blew out a loud sigh through my mouth.

Obviously, it was going to be a very long night.

By ten, probably thanks to the dose of medicine Elizabeth had given her before I arrived to their house, Lizzie's pain had waned enough that she'd fallen asleep curled up on my lap as I rubbed continuous circles along her back.

Elizabeth had said little, only quiet murmurings when she checked on her daughter, sweet words of reassurance and comfort.

Lizzie couldn't have had a better mother.

For the hundredth time that night, I looked to the beautiful woman beside me. She appeared exhausted, dark bags beginning to appear below her honey-colored eyes, her blond waves in disarray from the number of times she'd wrenched her fingers through them.

This time she must have felt me, and she lifted her eyes to meet mine as she smiled somewhat apologetically.

"Thanks for being here, Christian," she said as if she thought my being here was putting me out.

I inclined my head, turning so that I nearly spoke against her ear. "Would you be anywhere else right now, Elizabeth?"

She glanced at our sleeping child and then back at me, her brow furrowed. "Of course not."

I looked at her intensely. "Neither would I."

She blinked several times before she pursed her lips and nodded.

My mouth fell into a small, sad smile, knowing part of her still didn't believe it.

But that was okay because I knew another part of her did.

It was just another thing that only time would prove.

We sank back into silence. The passage of time dragged by as patients were called back and others arrived to take their place. Elizabeth yawned, her eyes drooping.

"This is ridiculous," she muttered under her breath as she scrubbed her palm over her face.

"Here." I shifted, laying Lizzie in her arms. Her eyes shot to my face, wild and pleading. *Don't leave me.*

She fell back into distrust so easily. It stung. "I'll be right back."

Less than five minutes later, I returned with two Styrofoam cups of steaming coffee. I had prepared Elizabeth's the way I remembered she liked it, one cream and two sugars.

She moaned in pleasure when I handed her the cup.

"Christian." She breathed in the aroma, and her eyes closed as she brought it to her lips. "You're a life saver."

Then she flashed me the first real smile she'd given me since I had come back into her life.

For what had to be the twentieth time in the last ten minutes, Elizabeth looked over her shoulder, checking to make sure Lizzie was comfortable. Lizzie had fallen back asleep almost the moment I'd put her in the car.

Elizabeth sighed as she faced forward, slumping deeper into the front passenger seat.

Her elbow rested against the door with her head in her palm. "I always overreact when it comes to her," she uttered, mostly to herself.

Glancing to my right, I smiled softly at the woman who owned my heart, who I now had come to know as one who questioned herself as a mother, worried that she was making mistakes, that she was too cautious or not cautious enough.

Apparently, parenthood did that to you.

She rolled her head across the headrest and turned to face me, her eyes tired but warm.

My smile grew.

"What?" she drawled, returning a lazy grin.

"I was just thinking what a good mother you are." I pulled into her driveway, cutting the engine and hoping I hadn't ruined the amicable mood we'd fallen into over the last several hours.

She laughed quietly. "Sometimes I feel like I have no clue what I'm doing."

Through the rearview mirror, I peered at the child she had raised, the little girl I had a hard time seeing as anything but perfect, and shook my head before turning back to Elizabeth. "You shouldn't doubt yourself so much."

The urge to reach out and touch her was almost too much to resist—the way her lips parted in response to my words as she stared across the small space at me, her body fatigued and mind weary.

It reminded me so much of the way she used to look just before she fell asleep in my arms.

I quickly removed myself from the car before I did something very stupid.

Carefully, I gathered Lizzie in my arms and followed Elizabeth into the dark house and upstairs to Lizzie's room where I laid our daughter on her small bed.

While Elizabeth dug in the dresser to find Lizzie's favorite nightgown, I pulled off her shoes and shorts. Guided by the dim light filtering in from the hall,

Elizabeth and I worked together to get Lizzie ready for bed by removing her shirt over the sling that protected her elbow and wrist, her tiny fingers now swollen.

"You have no idea how happy I am this isn't a cast," Elizabeth whispered as we coaxed the shirt from her head.

I nodded. I couldn't have agreed more.

Lizzie's injuries could have been so much worse, but she had escaped with only a sprained wrist and the cut on her head had only required a simple butterfly bandage.

Most important to Lizzie was the fact that it meant no shots.

She'd been so brave with the doctor and nurses, sitting still as they'd examined her and ran a series of x-rays and cooperating while they placed the bandage above her eye and rested her arm in a sling.

I was so proud of her.

Lizzie barely stirred as I held her up and Elizabeth dressed her, pulling the pink satin nightgown easily over her head. She took more time to carefully maneuver Lizzie's arm through the sleeve.

Elizabeth held the comforter back while I laid our daughter on the sheets, and for the first time in Lizzie's life, both of her parents tucked her into bed.

Even under the terrible circumstances, it felt amazing.

Pressing my lips to my daughter's head, I whispered against it, "I love you, Lizzie."

She groaned an unintelligible response that went straight to my heart.

Standing, I yawned and stretched. The small digital clock on Lizzie's nightstand glowed two-nineteen.

It was really late, but still I wasn't ready to go.

From the bedroom door, I watched as Elizabeth kissed our daughter and ran a tender hand through Lizzie's dark hair before she reluctantly stood and crossed the room.

I stepped out into the hallway and Elizabeth followed behind me, leaving the door ajar behind her.

We both breathed a simultaneous sigh of relief, the ordeal officially over.

Standing in the subdued light of Elizabeth's hallway, the two of us were frozen, unwilling to move. There were so many things I wanted to say—needed to say, the silence between us expectant. It stretched on and inevitably became uncomfortable.

"You'd better get some rest," I finally said, wishing I didn't have to say goodbye.

She fidgeted. "It's really late, Christian." She wrung her hands. "Why don't you stay? I don't have a guest room, but the couch is really comfortable . . . if you want."

The nervous edge to her words dissipated as she extended her hand, reaching out but not touching. "Lizzie will want to see you in the morning."

She seemed to think she needed to convince me. Didn't she understand I never wanted to leave? But as much as I wanted to stay, I understood this was a huge offering for Elizabeth to make.

"Are you sure?"

She nodded. "Yeah . . . stay."

Maybe she would never admit it, maybe she didn't even realize it herself, but as I peered down at her, I *knew* she wanted me to stay. The armor she wore in protection of herself wasn't enough to conceal the hope in her eyes.

I swallowed, searching for my voice. "Elizabeth—"

She held up a hand to stop me. "Please, Christian . . . don't."

On instinct, I stepped back and closed my eyes to keep myself from saying things she wasn't ready to hear.

Soon we would have to talk and lay it all out.

But I heard her plea, and tonight I wouldn't push her any farther than she was ready to go.

"Okay."

The tension between us dissolved, and she moved into action.

"Hang on a second." She turned and disappeared into her room at the end of the small hall before she returned less than two minutes later with a new toothbrush and a pair of pajama bottoms.

"Here." She handed the small pile to me. "Matthew left these here a long time ago."

I looked down at the things in my hand and then back at Elizabeth, incredulous. Did she really expect me to wear these? Matthew wasn't exactly my biggest fan.

She laughed and shook her head. "It's fine, Christian. Just wear them." She grinned and pointed toward the stairs. "There's a bathroom off the family room."

I chuckled at the confounding woman in front of me who amazed me at every turn. I shouldn't have been surprised. Elizabeth had always been the most caring, compassionate person I'd ever known, and she still was.

I just had to peel the layers back a little bit to see it.

How sad they were there because of me.

"Goodnight, Elizabeth." A gracious smile spread across my face.

"Goodnight, Christian." A moment was spent staring at each other, swimming in nostalgia and what could have been, before I turned and left her standing at the top of the stairs.

In the small bathroom, I shed my clothes and put on the blue flannel pajama bottoms, feeling a twinge of guilt as I did so.

I was tired, but there was an energy stirring in me, leaving me unsure of how much sleep I would actually get tonight. So many times, I'd imagined this, what it would be like to stay here, though the circumstances now were so different than what had taken place in my dreams.

I'd be sleeping on the couch—not with

Elizabeth.

Running dampened hands through my hair, I exhaled and hoped I'd at least catch a couple hours of sleep.

Opening the door and flipping off the light switch, I stepped into the dimly-lit family room and came face-to-face with Elizabeth.

I stopped mid-stride, surprised to find her waiting for me on the other side of the bathroom door.

Her eyes grew wide when they hit my bare chest before her face flushed red and she averted her gaze to the floor.

"Sorry . . . I . . . um . . . thought you might like to see these."

She extended her arms, snapping me from my shock as she brought attention to what she held in her hands.

There were three albums, the kind that were perfectly square and filled with hours upon hours of a mother's artwork.

Elizabeth held them out farther, encouraging me to take them. I shook as I reached a tentative hand out to accept them, my mouth dry and unable to express my gratitude for her gift.

As we both held the albums between us, she looked up at me with what could only be described as sympathy, a tenderness that broke my heart and healed it at the same time.

She nodded as she withdrew her hands and then turned and rushed upstairs.

Acute anxiety and severe longing filled my chest as I thought of facing what was inside, the albums an oppressive weight.

I slowly moved to the couch and placed five years of memories on my lap, memories I wasn't sure I was ready to face. I ran my fingertips over the brown cover and struggled to find the courage to open it. It took five full minutes before I did.

The muted glow from the lamp on the end table shed enough light to illuminate what the first page held—a birth announcement.

Elizabeth Grace Ayers
Born May 23rd at 4:37 am.
18.5" long
5 pounds 3 ounces

Breathtaking—heartbreaking.

Tears fell and there was nothing I could have done to stop them.

In my hands was the image of an infant child, her face red and new, her tiny mouth pursed. Even then, her gray-blue eyes were wide and expressive. A mass of shiny, black hair sat atop her head, my cleft marking her chin.

My daughter.

My fingers traced the picture.

So small.

I flashed back to the day I'd seen Elizabeth before she'd given birth—how thin, even sickly she'd appeared. Now to know Lizzie had been so small, it sent reality crashing down on me.

My stomach twisted, my head spun, and sweat broke out across my forehead.

Elizabeth hadn't just *looked* sick, she *was* sick.

I'd left her when she was sick.

I was a monster.

I forced myself to turn the page—snapshots of a swaddled baby asleep in the hospital nursery, rocking in Matthew's arms, pressed to her mother's breast. The last was by far the most beautiful, the way Elizabeth held her daughter as if she'd found the world because she knew she had.

And I had missed it.

Each page showcased my daughter's life, every milestone I had missed—first food, first step, first word, first birthday.

Lizzie grinned at the camera with a pointy cap on her head, two teeth on top and two on the bottom, and a round cake with one candle sitting in front of her—surrounded by those who loved her.

I wasn't there.

Images of a chubby-cheeked little girl, running, playing, always smiling filled the next pages. More birthdays, more Christmases, Easters, every celebration—five years of life.

And I wasn't there because I had abandoned my family.

But when I turned to last page of the last album, *I was.*

Lizzie sat on my lap with her arms around my neck, showering me in undeserved love as she thanked me for a birthday gift I'd had no idea if she'd even like.

Worse than seeing what I had missed was knowing what had to have been left out of those pages, what wasn't put on display.

Every sleepless night, every worry, every fear.

Failures and missed goals.

Heartache, every tear shed.

Swept away in grief, I tried to bury my regret in the pillow Elizabeth had left for me on the couch. It only smelled of her. I pressed my face deeper, trying to drown out years of sorrow and loss, to conceal the devastation tearing me apart.

It felt like death, five years slain by selfishness and stupidity.

Who of us had paid the biggest price? The beautiful child who shone like heaven on every page, her smile joy—her face peace?

Her mother, the one betrayed, the one who had worked so hard, loved so much that she had raised a child such as this?

In the end, I knew it had to be me. I was the

one who had lost, the one who had lived without, the one who was a fool to have ever imagined *anything* could have been better than this.

Without a doubt, I didn't deserve to be here, to wrap myself up in the comfort of the blanket Elizabeth provided, to rest my head on the pillow that could only have come from her bed, to accept her kindness as she allowed me into her home.

Most of all, I didn't deserve the love of Lizzie.

The night I'd fallen apart after Elizabeth had first allowed me to see Lizzie, I'd thought I'd understood, but I'd had no idea.

The truth was, I never would.

I wasn't there and I would never really know. And there was nothing I could do to earn that time back.

Even if Elizabeth forgave me, I didn't think I could ever forgive myself.

As much sorrow as these stilled memories brought me, I couldn't help but cherish the veiled experience, thankful to have a glimpse into life while I wasn't really living at all.

I lamented those years and hugged Elizabeth's pillow close as I took comfort in her scent, took comfort in her presence as I praised her for sharing the life I'd chosen not to be a part of—praised her for being brave enough to allow me to be a part of it now.

That presence grew stronger, palpable.

I jerked up when I realized I wasn't alone, my eyes drawn to her.

Elizabeth stood clinging to the railing at the top of the stairs, watching down over me, tears staining her face.

Neither of us said anything aloud, though my heart spoke a thousand regrets, every one of them a plea for forgiveness I could never deserve.

In her eyes, I saw what I desired most.

Elizabeth cared for me—hurt for me—loved me.

I stared back and poured everything I had into that moment, praying for once she wouldn't question that I did too.

She closed her eyes and took two steps back, uncertainty and fear flowing from the corners, exposing a wounded heart that had forgotten how to trust but hadn't forgotten how to love.

———

I shifted deeper into the warmth, refusing to let go of the comfort of Elizabeth's lingering presence as I buried my face in her pillow and pulled the blanket tighter around my body.

An unfamiliar nudging stirred me, dragging me from what I was sure were the two best hours of sleep I'd ever had.

"Wake up, Daddy." A tiny giggle sounded close to my ear.

I rolled from my stomach to my side and then opened my eyes to paradise.

Lizzie leaned over me, grinning.

I blinked the sleep away, smiling as I focused in on the precious child in front of me. She still wore her nightgown but none of the pain from the night before.

"Hi, baby girl," I rasped out, my throat raw from lack of sleep and hours of uncontained remorse. "Come here."

I lifted the blanket, inviting her to crawl in beside me.

After last night, I needed to hold my daughter.

She felt perfect as she settled next to me and rested her head on the pillow. I placed a kiss on her forehead before ghosting fingertips over the now bruised skin over her eye.

"How are you feeling, sweetheart?"

"I'm almost all better. My arm only hurts a little bit." Her fingers grazed over my chest as she flexed and extended her fingers in a show of recovery.

My chest swelled with emotion, her nearness eliciting a haunting sadness from the night before and an overwhelming appreciation for the grace I'd been given that allowed me to hold her this way today.

Her eyes burned, her child-like innocence overshadowed by a sudden deep awareness.

"Daddy, what's wrong?" The same swollen fingers reached out to caress my cheek in undeserved affection I would never take for granted.

"Nothing's wrong, princess. Everything is perfect."

And just like that, the child was back. Her eyes were alight as she wiggled out of my grasp and onto her feet. "Come on, Daddy. Breakfast is almost ready," she said, attempting to drag me from the couch with her good arm

Her statement set my senses in motion. The smell coming from the kitchen aroused memories from long ago—bacon, eggs, and biscuits. My mouth watered and my stomach growled. Nobody made breakfast like Elizabeth.

Lizzie tugged on my hand again, clearly as excited over her mother's breakfast as I was. With no resistance, I allowed Lizzie to lead me into the kitchen only to have my footsteps falter at the sight in front of me.

Elizabeth stood at the stove with her back to us, wearing black pajama bottoms and a matching tank top. Her blonde hair was pinned up in a messy bun at the base of her neck. Errant pieces had fallen out and toppled down her back.

She was barefoot, glowing, and gorgeous.

I struggled to breathe through the intense longing that coursed through my body.

She threw a quick glance over her shoulder,

flashing another genuine smile. "Good morning."

She turned back to her work, leaving me to whisper a barely audible good morning in return when really I wanted to sing.

Elizabeth spooned what looked to be more than a dozen scrambled eggs into a bowl from a frying pan. "You'd better be hungry. I made enough food to feed an army."

Her tone was light, maybe even cheerful, as if the intensity from last night had long since been forgotten.

It struck me how natural it would seem to walk up behind her and wrap my arms around her waist, to lean over her shoulder and place a good morning kiss on her cheek, to tell her I loved her.

Instead, I said, "Starving."

"Good." She opened the oven door and leaned over to pull out a pan of homemade biscuits.

I had to look away, and my roving eyes drifted to the small table in the kitchen nook. It was set for five. Suddenly, I became very uncomfortable.

"Uh, Elizabeth?"

"Yeah?" She stopped placing biscuits in a basket to look in my direction.

I gestured toward the table with my head. "Are you expecting company?"

Understanding dawned on her face. "Yeah, Matthew and Natalie come for breakfast every Sunday morning."

I roughed a hand through my hair. No further confrontations had taken place between Matthew and me since Lizzie's birthday, but I wouldn't say we were exactly friendly, either.

I'd only seen him a handful of times in passing as I'd been picking up Lizzie or dropping her off, but each time he'd watched me with both suspicion and disdain.

Elizabeth looked at me as if she knew exactly what I was thinking. She pointed toward the bathroom. "You'd better hurry up and get changed. They'll be here any minute."

I knew then that I'd better get over it if I was going to be a part of Lizzie's life.

I was only in the small bathroom long enough to change into the clothes I'd worn the day before, brush my teeth, and to run wet hands through my hair in an attempt to tame the disaster on my head, but when I stepped out, Matthew and Natalie were already there.

From the archway, I watched the profuse apology Matthew gave Elizabeth while he held Lizzie in his arms, almost breathless in his explanation.

"Elizabeth, I'm so sorry. Nat and I were at the movies last night and I'd turned off my phone. I didn't get the message until just before we got over here."

Elizabeth tried to stop him. "Matthew . . .

honestly . . . It was fine. Don't worry about it."

Elizabeth's reassurance did nothing to ease his remorse. He hugged Lizzie to him. "I'm so sorry, Lizzie."

"It's okay, Uncle Maffew," Lizzie promised as she nuzzled against his neck before sitting back and looking between Elizabeth and me. "My Mommy and Daddy took care of me."

For the briefest moment, Matthew's attention shifted from Lizzie to me. His expression was wary, but for the first time it lacked the contempt it normally held. He opened his mouth as if to say something but turned away as Elizabeth made the call to breakfast.

I couldn't help but feel out of place as the four of them settled into their usual spots without a thought.

Matthew and Lizzie dove right into conversation as he asked for a play-by-play of the night before while he dug into the food spread out on the table in front of him.

My feet were glued to the floor as I watched them with benevolent envy, without spite or resentment, but covetous of the bond they had formed.

Elizabeth looked up from her seat, smothering me in the warmth in her gaze. She inclined her head, beckoning me to take the spot beside her.

As much as I felt like an outsider, my need to be

a part of this family outweighed the discomfort I experienced as I walked across the room and pulled out the chair between Elizabeth and Lizzie.

Three pairs of eyes watched as I settled into my place, Natalie as if she'd always believed I belonged there, Matthew cautious, and Elizabeth with a hint of red on her cheeks.

Apparently, I wasn't the only one feeling self-conscious.

But even if it was new and filled with uncertainty, it didn't make it any less right.

Lizzie was the only one who didn't seem to notice anything out of the ordinary and continued with the animated description of the previous night, relieving some of the awkwardness.

With a quiet grin on my face, I listened to my daughter prattle on and was unable to contain the pleasure I felt as I filled my plate from the bowls Elizabeth passed my way.

If Lizzie had been in distress the night before, I never would have known.

Matthew and Natalie hung on her every word as they showered her with sympathy and cheered her for being such a brave girl as she recounted her experience.

By the look of my plate, I knew I appeared to be a glutton. The homemade breakfast was piled high, but I couldn't resist.

How many mornings had I woken up to

Elizabeth cooking in that small kitchen of my apartment back in New York? I was salivating by the time I bit into a biscuit dripping with butter and raspberry jam.

A moan escaped me before I could stop it.

The voice beside me was so quiet I wasn't sure if I'd imagined it. "They were always your favorite."

I tilted my head toward her, smiled softly, wished I had the freedom to reach out and touch her face, and whispered, "Thank you for making them."

I realized we were being watched, but I didn't care. I'd chosen to stop being a coward the day I'd finally sought Elizabeth out, and if I had to lay my heart out in front of her family to show her I cared for her, that I had never forgotten her, through something as simple has homemade biscuits, I would do it.

"So, Christian . . . ," Natalie said, cutting in before placing a forkful of eggs in her mouth. She chewed and swallowed before she continued. "What do you think of living in San Diego?"

I looked across the table at her, aware she was trying to make me comfortable and welcome me into their circle. She'd always been kind to me, giving me the benefit while everyone else had remained in doubt.

My gaze flickered between the girls on my left

and right before returning to rest on her. "I love it here."

"Me too," Lizzie added as she shoved half of a piece of bacon into her mouth.

Yes. I *absolutely* loved it here.

"And work?" Natalie asked.

"Uh . . ." Honestly, I really didn't know how to answer her. I knew I had a dream job and I wished I could appreciate it more, but in the end, it really only served to remind me of what I'd walked away from to attain it.

Natalie laughed. "Work's work, right?"

I chuckled at her observation even though it went much deeper than the obvious. "Yeah, I guess you could say that."

Elizabeth tensed beside me as we broached what I knew was going to be a very touchy subject for us. Elizabeth had never been in it for the money, but that didn't mean she didn't have aspirations. And she was right, what she'd said that afternoon—we could have figured it out.

Lizzie jumped on the topic. "At my Daddy's work you can see the ocean *and* at his house too," she said with wide-eyed exuberance.

Months before, I'd taken Lizzie to my office to show her where I worked, and of course, she'd been to my condo a number of times.

She'd clearly been impressed by the fact that they looked over the water and had declared that one day she'd live by the ocean, too. It was a wish I'd be all too happy to grant.

Elizabeth joining the conversation caught me off guard. "So, what's it like working for your dad?"

She studied me with a genuine concern-filled gaze. She'd known how turbulent my relationship with my father had been, and he'd been nothing but a self-righteous asshole to her.

I was surprised she'd even mention him.

I looked directly at her and expelled a weighty breath before I answered truthfully. "Miserable." I shoveled some scrambled eggs into my mouth to cover up the disdain I felt for my father.

He ruled his company with an iron fist and treated every single one of his employees like garbage, including me.

Why he'd asked me to "head" the San Diego office when he thought me incapable of doing anything right was beyond me.

She nodded softly as if she'd expected it. "I'm sorry."

"Me too."

For everything.

Her attention dropped to her plate, absorbed with spearing eggs onto her fork.

It was all so disconcerting, the way Elizabeth and I had to tiptoe around each other as if every simple comment came with a threat to sweep us away in the undertow and to drown us in our past.

I turned back to Natalie in hope of a safer topic. "What do you do, Natalie?"

Her brown eyes lit up as she jumped into a detailed account of the last four years of her life— her goals, school, meeting Matthew.

While she was young and viewed the world through an almost childlike awe, there was still a depth to her. I liked her and could easily count her as a friend.

"So right now, I'm taking classes in the mornings to finish up my bachelor's and taking care of this sweet little thing in the afternoons." She poked Lizzie in the belly with her finger, causing Lizzie to squeal.

Matthew watched his wife with tenderness, his face glowing as she spoke.

I glanced at Elizabeth, then back at him, searching for any sort of unease with the interaction while wondering how their lives seemed so simple when the situation was anything but. Elizabeth merely watched them both with fondness.

Maybe when I had seen Matthew at Elizabeth's side that night I'd been too blinded by my own self-pity to see clearly, but I could plainly see it now.

He'd stood beside Elizabeth devoted as a protector, her guardian, but his touch had lacked what poured from him when he looked at his wife.

He'd never *loved* Elizabeth—not the way I did, not the way he loved Natalie.

I was such fool, every realization an amplification of the mistakes I'd made.

For the remainder of breakfast, I listened and learned. Matthew directed nothing toward me other than an occasional penetrating stare as if he would give anything to know my thoughts.

Elizabeth's little family carried on the way I imagined they always did, relaxed, enjoying each other, and chatting about what had happened throughout their week.

Elizabeth laughed.

And the world was right.

"Can I help with anything?" I stood in the doorway of Elizabeth's kitchen as she loaded the dishwasher with the aftermath of Sunday morning.

I'd just come downstairs from Lizzie's room where I'd spent the last hour playing with her on the floor—everything from dolls, to cars, to a game that required me to wear plastic earrings and a princess tiara.

I won.

Elizabeth smiled over her shoulder. "Nope, just finishing up." She closed the dishwasher and twisted the dial to start.

"This was great, Elizabeth. Thank you."

She shook her head indicating it wasn't a problem. "I'm glad you were here."

"I'm glad I was, too." More than she could ever know.

Seeing Lizzie three days in a row had been wonderful, and even though I was aware this request would count as pushing again, I couldn't imagine not seeing her for an entire week.

"So, I was thinking . . . maybe I could pick Lizzie up on Tuesday from school to take her to lunch?"

I felt nervous, shifting my feet, worried of her reaction. So I rambled. "I'd only keep her for a couple of hours and I could bring her back to Natalie. You wouldn't even know she was gone."

She didn't hesitate. "I don't see why not. Just let me check with Nat."

Natalie agreed, which didn't surprise me. She seemed thrilled with the idea. The arrangement would be for me to pick Lizzie up from school and then drop her back at Natalie and Matthew's house afterward.

I typed the address Natalie had given me into my phone while she and Matthew hugged and kissed Elizabeth and Lizzie goodbye, their affection great as they promised they'd see each other tomorrow.

Natalie hugged me. At first it caught me off

guard, but I was quick to reciprocate with a murmured, "Thank you," low against her ear.

She nodded and squeezed me harder in return, a clear understanding taking place between us.

The greater shock was when Matthew stepped forward and extended his hand. I accepted it, though my grip was weak and unsure. He shook it, firm and without reproach. "Thanks for being there last night."

I nodded even though I didn't want his thanks. No father should need to be thanked for participating in what was his responsibility, but I had to accept that my past choices resulted in the judgment of my actions now.

"All right, we're outta here." Natalie tugged on Matthew's arm, taking his hand. With a final goodbye, they filed out the front door, their departure signaling that my time here today had ended as well.

"I guess I'd better head out, too." My tone was less than enthusiastic.

I knelt in front of my daughter and gathered her in my arms. There was nothing worse than telling her goodbye.

"I love you, baby girl. Daddy's going to pick you up from school on Tuesday." I smoothed her hair and drank in her eyes. "Would you like that?"

"Yes!" She squeezed her arms around my neck. "You're the best daddy in the world!"

Her perception of me was so skewed, so far removed from the truth, but there would be no good purpose in correcting her now.

I needed to talk to her about it, I knew, just as much as I needed to talk to her mother, but not as I was walking out the door.

So, I drew her closer, held her tight.

"Goodbye, princess." In disinclination, I let her go and stood to leave.

"Bye, Daddy."

Elizabeth regarded us from where she stood, leaning against the wall under the stairs, a new sadness on her face. It was a sadness I knew all too well. I wore it all the time.

"Goodbye, Elizabeth. Thanks for everything."

"Goodbye, Christian."

I opened the door and stepped out into the warmth of the summer sun.

Elizabeth followed me to the doorway to see me out.

"Elizabeth?" I turned to her, pausing on her stoop. This wasn't an afterthought. It'd been on my mind, weighing on me since last night. "Why didn't you come back to class?"

She stilled as the meaning of my question dawned on her face. Her voice was quiet and cracked when she answered. "I was sick."

Closing my eyes, I nodded as I rode out the suffocating wave of guilt, and in my shame, I turned and left Elizabeth with no further words.

The preschool was a large, white building with colorful letters splashed across the front and shrubs growing against its walls.

A wrought iron fence painted bright blue encompassed the grounds, and playground equipment filled the yard that was protected from the heat by a matching blue sunshade.

At exactly noon, I walked through the door and into the office, feeling a bit out of sorts and nervous. The room was mostly quiet, only the distorted sound of children playing seeping through the thin walls. The young woman behind the counter asked if she could help me.

"Yes, I'm here to pick up Lizzie Ayers."

Her face lit in recognition. "Oh, yes, we were told to expect you."

She thumbed through a stack of files on her desk and produced a folder with Lizzie's name on the tab.

She pulled a sheet from it, passed it across to me, and set a pen on top of it. "I just need you to fill this out and I need your driver's license for verification."

Most of the form had been filled out by Elizabeth, her distinct handwriting adding me to the list of people authorized to pick Lizzie up from school.

There was only a small section where I needed to add my personal information.

My heart palpitated as I realized the huge leap of faith Elizabeth had taken in me.

I now had control of signing my daughter in and out of school.

With a shaky hand, I added the information and passed the form back to the receptionist along with my license.

She looked it over, put up a finger, and said, "Just a minute."

She made a photocopy, added it to the file, and showed me where to sign out my daughter. Then she led me down the hall to Lizzie's classroom.

"Daddy!" Lizzie spotted me the second we walked through the door and ran across the room with outstretched arms.

"Hi, sweetheart." I picked her up and kissed her on the forehead, rocking her as I held her to my chest. "I missed you."

"I missed you too, Daddy."

"Come on, let's get your things."

Lizzie showed me her cubby stuffed with her day's work, proud as she presented me with a picture she'd painted.

Although the picture had been drawn with the crudeness of the hand of a five-year-old, the two adults and one child standing hand-in-hand, one with yellow and two with black hair, made it clear who she'd drawn.

"This is beautiful, Lizzie."

So damned beautiful.

I helped her wriggle her backpack over the sling she still wore on her arm and then took her good hand and led her out.

"Where to, Lizzie?" I looked at her through the rearview mirror where she was buckled in her booster in the backseat of my car.

"I want pizza!"

Then pizza it was.

Soon we were seated at a round table for two at the small pizza parlor I'd looked up on my phone. It was the kind of place where the owner cooked in the back while he yelled orders to his employees up front, a place where a person could order pizza by the slice and sit at tables covered in red and white checked cloths, a place where the intoxicating smell of fresh-baked dough hung in the air.

Lizzie sat on her knees, sipping a clear, bubbly soda through a straw, the two of us conversing about our day. She told me of the fight between two little boys on the playground, her voice disapproving as she described how they had to sit in time out for the *whole* recess.

I chuckled and then told her about the board meeting I'd had to sit through the entire morning, leaving out all the boring details, instead telling her how I'd spent the entire time gazing out on the sailboats on the water while thinking of only her.

The server arrived with our food and refilled our drinks. The slices of pizza were huge and dripping with grease, and I convinced Lizzie to allow me to cut it into pieces so she could eat it with a fork rather than trying to balance it with her one good hand.

"Thank you, Daddy," she said with a soft expression of appreciation on her face as I set her plate back in front of her and handed her a fork.

"You're welcome, sweetheart." I smiled as she speared a piece of her cheese pizza and popped it into her mouth. Only then did I turn to wrestle the huge piece in front of me.

We ate in peace for a couple of minutes while I contemplated the best way to bring up a discussion I was certain would be one of the hardest of my life, but one I couldn't put off any longer.

"Lizzie, honey?"

Grinning, she looked up from her plate and across the table at me.

"Are you happy Daddy's here . . . now?" Really, I knew what she would say. I just didn't know a better way to break into the conversation.

She nodded as she took another bite. "Uh-huh."

"Did your mom ever talk to you about why I wasn't with you when you were younger?"

She shrugged one shoulder as if it didn't matter

at all. "You didn't want me."

I wanted to pass out from the dizzying pain her answer brought me.

Swallowing the lump in my throat, I held onto the table in front of me, forcing myself to speak. "Lizzie, I'm so sorry."

Even if it hadn't always been the case, even if I'd spent the first five years of her life wondering about her, longing for her, there *had* been a day I'd believed *this* child would ruin my life.

"It's okay, Daddy."

There was nothing *okay* about what I'd done, but I accepted it as her way of telling me she'd already forgiven me.

I leaned heavily against the table, lowering myself so I could look up at my child's face. "I need you to know, Lizzie, that as long as I live, I will *never* leave you again. Do you understand?"

She smiled a simple smile, one of sincerity and trust. "I know that, Daddy."

Then she grinned and asked if she could have another soda.

It was just after three when I pulled into the spot with my name engraved on a silver plaque in the parking garage of my building. I jammed the up button several times, willing the elevator to hurry.

I'd been due for another round of board

meetings at three o'clock. After spending the hour after lunch at a nearby park, I'd dropped Lizzie off at the small, one-level house Natalie and Matthew shared.

With a smile, Natalie had invited me in. She'd enveloped me in an encouraging embrace when I explained I had to get back to the office.

What felt like five minutes passed, which in reality was only about thirty seconds, before the elevator doors slid open.

I breathed a sigh of relief when I stepped out onto our floor a minute later, rushing to my office to grab the files I needed for the meeting.

I nearly tripped over my feet when I found my father sitting at my desk, his face twisted in disapproval.

"So very nice of you to show up, Christian."

Recovering from my surprise, I shook my head and crossed the room to find the paperwork.

"Nice of you to let me know you were coming into town," I threw back at him.

Standing at the front of my desk facing my father, I rummaged through the files, grabbed what I needed, and shoved them into my briefcase.

"I just thought I'd pop in to see how things were coming along here." He waved his hand around the room.

"They're coming just *fine*." He was already well aware of this. Sure, we'd had a few snags in the beginning but nothing that wouldn't have been expected.

"Doesn't look that way to me."

I stilled my frenzied activity and stared down at the man sitting in my chair, staring back at me, his dark eyes gleaming with contention.

"Care to tell me why I've been sitting in this very spot for . . ." He glanced at the Cartier around his wrist. "The last three hours while you were nowhere to be found?"

I knew my father expected me to live my life the same way as he, tied to the office with concern for nothing but the elevated title he'd given me.

I refused.

"I was with my daughter. Do you have a problem with that?"

He looked as if I'd just smashed a paperweight against the side of his head, reeling with the blow I'd struck him with.

The shock was quick to morph into fury. He jumped up, his palms pressed flat on the desk. "You hooked back up with that money-hungry little whore? Are you really that stupid, Christian?"

The briefcase I held smashed against the wall when I threw it across the room, glass shattering on the impact, frames falling to the floor.

I'd just told the asshole he had a granddaughter, and instead of thinking to ask her name, he thought of money?

I couldn't stand to look at the pathetic man in front of me—his black hair salt and peppered around his ears, only worn that way because he believed it gave him a look of distinction— couldn't stand to watch him trembling with rage over what I knew was his embarrassment over my bastard child.

I hated him for it.

With a shaky hand, I pulled my wallet from my back pocket and dug out the small picture of Lizzie I kept there.

I slammed it down on the desk in front of him and made a decision I was sure I would never regret. "You can count that as my resignation."

Ten

I had no idea what I believed anymore or where I stood. A door had been opened, a line crossed, and I couldn't decide how I felt about it.

I knew I'd let it happen, had been a partner to it, had even pushed for it.

How easy it would have been to call my mother or my older sister when Matthew's phone had gone to voicemail.

But no, I'd called Christian.

In the time it had taken him to drive to our house, I'd agonized over that decision, what kind of mistake I was making, and its ultimate effect on my daughter.

Did I still believe he would harm her?

Then when he'd knelt before her, his worry and tenderness enough to engulf us both, enough to chase away my baby's fears and assuage the panic pounding against my chest, I'd thought, *No. He never would.*

It wasn't difficult to trace it back to its origin, to the moment I'd sat beside Claire and she'd made me question everything I'd held onto for so long, everything I thought I understood.

I shook my head and tried to focus on work, only to tense when a too intimate hand ran down my upper arm and rested on the small of my back.

"Hey, Elizabeth, Anita asked me to finish up for her today. Do you need any help with anything?"

Scott leaned over my shoulder and looked at my computer screen. He was so close I could feel his breath against my neck.

I shrank forward, the movement minute. With mouse in hand, I clicked through the daily closing procedures, brought up my reports for the day, and pressed print.

"I'm just finishing up here." I handed him the small stack of papers, ending drawer, and key. "Here you go."

Scott was my friend, and I smiled at him in a way to indicate that was the only thing he was. His green eyes glimmered with misunderstanding.

He'd been bold of late, his touch no longer a hint of desire, but overt want.

He examined the documents for what seemed like minutes when it should have only taken seconds—stalling.

Shifting my feet, I tried to remain patient under his scrutiny of both my work and my body while he stood inappropriately close.

All I wanted to do was rush out, grab my phone, dial Natalie, and ask her how the day had gone.

Today had been Christian's first day to pick Lizzie up from school.

"Looks good, Elizabeth," Scott said as he nodded and took a step back, still lingering.

"Great." I glanced around, hoping for an easy escape.

"So, uh . . ." He looked back at the papers in his hands before looking back at me. "Do you have any plans Friday night?"

I grimaced, wishing he would stop continually putting me in this position, the one where I had to let him down. He was starting to make things uncomfortable between us.

"Scott . . ." I sighed and looked away, pushing my bangs from my face in exasperation.

"Elizabeth," he pled low as a whisper. "I'm tired of waiting." His dipped his eyes, searched my face. "Please, give me a chance to prove how good we could be together."

"I can't."

His voice raised a fraction in frustration. "Why not?"

"Please, Scott, you're my friend."

Don't ruin that, I wanted to beg.

He stepped back and huffed before he turned and left me staring at his back as he stalked away and into the break room.

I placed my hands flat against my counter, sighed, and flipped off my computer monitor while I wondered why I couldn't force myself to say yes.

It was *just* dinner.

Why did it have to be such a big deal?

In the break room, I gathered my things from my locker and powered my phone, anxious to be in the privacy of my car so I could make the call.

Tension filled the room, radiating from Scott as he trained his attention ahead, brooding as he refused to look my way.

Selina offered a small understanding smile, a sympathetic shrug.

"Night everyone," I called as I slung my purse over my shoulder and rushed from the room, through the lobby, and out into the cool evening air, the sky gray with overcast.

I breathed it in and wondered when things had become so complicated.

Walking along the side of the building, I studied my feet, counted my steps, and tried not to think of Christian and his pain that had echoed through my house, called to me, almost caused me to cave.

It was pointless. He pursued me in my thoughts and dreams—waited against my car.

I froze when I saw him, and a deep ache stirred in my stomach.

He leaned against my trunk, slouched with his hands deep in the pockets of his dark gray suit, his focus intent on the spot where he dug the toe of his shoe into a small divot in the pavement.

"Christian?" I called, startling him, and his anxious face whipped up to meet mine.

In two seconds, I crossed the lot and stopped a foot away from him. "What's going on?"

My first thought had been worry for my daughter but knew I would have heard from Natalie had something been wrong.

Christian sat up taller, crossed his arms over his chest, and jerked a hand through his hair as he bounced in agitation.

His demeanor caused the ache in my stomach to swell, transform, and rise in apprehension. The doll he'd given Lizzie lay beside him on the trunk of my car, and he picked it up and handed it to me.

"Lizzie left this in my car today. I thought she might miss it." He feigned calm, though the tight creases at the corners of his eyes served to belie it.

I studied the toy with narrowed eyes as if it held some sort of answer. I looked back at him.

"Christian?"

It was obvious the doll had nothing to do with the reason he sat against my car.

He groaned and ran his hand through his hair again, the movement causing it to fall in his face.

"I had a fight with my dad." He quaked as he spoke the words, appearing as if his world had been rocked.

Shattered.

I shook my head, trying to process why this seemed so pivotal.

"I quit," he clarified with a tight nod as if he were trying to convince himself that his action had been the correct one.

He quit.

Tears sprang to my eyes and I stepped away.

"You're leaving?" slipped from my mouth, slow and hurt, more an accusation than a question.

I couldn't believe he would do this, not after everything, after I'd welcomed him into my home.

I was such a fool.

Christian appeared confused, which then bled into the same sadness he'd watched me with for the last three months.

"God, no, Elizabeth. Of course not."

That sadness thickened as he watched me come to comprehension, watched me wipe away tears of perpetual distrust and then the ones that followed that fell with the relief that he was staying.

"I'm not going anywhere." His eyes shone deep with the promise, intense as they seemed to search mine for understanding—for acceptance.

I bowed my head and closed my eyes as I clutched Lizzie's doll to my chest. Would there ever be a day when I would believe, when I'd stop waiting for him to leave?

I lifted my face to find his. "I'm sorry, Christian."

I regretted my assumption, my knee-jerk reaction, and wished I could take it back and put the focus back on him.

Once I finally stopped thinking about myself, I realized he'd come here for a reason.

He needed support and comfort as he confided in me that he'd quit his job.

Since the day I'd met Christian, I'd known that working for his father had been what he'd strived for, what had pushed him further, made him work to be the best. While I never agreed with the reasons behind it, I knew how important it was to him.

And now he'd walked away.

I felt like a complete jerk.

Christian cringed with my apology, blowing air through his nose while he shook his head. "Don't apologize to me, Elizabeth," he commanded softly as he looked back at me in what appeared complete understanding, his grievance only with himself.

Taking an unsure step forward, I looked up at him under his partially bowed head. He had slunk further down against my car, his hands shoved even deeper in his pockets as he kicked at small pebbles with his shoe.

"Are you okay?" I asked carefully, searching his face.

Frowning, Christian pursed his lips as if he were asking himself the same question.

Finally he shrugged and offered a feeble, "I guess," though it was clear he didn't believe it any more than I did.

"Do you want to talk about it?"

Richard Davison was probably the least kind, most difficult person I'd ever encountered in my life, but Christian had always just dealt with it. I couldn't imagine what would cause him to throw it all away now.

A fiery anger flashed across Christian's face as he held his jaw rigid. "No, I think I'll spare you those details."

He released a heavy breath, slumped his shoulders and he stared at his feet. "I don't know what I'm supposed to do now. I've spent my entire life working toward a place in my father's firm, and now . . ."

He looked up at me, lost.

I wrestled back the urge to comfort him, to

bestride his legs crossed at the ankles in front of him, to wrap my arms around his neck, and to promise him it would be okay.

Instead, I shuffled a little closer and tapped the side of his shoe with the tip of mine.

"Hey," I urged softly, "You'll figure it out. It's going to be okay."

He glanced down at our feet and then back at me with a frown still marring his mouth. "I'll never make as much working in another firm as I was for my father."

He looked at me as if he were waiting for my reaction, how I felt about this news.

"Is money really that important to you?" The question came out low, probing, as if his answer meant everything—as if it would somehow change something inside of me.

Because almost six years ago, his answer had been yes.

He shook his head, so slow, the movement filled with comprehension of the root of my question. "No, Elizabeth . . . not anymore. I just need you to know things might be different now."

Once again, Christian blurred the lines of who we were as my mind finally caught up to why he was here, where his concern laid.

He wanted my approval as if we were a family and there was a family decision to be made.

The step I took back was slight, almost

imperceptible, but enough to place some distance between us before I completely lost myself in this man.

I swallowed down some of the emotion, desperate to lighten Christian's distress and at the same time desperate to distract myself from the need I felt to reach out and comfort him.

"Are you asking me for a loan, Christian?" It came out rough, ill timed, though I couldn't help but giggle over how ridiculous my attempt at cheering him up sounded.

A smile tugged at the corner of his mouth and he chuckled through his nose. "You never know, Elizabeth, you never know."

A full smile broke through as he looked up at me, his expression relieved. "Thank you."

I smiled back at him softly, it becoming harder and harder to hide the love I'd kept for him for so long. I chewed on my bottom lip and nodded, wishing I could offer him something more than another exhausted *goodnight, Christian.*

"Goodnight, Elizabeth," he whispered, his eyes warm as he stood up. He reached out in a small wave before he turned and got into his car parked next to mine.

I couldn't move as I watched him go.

"That's the reason you won't say yes?"

I jumped when the harsh, hurt voice hit my ears. I twisted to look over my shoulder to find Scott standing near the wall of the building, shaking his head in injured disappointment.

"You're taking that asshole back, aren't you, Elizabeth? After everything he's done to you?"

I gaped at Scott, his face flushed with anger and disbelief.

I swallowed down my urge to defend Christian, remembering how many times I'd maligned Christian as I'd cried on Scott's shoulder.

Did I really expect him to think well of Christian now?

"No." I shook my head, quick to counter Scott's assertion. I knew what it must have looked like to him—what it had *felt* like to me.

"No," I said again to convince both Scott and myself.

I *wasn't* taking Christian back.

I couldn't.

He'd caused me too much hurt, and I'd never survive another broken heart like that.

"No?" Scott asked, his tone skeptical, challenging, "Then have dinner with me."

He pushed away from the wall and stepped forward. His voice lost its bite as he implored, "Just once, Elizabeth. If you don't enjoy yourself, then I promise I'll never ask again."

I wanted to tell him to go to hell, to ask him how he thought he had the right to manipulate me this way.

Instead, I gave in. I persuaded myself that it was only dinner, that it wasn't that big of a deal, that there could never be anything between Christian and me again—and I told Scott yes.

⁂

The full-length mirror in the corner of my bedroom mocked my stupidity as I stood before it smoothing out the white blouse and black skirt that fell just above my knees.

I was anxious, agitated.

My thick, blond waves had been transformed into a mound of curls, my eyes lined and lashes coated, and a thick sheen of clear gloss was smeared across my lips.

"You look pretty, Mommy," Lizzie said. She sat with her legs crisscrossed on my bed and grinned while she watched me get ready.

I smiled halfheartedly back at her through the mirror and slipped my feet into a pair of black pumps, fighting off another wave of guilt.

As the last three days had passed, realization had slowly seeped in, acceptance of the *real* reason I'd agreed to this date.

For two years, I'd been successful at dodging Scott's affections, at putting him off, and in one weak moment at Christian's feet, I'd panicked. I'd felt the need to prove to myself that I was stronger than the surging emotions I felt for Christian, stronger than the need for him that was threatening to boil over.

Now I readied myself for a date I didn't want to go on—prepared myself to lead on a man who'd only ever cared for me and been my friend.

The doorbell rang. Lizzie jumped from my bed and flew downstairs in anticipation of her father.

I grabbed a light jacket and my purse, my hands shaking as I shrugged the coat onto my shoulders. Ill at ease, I sighed and glanced one last time in the mirror before forcing myself to leave my room.

Hovering at the top of the stairs, I watched Christian kneeling in the foyer with our daughter in his arms, his face buried in her hair.

For the first time on a Friday evening, he was not wearing a suit but rather jeans and a T-shirt, a stark reminder of his choice to leave his father's firm just days before.

Taking a shuddering breath, I descended the stairs, tentative and slow, as if my subconscious believed if I were quiet enough, I'd go unnoticed, my compulsive, irrational actions overlooked and unseen.

Of course, Christian looked my direction. His face spread into a timid smile, his eyes appraising as he took in my appearance. "Hey, Elizabeth."

"Hi." I held onto the banister, reticent to take another step. I felt so exposed, as if he could see right through me and decipher my intentions.

"You look really nice." His face flushed with the compliment, self-conscious, but he pressed on. "Are you going out?"

Maybe he could.

Swallowing, I nodded and took the last step onto the tiled foyer, my mind working for a way to explain myself, a way to justify what I was getting ready to do.

Another part of me insisted I didn't need to give him an account of myself, but somehow tonight that line of reasoning felt wrong.

Before I could answer him, there was a light tapping on the front door that sat only partially closed.

Scott peeked through the crack, pushing the door the rest of the way open with a small bouquet of handpicked flowers in his hand.

"Hey," Scott said almost breathless when he realized what he'd just walked in on.

While I felt Scott surveying the room, wary of its occupants and the distinct tension that had just set in the air, I couldn't even look at him.

My attention was on Christian.

His face paled when recognition dawned, and his eyes flashed to mine, grieved, and then fell to the floor. His hands shook as he stooped in front of Lizzie and helped her into her thin coat.

"You ready, sweetheart?" he murmured to her as he used both hands to free her long hair that was trapped inside her jacket, his tenderness for our daughter unaltered in his distress.

It was clear Lizzie was not immune to the intensity of the room, of the sadness in the quiet of her father's voice, or my discomfort for causing the whole situation.

Her focus darted between her father and me, her worry salient.

I took a step forward and placed a hand on her shoulder as I leaned down to her. "You have a great time with your daddy tonight, Lizzie. I'll be home before you are."

My words were meant as a reassurance for them both, an attempt to pacify my daughter's concern and a promise to Christian that I would be back.

"Okay, Momma." Lizzie took her father's waiting hand, and he led her out without a parting word.

Christian paused for a passing second when he encountered the smug demeanor Scott wore. Every slanderous word I'd said against Christian played across Scott's face, a gauntlet thrown.

It was as if Christian watched it fall to the ground, an unreciprocated provocation, unarmed for battle, his feet treading my sidewalk in surrender.

The heavy breath I released was not in relief the way Scott interpreted it.

"You're not kidding," Scott said as he stepped

through the threshold. His expression was sympathetic as if he felt bad for me.

"That was really . . . uncomfortable. You're a saint for putting up with all of that."

He waved toward the sidewalk in the direction Christian and Lizzie had just departed, as if he understood everything, how I felt, how hard it was to watch my daughter leave with the man I loved every Friday night and act as if it didn't affect me.

His assumptions roused a spark of bitterness, an irritation with him for goading me into this date. But I knew I couldn't blame him for this.

This was my mistake.

Yes, he'd badgered me into it, pestered me until I'd given in, but that was only because I'd never been clear with him.

So many times, I'd told him we could only be friends, though my reasoning had come weak, given with a false hope that maybe in the future I'd be ready, even though I'd known I'd never be.

I'd just never wanted to hurt my friend's feelings.

Scott handed me the small bundle of purple, pink, and white flowers, which I thanked him for and took to the kitchen to place in a vase of water. I used that moment to regroup, to remind myself that it was only dinner.

It was *only* dinner.

By the time I'd placed the vase in the center of

the table and locked the door, Christian was about to get into his car, having already buckled Lizzie in the back.

This time his eyes didn't fall.

They burned into me, blue anguish following me to the curb where Scott was parked on the street, unwavering as Scott settled me into the passenger seat of his black sedan.

Did this hurt him as much as he'd hurt me?

Could he feel anything close to the devastation I'd felt the night he'd thrown me from his apartment?

His expression told me yes, at least some of it.

I found no satisfaction in it, no triumph in his misery. Instead, I wanted to call out to him that I was sorry.

"Ready?" Scott asked as he dropped into his seat and started his car.

Forcing a smile, I lied with a nod, hating the person I'd become.

***

I ran upstairs, rushed through the buttons of my blouse, the zipper on my skirt, and kicked out of my heels, trying to shake off my guilt.

It didn't work.

I was a terrible person, plain and simple.

I'd used my friend.

Digging through my dresser, I pulled on a pair

of sweatpants and a tank top.

Aggressively, I pulled a brush through my head full of product and ironed in curls and twisted my hair into a loose ponytail, wishing the action could somehow erase every memory of this night.

Scott had been so eager, excited even. He seemed sure I'd finally crossed that bridge and I would be his at last.

It had been there in his eyes, in the way they gleamed when they'd wash over me, in the light brushes of his leg against mine under the table—in the kiss I'd avoided with a jerk of my head, the one that had landed in rejection against my jaw.

I'd felt it then, standing at my doorstep, the way Scott withdrew his unreturned affections, his hands still firm in their hold on my shoulders while he tore the rest of himself away.

His eyes had been kind, lacking the reproach they should have held when he stepped back and uttered an apology.

"I'm sorry, Elizabeth, I shouldn't have forced you into this."

I'd choked on his apology, angry that I'd caused him to feel the need, and insisted that I was the one who should be sorry.

He'd shifted in discomfort and tried to hide the wounded look on his face, as the idea of us became a firm disenchantment in his mind.

He'd shrugged in indifference and said, "It's

okay."

We both knew it wasn't.

We both knew what I'd done.

He'd left with embarrassment on his face and a halfhearted, "See you on Monday."

In my bathroom, I scrubbed the makeup from my face, blotting out the last bit of physical evidence of this self-inflicted fiasco.

Five seconds later, the doorbell rang, and it almost sent me spiraling to the floor in confusion.

I no longer knew up from down, what I wanted and what I should run from, what to fear and what to embrace.

When it rang the second time, I realized Christian probably thought I hadn't yet made it home.

I rushed downstairs, my bare feet landing with a heavy thud with each step I took.

I fumbled as I raced through the locks to open the door.

Christian seemed surprised by the sudden movement, even more so when he took in my disheveled appearance, my pajamas and frazzled hair, I could only guess the expression on my face to match.

Lizzie danced in, her voice a sweet melody, singing praises for her and her father's night. She crooned about how they'd made dinner together at his apartment, shared it while they counted the lights of the boats floating out upon the water, how she wished I could have been there to see it.

The entire time Christian stood in my doorway, his face flat, mouth slack in surrender.

I leaned against the edge of the door, gripping it for support as I prepared to cross another line. "Will you stay?"

His eyes flitted over my face, searching, seeking answers that neither of us had.

The only thing I *did* know was I wanted him here with Lizzie, with me—that I couldn't bear to watch him walk away, that I *needed* him to stay— that I wished I didn't fear that need so much.

"Please," I said, all but begging.

His brow furrowed when my plea seemed to break through his numb defeat. His hands pressed into fists at his thighs, his mouth trembling as he looked over my shoulder, probed my family room to find it empty.

His eyes bore into mine, molten anguish.

"I *hate* this, Elizabeth," his words abraded, his breathing labored. "It *shouldn't* have been like *this*."

I had no words in response to that truth. I only widened the door and stepped back in inferred summons.

Please.

Even if it were only for tonight, I wanted to pretend that it wasn't like *this*, that he hadn't hurt me and in turn, I didn't have to hurt him—that I hadn't hurt Scott in the process.

I wanted to pretend as Christian relented and stepped through the door that he wasn't unsure of his welcome.

Pretend as we dimmed the lights and the animated fairy tale sprang to life across the screen that we didn't look at each other with uncertainty, rattled nerves, and pounding chests.

Pretend as the three of us gathered on the couch that we did it every day and that it was normal for Lizzie to sit between us snuggled into her daddy's side to share a bowl of popcorn and a blanket spread over our laps.

Pretend that together we'd seen this movie a hundred times just as Lizzie and I had, that he'd been there when we'd seen it the first time more than two years before.

Pretend that later this thirst would be slaked, that Christian would lay me down, that I would be his and he would be mine.

The way it *should* have been.

But make-believe could only get me so far, and I knew it was time I measured my strength and resolved how far I'd allow my heart to go.

I glanced across at him.

His arm was draped over Lizzie's shoulder and he played with strands of her hair. His attention was not on the television but on her, attentive to the way her face lit up in laughter, the way she sang along, the way she hid her eyes when the film turned dark even though she already knew the result and her hero would live.

He leaned down, nuzzled his mouth against her hair, and looked up at me as he held her close.

And I knew I wanted him a permanent a part of my life, not as lovers, but in a partnership for our daughter, for him to take a place as a part of this family.

eleven

Switching lanes, I accelerated through traffic, thankful the I-five flowed free. The Saturday mid-morning traffic was light as I traveled north.

Wind pounded my hair, windows and sunroof wide open.

The trip flew by, and faster than I could have imagined, the GPS instructed me to exit and I was hunting for an open parking spot.

I slipped into the first one I could find, cut the engine, and jumped from my car. Black flip-flops that just months ago I'd sworn to never wear crunched against the loose pavement under my feet, flinging sand as I followed the walkway up and over the embankment.

I shielded my eyes, scanning the beachgoers dotting the shore below.

They weren't hard to spot.

Elizabeth sat on a blanket in beige shorts and a red tank top, long legs stretched out in front of her as she reclined against her elbows, hair whipping around as she watched our child playing in the sand. She attempted to tuck a thick tress behind her ear before it was thrashed with another gust of wind.

Hurrying, I wound down the path and hit the heavy sand, sinking with each step I took.

Lizzie noticed me first.

"Daddy!" she cried out, dropping a plastic bucket and waving wildly. Elizabeth sat up and turned toward me, her lips stretching into a smile I was certain could bring any man to his knees.

I waved as I increased my speed, meeting Lizzie halfway when she ran to me. "Lizzie," I sang as I lifted her, swung her around, and brought her to my chest in a playful squeeze. "How's my baby girl today?"

She wrapped herself around my neck, kissed me there. "I missed you, Daddy," she said against my ear.

I'd seen her only last night, yet I'd missed her too. So much.

I set her down and took her hand. She skipped beside me as we made our way to her mother, Elizabeth's face aglow and peaceful as she watched the two of us approach.

"Good morning, Elizabeth."

She pushed the hair from her face and squinted against the sun as she looked up at me. "Hey, Christian. Did you find it okay?"

"Yep." I contemplated for only a second before I plopped down on the blanket beside Elizabeth and pulled Lizzie down with me. I nestled her between my legs and held her around her small shoulders.

I shook off my shoes, buried my toes in the cool, damp sand, and took in the beach that both Elizabeth and Lizzie had so many fond memories of.

This place was something sacred shared between the two of them, and I felt honored to be included. I knew it was rare for even Matthew and Natalie to be a part of it.

And to think only last night I'd felt the bottom dropping out of my world.

Something had touched us in the parking lot of Elizabeth's work Tuesday afternoon, a new connection after I'd walked headlong from my father's firm.

I'd been so sure of it that on the drive over to pick Lizzie up, I'd planned to ask Elizabeth to join us, daydreamed of her in my kitchen preparing dinner with Lizzie and me, saw her sitting next to me at my kitchen table.

I'd gone weak when I'd caught sight of her on her staircase, the reaction she invoked from my body, the things I envisioned doing to hers.

It had taken a few seconds for my mind to catch up with my flesh, and I'd realized she wasn't dressed for an evening spent on the couch alone.

She was going out.

Then that touchy bastard from Lizzie's birthday party had shown up.

It'd felt like she'd run me over, the sharp sting of Elizabeth's hand as it struck me across the cheek, spat in my face. I couldn't help but turn to her, desperate to ask her why.

All I found there were the results of my spoil, as if she'd received the same blow, one I'd inflicted, a reminder that I had done this.

Dinner with Lizzie had been difficult, but I'd forged through it, loved her and made her smile, unwilling to allow my mistakes to steal any more of the precious little time I had with my daughter.

Then Elizabeth had asked me to *stay*.

"Are you hungry?" Elizabeth shifted to her knees and began unpacking the picnic basket, sandwiches wrapped in plastic, whole pieces of fruit, bottles of soda and water.

She glanced at me with a timid smile as she set

them between us.

"Yeah," I answered, helping Lizzie with the wrapper of a sandwich. I twisted the cap from a bottle of water for her and did the same for myself, and then I shared lunch with the two girls who owned me heart and soul.

Lizzie rested against my chest between my bent knees, peeking up at me as I gazed down at her, grinning as she chewed her ham and cheese sandwich.

Her hair flew around us, licking my arms, kissing my chin—it scared me that I might love her too much.

Sated and relaxed, Elizabeth and I sat in silence as Lizzie jogged back to her playthings, far enough away that she submerged herself in her own imaginary world of castles and dragons and princesses but not close enough to the water to cause us alarm.

The sun washed over us, its heat the perfect contradiction to the coolness of the ocean breeze.

Elizabeth stared ahead, but I could almost hear the click, the quickening of her pulse, triggering the same reaction in my own, the rush of nerves as she hugged her knees to her chest.

"Did you think of us?" Her voice was pained, and her question hung in the air as a doorway to our past, one she finally asked me to step through.

Up until now, every time I'd tried to talk to her,

she'd shut me down.

But now it came without provocation, her own instigation.

As much relief as it brought me, I knew there was no way this conversation would be easy.

"Every day." I looked over at her and watched the pain gather in the creases at the corner of her eyes.

She turned and rested the side of her face against her knees as tears pooled in the honeyed amber. "Why didn't you come for us?"

A solicitation for me to finally account for what I'd done.

No. There would be nothing easy about this.

I squirmed while I debated how to explain myself, knowing there would never be any justification.

My conscience assaulted me and I looked to my daughter for strength.

I brought a knee to my chest and anchored myself to it as I dug my other hand in the sand, pulling out a handful and watching it fall through my fist as an hourglass.

Exposed in all my shame, I turned back to Elizabeth in confession. "I did."

I watched her as my words sank in. Her irises widened and a tremor shook her body.

"What?" The word fell as a small cry from her lips.

Exhaling some of the pressure in my chest, I focused on Lizzie, knowing I wouldn't be strong enough to handle the disappointment on Elizabeth's face while I described to her how I'd not only walked out on her once, but twice.

"The night after Lizzie was born. I came to the hospital. I planned on apologizing to you, asking you to take me back." I swallowed the lump in my throat and pressed on. "But Matthew was there . . . and I . . . left."

I mustered enough courage to look at her, to watch her have her heart broken all over again. She turned from me and buried her face in her knees, her body convulsing as she tried to still her racking sobs.

She jerked up, burning with anger, unable to speak, and then closed her eyes, tripped back into sadness.

"That's how you knew about Matthew," she said under her breath. She seemed disoriented as she tried to acclimate herself to this most dishonorable revelation.

I couldn't stop now, even when I was certain my words would do more damage than good, but when I came back into this, I'd promised myself I would always be truthful with her.

"That night, I convinced myself I was doing the right thing . . . sacrificing for you so you could have a normal life with Matthew. I realize now it was just an excuse, Elizabeth. I walked away from *my child* because I thought I couldn't have *you*. I never even knew if she was a boy or a girl." This admission flowed like poison from my mouth, vile in its offense.

"I regretted it every day. I'd always expected to hear from you with a request for child support or . . . something. I waited, but none ever came." No apology could ever rectify this wrong, but still I needed her to understand.

Elizabeth's bottom lip quivered, and she shook her head, a clear dismissal of my reasoning. "That doesn't make it any better, Christian."

She looked out upon Lizzie, and then leveled her eyes back on me.

"Maybe it makes it worse. For so long I believed we never even crossed your mind, that the moment I'd walked out of your apartment we'd been forgotten, and to find out you . . . you waited for me to *come to you*," she stressed the words.

"It's just . . ." she said, at a loss for what to say as her voice trailed off.

"I thought you were happy."

She sniffled and rocked herself. "How could you think that? Did you not believe that I *loved* you? That I wanted to spend my life with you?"

"Of course, I knew you loved me." My voice rose in frustration. "There's nothing I can say that can make any sense of the decisions I made.

Bottom line, I was a selfish asshole."

I splayed my hand through my hair, helpless, losing the grip I'd had on my control.

I angled toward her, capturing her face with my eyes as I pled with her. "It doesn't change anything, Elizabeth, but I *truly* am sorry. If I could, I'd take it back, right back to the moment I made you choose between me and our child. That was the worst decision I've ever made."

She turned away and sat silent while she listened to my explanation, watching the waves race in against the sand, their constant ebb and flow but still steady progress as they claimed a stake further up the bank, just like us, the low necessary to reach the high.

I looked out at the horizon, unable to discern where the ocean met the sky, and settled into her quiet as I continued to speak.

"My mother . . ." I felt her eyes fall on me. "She always pushed me to find you, told me I was wrong in staying away. I never believed her until I saw Lizzie in that store."

I looked at Elizabeth who was staring at me as my words turned to desperation. "She means everything to me, Elizabeth."

You mean everything to me.

I didn't say it aloud. She wasn't ready to hear it yet.

Even under the weight of the conversation, I

saw in her expression that she at least understood *this*, accepted that I adored Lizzie.

That expression shifted as if something had just occurred to her, her words flowing with the quiet shock of her realization. "You left your father's firm because of her."

I didn't respond. I didn't have to. I'd give up anything for my child.

Elizabeth glanced at Lizzie and then back at me. "I'm so sorry, Christian."

"I'm not," I said with complete conviction, because it was true.

I couldn't go on working for a man who would say such unfounded, disgusting words about Elizabeth and my child.

I should have walked away six years ago.

She chuckled quietly, and I could tell by the softness that settled on her face that it was not at my expense, but in her own surprise with my actions.

"You are a mystery, Christian Davison."

I shook my head at her notion. "No, Elizabeth. I've just changed."

She nodded almost imperceptibly, her lips parting as the idea seemed to penetrate her, her eyes setting in agreement. I hoped she believed that change was for the better.

Taking a collective breath, we turned our attention back to Lizzie and watched while she filled bucketfuls of sand with a small plastic shovel, tipped them over into towers that housed the captive of her fairy tales, her mouth moving without voice as she played out the scene unfolding in her head.

It was as if we had called a time-out, a reprieve from the past, needing a moment to regain a measure of equilibrium before pressing forward.

Finally, I broached the topic I was sure neither of wanted to discuss. "Will you tell me about Matthew?"

She emitted a heavy breath, though didn't seem surprised by my line of questioning.

"Matthew." She released an affectionate huff. "We tried so hard to fall in love. The first time I slept with him, I was four months pregnant with Lizzie."

I flinched at her brutal honesty, but that's exactly what the last six years had been—brutal.

Swallowing, she seemed to get lost in the memory.

"I cried the whole time." Her voice dropped in slow ruefulness. "Matthew was so good to me. He kissed away my tears and promised that it would be okay, that somehow we would make it work."

She glanced at me askance, not meeting my face.

I realized I was holding my breath.

"But it was always forced. We loved each other, but not like that. The day after we got to San

Diego, Natalie showed up at our doorstep to meet my new daughter and boyfriend, and it was like . . . like . . ."

She looked up at me as if she were wondering if I could understand. "Like they could touch each other from across the room."

"I let him go that night." She laughed without humor and shook her head. "Of course, he tried to refuse, adamant that Lizzie and I were his family, and he'd never leave us like that."

We cringed at the same time, cutting words that hadn't been her intention. Her eyes flashed to mine. "I'm sorry, Christian, I didn't mean—"

I shook my head, stopping her. "It's okay, Elizabeth."

She shouldn't apologize for my deficiencies. The truth was that I'd left her.

"Anyway," she went on, "we talked the entire night, and we both decided if he stayed, we were only prolonging the inevitable. He packed a small bag and checked into a hotel down the street from my apartment. Within two weeks he had moved in with Natalie."

She sighed with a shrug. "When it didn't hurt, I knew we'd made the right decision."

She looked at me with a grimace etched into her beautiful face. "All I felt was relief."

I had no clue what to say—if I should say anything at all.

All I knew was that I owed more gratitude to Matthew than I had ever imagined.

"But he continued to take care of you?" I inclined my head toward Lizzie while still holding her gaze, unwilling to break this free flow of trust.

She smiled, the warmth of her face the same as if it were directly focused on Matthew. "Yeah, he did everything he could for us. That first year after he and Natalie got together, I hated being a constant burden on him, so I tried to hide things from him."

From this came the first amount of regret I'd seen from Elizabeth when she talked of Matthew, and she shifted in discomfort. "All it did was cause him more worry, so we ended up becoming this strange little family that we are."

Running a hand through my windblown hair, I deliberated for a second before I decided that since we'd finally found ourselves being so candid, I should take it as far as it would go.

"Was there ever anyone else?" I asked, worried I might not be able to stomach her answer.

She bit her bottom lip, shaking off what must have been an involuntary shudder. "There was this guy . . . Shawn." She gulped for air. "He was an asshole."

She shook her head again and looked at me, almost pleading. "I really don't want to talk about him."

Now *I* felt like the asshole, but still I pushed. "Did you love him?"

"No," she said, the word flying from her mouth before I could finish the sentence.

From the look of disgust set deep at the core of her eyes, I knew she was speaking the truth. While I wanted to ask more about him, I could see that it was a shut door, one that needn't be pried open by my jealousy.

"And Scott?" I asked, again feeling guilty for digging so deep, but unable to stop myself when I found myself so close to Elizabeth's heart, to her soul that been laid bare, taking just a little more.

She appeared to be almost amused by my prodding, embracing me in the warmth of her small, knowing smile.

"No, Christian. Last night was . . ." The levity from seconds before was replaced with total resolution and a tinge of remorse. "A mistake."

The relief that escaped me was audible, and I ducked my head, chuckling at just how obvious I was.

She nudged me with her elbow, the heat of her arm spurring a reaction in me that was becoming harder and harder to suppress.

I hadn't realized we'd gravitated to each other, our bodies now just inches apart. "So, what about you?"

It came out as almost a tease, though I could

feel the pain simmering just below the surface.

I brought my face up to meet hers and saw the fear in the way her eyes, never at ease, skittered across my face, her sun-kissed skin blanching where she dug her nails into her legs.

"God, Elizabeth, do you really want to know?"

She averted her eyes, contemplative, before raising them back to mine and nodding.

"I think I do," she said as she seemed to come to a resolution, her gaze becoming firm as she stared at me across the small space.

There was a moment that I considered lying to her, sparing her the obscene, especially in light of the divulgence of her not-so-scandalous past, but I just couldn't bring myself to that type of dishonesty.

I searched for air and my voice.

Finally, I just forced myself to speak. "That first year"—*when you were pregnant and sick and needed me*—"I tried to forget you."

I snorted in revulsion at the memory. "I slept with any girl who'd let me."

Elizabeth whimpered and her eyes glistened, but she lifted her chin and waited for me to continue.

"Then after seeing you at the hospital, I realized that who I'd become made me sick, and I couldn't continue on that way."

That brave chin quivered, but I didn't stop.

I just looked away and let the words bleed from

my mouth, low and monotone. "I dated a little bit but pretty much filled my time with school. Then I met Brittany."

I felt Elizabeth tense at my side, heard the sharp intake of air.

"We lived together for almost two years."

I could sense that Elizabeth had begun to cry again, but I continued with my attention trained on the ground, wishing I could somehow find a way to bury my shame there.

"She wanted to get married, and when I couldn't make that commitment, she left me."

While it had been sad to see my friend go, watching Brittany pack her things and leave had been so much like Elizabeth's depiction of when Matthew had gone.

The winning emotion had been one of intense relief.

"You didn't love her?" Elizabeth choked as she squeezed the words out one by one.

"Yes . . . in a way. I mean, I cared for her. She was kind and sweet but . . ."

But just like she and Matthew, I never loved Brittany that way.

"But what?"

Without hesitation, I looked up to meet Elizabeth's face, her cheeks wet and blotchy.

"She wasn't you."

She squeezed her eyes shut, sending more tears

racing down her beautiful face.

The hurt she wore broke me, and I couldn't stand the distance any longer.

"Elizabeth," I said so slowly, so softly as I reached out to cup her face to give her comfort for all the pain I had caused her, to show her how much I still loved her.

She winced with the contact and pulled away as her eyes fluttered open, leaving my hand suspended midair.

"Don't." She shook her head and swallowed. "It's too late for us, Christian."

I didn't miss the doubt that washed over her when she spoke those words, though she continued in delusive determination.

"I can't do this," she said as she gestured rapidly between the two of us, squeezing her eyes shut again as if she didn't believe it herself.

When she opened her eyes again, she amended the motion to include Lizzie and an expectant smile displaced the despondent resignation of seconds before. "But I *can* do this . . . I *want* to do this."

She nodded vigorously, and her soggy smile spread, hopeful of my response.

I smiled slow, allowing it to smolder and then light with the joy that surged through my veins with her request, wishing nothing more than the freedom to kiss the sweetness of her wet mouth as it grew with reception.

Instead, I captured the last tear that slid down her face and then wound my finger in the lock of hair matted on her cheek, giving it a slight tug of affection in anticipation of what I knew was to come.

Because while she said never, what I heard her say was she wasn't ready yet.

I stood, dusted off the sand clinging to my shorts, and extended my hand out to her.

"Come on, let's go play and with our daughter."

She laughed and wiped her face with the back of her hand before reaching up to take it.

I had spent nearly the entire weekend with Lizzie and Elizabeth. The three of us had played on the beach until the sun finally dipped into the horizon and brought a chill to the air, and we'd ended the almost perfect day with dinner and ice cream cones.

With Sunday morning had come a text inviting me to breakfast, a meal shared over a table of laughter and ease, one that seemed to shape a sort of truce between Matthew and me.

While a vestige of his distrust still lingered, he seemed to slowly be warming to the idea of me being a part of Elizabeth and Lizzie's lives.

I'd wished the weekend would never end, but

unfortunately, Monday had come, and with it, the ball of nerves I currently found myself in.

I straightened my tie, grabbed my briefcase, and took one last glance at myself in the mirror before walking out my front door and to the elevator.

Looking for a position at another law firm had been the last thing I'd ever thought I'd have to do. I'd always believed that one day I'd be my father's successor.

Funny how things changed in the blink of an eye.

The elevator opened to the parking garage below and I rushed toward my car. Just as I opened the door, someone called out my name.

"Christian Davison?" It was posed as a question.

I paused to look over my shoulder at the man in a baseball cap and jacket approaching from across the garage.

"Yes?"

With my confirmation, he pulled a thick envelope from his jacket. I closed my eyes in fruitless defense as his intent became clear.

I supposed this was inevitable, but I'd hoped that once, *just once*, family would come first.

I took the package without dispute and sank into my car, wondering how he could do this to me.

With a heavy heart, I ran my finger under the flap and freed its bond.

It was exactly as I'd expected.

My father was suing me.

I drove aimlessly around the city, passing time, trying not to focus on the envelope sitting on my passenger seat.

I couldn't believe the man could be so cold.

He was suing me for essentially everything, as if he'd tracked my every asset and every deficit— every venture and every loss.

The only thing he hadn't accounted for was the money I'd socked away for Lizzie before I'd even known her name.

At least that was hidden, protected from his greed.

Beyond that, my father hoped to wipe me out.

At five thirty, I pulled up to Elizabeth and Lizzie's house unannounced and agitated, desperate for the solace that could only be found in them.

I was hit by a staggering wave of relief when Elizabeth opened the door and, with an understanding smile, welcomed me inside.

As long as I had these two, I could take whatever else was thrown my way.

I pulled Lizzie's blanket up tighter over her body, nuzzling my nose in her hair as I wished her a good night.

Elizabeth had already gone downstairs to give me a few minutes alone with our child.

Lizzie snuggled deeper into her pillow and murmured a tired, "Night, Daddy."

With a slow grin, she added, "Love you."

Every time she said it, I felt like my heart would burst through my chest.

I pressed my lips to her forehead and whispered, "I love you, princess."

I stood and crossed the room, pausing at the doorway to take in a few more seconds of my precious daughter. Then I switched off the light and left the door cracked open the same way Elizabeth did.

As I crept downstairs, my heart picked up a notch, the way it always did when I knew I was going to be alone with Elizabeth.

Since our talk on the beach two months ago, I'd spent nearly every day with them. Each one had brought me closer to Lizzie, closer to Elizabeth, as our lives merged and slowly became one.

Being with them this way as a family brought me more joy than I'd ever believed possible. Not even the lawsuit looming in the distance could do anything to dampen my spirits.

But even with as close as we had grown, there

was a part of herself that Elizabeth kept closed off.

It was the part that was found in the tension that filled the room and fought for release each and every time we were alone.

She *wanted* me, I knew, but she wasn't ready.

I hadn't pushed, though that was becoming harder and harder to do. I ached for her, a physical need that kept me awake through the long hours of the night and often woke me just as soon as I'd finally drift to sleep.

My body craved attention, something it had gone so long without. The need she created in me had not gone unnoticed but remained unheeded, just as she continued to ignore her own desire.

I knew it was just a matter of time before one of us cracked.

I took a steeling breath in preparation of Elizabeth's presence before I made my way across her living room and toward the kitchen.

At the archway, I peeked in and was going to say something to make myself known but stopped short when she came into view.

Elizabeth sat at the table surrounded by a stack of mail. Her face was wet with tears as she read what she held in her hand.

I didn't have to ask her what it was.

I stepped forward, tentative, praying this wouldn't cause us another setback. I wasn't sure I could handle her running away from me again.

She looked up when she heard me, her brown eyes watery, confused—maybe even hurt.

"What is *this*?" she asked, searching my face.

I closed my eyes and ran my hands through my hair, struggling to find a way to explain.

So many times, I'd wanted to tell her, to warn her of what I was about to do, but it had never seemed to be the right time to broach the subject.

At least that's what I'd been telling myself. In reality, it had only been left unsaid because I was afraid of Elizabeth's reaction—the reaction I now saw on her face.

Gathering my courage, I took the few steps needed to bring me to Elizabeth's side, knelt beside her, and whispered her name. It sounded like an apology.

"Why?" She shook her head as she sat back, refusing to look at me and staring at the papers in front of her.

With a shaky hand, I took them from her and set them aside. Elizabeth only watched the movement, still not meeting my eyes.

I looked up at her and tried to get her to see me, to understand. "It was always hers, Elizabeth."

I touched the edge of the document that authorized the transfer of funds from my name to Elizabeth's. The money was to be used for the care of Lizzie and only Elizabeth's signature was required to finalize it.

The sum was significant, but as far as I was concerned, not nearly enough.

Even though I couldn't see it, I knew the sheet below described the payments that would come out of my checks and deposited into Elizabeth's bank account now that I had started with the new firm.

Even if my father took everything else, Lizzie would have what was rightfully hers.

I knew well enough that the lawsuit would never yield what it asked, that the huge number was there as a threat, a way for my father to hold his hand over me just for a little while longer.

Even so, both my attorney and I thought it safest if it officially rested in Elizabeth's hands, in the hands that now shook as she fisted them and pressed them into her thighs.

"You can't buy us, Christian," she finally said as she pushed the papers away.

I rubbed a hand over my face, frustrated with the situation but not surprised by the backlash. This was exactly why I had said nothing, why I would have kept the money in my name had I been given any other choice.

Leaning in closer on my knee, I turned to face her while she tried to hide her sadness behind the wall of blond waves that concealed her face.

With an unsteady hand, I reached out and brushed them back, hoping to coax her from her anger. "Elizabeth, baby, look at me."

She flinched at the affection, at the touch of my hand, at the endearment that fell from my lips so easily. It was one that had been uttered so many times before but never since she'd walked from my door years ago.

I withdrew my hand, cursing myself for the act that had felt so natural—comforting Elizabeth, loving her.

I shrank away from the rejection and looked to the floor as I choked through the words, offered more of my regret. "I just want to take care of my daughter."

To take care of you.

She chewed on her bottom lip, fighting another round of tears, her jaw quivering. She looked at the papers on the table and then finally back at me when she asked, "How long?" It was an accusation.

"I don't know." I shrugged with vagueness. "A while now."

She shook her head in clear irritation. "I asked how long, Christian."

Sighing, I looked away and answered quietly, almost wishing she wouldn't hear. "Five years."

Her expression raged from confused to hurt to bitter to broken.

Like an idiot, I reached for her again.

This time she jerked away and put a hand out to

stop me.

She closed her eyes, guarded herself, put the wall back in place. "I need you to leave."

I opened my mouth, desperate to reason with her, to make her understand what my intentions had been, but nothing would come.

Swallowing, I nodded and stood as it hit me just how badly her refusal had stung.

While there were so many things I had to apologize for, providing for my daughter wasn't one of them.

I paused in the archway to look back at her, my voice sounding just as despondent as I felt.

"If you don't want the money, Elizabeth, then fine, don't touch it. Save it until Lizzie turns eighteen. But one way or the other, it belongs to her."

I *knew* she'd be upset, that every time money was mentioned, Elizabeth would tense, that she fought ferociously to be independent because she'd had to do it for so long.

Even so, I'd believed we'd talk through it and together we'd make a plan for Lizzie's future, for *our* future.

I guess I'd been a fool to think we'd come so far.

With my hopes crushed, I started my car and backed out of Elizabeth's driveway.

I was halfway home when my phone rang.

Elizabeth was on the other end sobbing. The only thing I understood her say was, "Please come back."

twelve

ELIZABETH

As I weaved my small car through the traffic heading downtown, I felt a bit nervous, though I wasn't quite sure why.

It wasn't as if I hadn't spent almost every day with Christian for the past two months or more.

I'd just never been to his place before.

Lizzie, on the other hand, could hardly contain herself.

"Mommy, look!" Lizzie squealed from the backseat. I glanced in the rearview mirror to see her pointing at one of the towering buildings ahead.

"There's Daddy's house." Her eyes were wide in anticipation, her body humming in excitement as she squirmed in her booster seat.

Tonight would be the first night she'd ever slept over at her father's house.

Switching lanes, I pulled into the underground parking lot and entered the code Christian had given me.

Chuckling, I rushed to keep up with Lizzie as she unbuckled her seat belt and grabbed her things. She swung her door open wide and stood impatiently at mine.

"Come on, Mommy!" She ran ahead, her backpack bouncing with each step, her doll tucked under her arm.

Adorable.

She pressed the button to the side of the elevator; it was obvious she was familiar with the routine. She was grinning as she yelled, "Hurry up, Mommy!"

She was forever excited to be with her father.

I wondered when that had stopped hurting.

I caught up to her and entered the elevator. We rode it the ten floors to Christian's condo, and I followed her down the hallway to his door.

I went to knock, but Lizzie turned the knob before I could. She ran in unannounced, squealing her delight as she called out for her father.

Christian didn't seem surprised by her entrance,

but turned from where he sat on the couch, a computer resting on his lap, black-framed glasses on his eyes, and a welcome on his face.

Breathtaking.

I shook away the thought and instead, focused on my daughter's joy.

Christian set his computer aside just in time for her to jump on his lap. "Hi, Daddy!"

"Hi, princess." He nuzzled his nose in her hair, held her.

My chest swelled as I watched them and internally celebrated their reunion, thankful my daughter had this.

Christian looked over his shoulder and smiled at me from where I still stood in his doorway. "Hey, Elizabeth."

"Hey." I offered a small smile and stepped forward.

For the first time I took in my surroundings.

There was one large room that served as living space and kitchen. There was a hall off to the right that I assumed led to the bedrooms.

The view of the ocean was beautiful, but the home on scale was much smaller than I'd expected.

Less assuming.

Warmer.

It surprised me, much as everything seemed to where Christian was concerned.

As I crossed the room, Christian watched me as

if he relished each step that brought me closer to him.

I still hadn't come to terms with the revelation of last weekend—a savings account in my name that held more money than I'd make in five years at the bank.

The amount of anger I'd felt when I'd opened the fattened envelope had been blinding, enough to make my head spin and my blood boil.

Of course I understood what Christian was trying to do, that he desired to provide for his daughter and, though he never said it, provide for me as well.

What he couldn't understand was how in the process he had trivialized the trials *I* had overcome, the difficulties I'd faced, and the hardships I'd endured.

It made light of the nights I'd spent awake while I'd worried for my daughter's future and wondered how we would survive.

Part of me had argued that I couldn't blame him, that he didn't know what I'd been through.

But, really, that was the issue; he didn't know because he had never been man enough to check.

I still didn't know if I could ever forgive him for that.

As deep as my resentment went, that anger paled in comparison to the void his absence had left, and I was on the phone begging him back before I'd even realized what I was doing, before I could comprehend the hold he had on me.

It scared me to feel my resolve slip as Christian chipped away at my heart, a little here and a little there, slowly rendering me weak, just as he had done so many years before.

Sometimes I wondered why I fought it, fought him, that no matter how hard I tried, we'd end up in the same place—the place where he had control of my heart, the place where he could shatter it just as easily as he could make it whole.

That pain was fresh enough to know it was not a place I wanted to be.

I remembered it as I sank down beside the two of them on his couch, conscious to leave a small amount of space between us—distance.

It didn't stop his eyes from their touch, from the embrace of his gaze as it washed over me, lingering on my mouth.

I closed my eyes to shield myself from it, my only defense. Even then, I *felt* him.

I opened them when I felt his attention shift and the weight of his gaze subside, his voice only for our child. "So, what do you want to do tonight, sweetheart?"

It was easy to regret that I wouldn't be spending the evening with them as I listened to them make their plans, an evening of games, stories, a quiet night in. Having watched them play enough, I was sure there would be lots laughter, plenty of hugs, tender embraces.

The clock against the wall indicated it was getting late, so with reluctance, I declared that I needed to go.

At the door, I knelt to hug my daughter to my chest and whispered for her to have a great time with her dad.

She nodded and squeezed me tighter. "I'll miss you, Mommy."

I released a heavy breath against the side of her head. "I'll miss you, too, sweetheart."

Even if I was looking forward to the evening, there was a part of me that hated any time spent away from her, the part that would always rather stay.

Christian stood to the side of us, his hands burrowed deep in the pockets of his jeans, his eyes soft as he watched us say our goodbyes.

I wondered if he felt anything like I did when I watched them say goodbye.

When I rose, I brushed his arm, and I hoped it wasn't too obvious when I pulled away.

Other than by chance, I'd only reached for him once, the day at the beach when he'd extended his hand. It was a connection that had proven to be too much, and I'd released his hold just as quickly as I had taken it.

If he noticed it now, he didn't acknowledge it.

Instead he smiled. "Thanks, Elizabeth."

I shook my head and released a small laugh at his needless thanks. "I asked you to keep her tonight, remember?"

"I know." He inclined his head toward Lizzie. "This just means a lot."

I nodded. I had long since accepted his devotion to our daughter, though I still couldn't keep myself from praying that trust wasn't a mistake.

But even if it were, I wouldn't steal this time from Lizzie.

It was hers, and for now, she was adored. And as long as she was, I wouldn't let my fears get in the way.

I smiled down at my wide-eyed daughter and then directed it at Christian. "You two have a great time tonight."

Christian looked at his feet and then back at me. "Wish you were staying with us."

Me too.

Instead of admitting it, I nodded and started out the door, waving over my shoulder with a laugh as Christian's tone turned teasing when he called out, "You girls don't get into too much trouble tonight."

There wasn't much risk of that.

I drove across town and pulled up to Mom's house a couple of minutes after six. The street was already lined with the cars of those I loved.

Mom had called a *girls' night* as these nights were so aptly referred to, a night of reprieve from the everyday stressors of life.

This was a night to laugh and unwind, to joke, to uplift, to renew the everlasting bonds of the women of this family.

It served to remind us of why we'd flocked back to this city.

I always appreciated the time set aside to remember just how much we needed each other.

I walked up the narrow sidewalk to the small house I'd grown up in. The neighborhood was old but valued by its residents, well-kept and well-maintained.

The dark green shutters showed evidence of a fresh coat of paint, and the planters under the windows were bursting with fall color. Lush trees grew along the house, tall and proud.

With my overnight bag slung over my shoulder, I walked through my mother's front door without a knock. I was hit with the sound of high-pitched laughter coming from the kitchen.

It was apparent girls' night was already in full swing. Grinning, I set my bag aside, made my way across the family room, and swung the door open to the kitchen.

Immediately, everyone welcomed me, a resounding *Elizabeth* engulfing me as I entered the room.

Mom and Aunt Donna, the family matriarchs, our cornerstones, sat at the small kitchen table. They were laughing as they drank beer from cans and ate potato chips.

Both of their voices were a deep alto, a rich vibration that spoke of security and stability.

I went straight to Mom, kissed her cheek, and told her how happy I was to see her.

Next, I hugged Aunt Donna and then her daughter, Kelly, Natalie's older sister.

Kelly was two years my junior, sweet and shy. She always seemed to linger on the outskirts of conversation with not much to say but always had a permanent smile on her face.

Their sister-in-law, Samantha, stood at the end of the bar that separated the kitchen and breakfast nook, her belly round with her first child.

She sipped from a glass of lemon-mint water I was sure my sister Sarah had been thoughtful enough to prepare for her.

I went to her, pressed my hands to her stomach, and told her how I excited I was to meet her baby boy.

She held her hands over mine, her smile endless, exuding joy.

On the other side of the bar at the kitchen counter, Sarah was arranging cheese and crackers on a tray, mixing dips, and slicing vegetables.

True to form, her hands were never idle. She

only paused long enough to offer me a tight hug and tell me she was glad I was here, before she was hard at work again.

We'd long since given up trying to get her to relax.

Natalie and Carrie sat on barstools that were swiveled around to face the table.

I leaned in to place a kiss on their cheeks, raising my eyebrows and shaking my head in mock disapproval as it became quite clear the two of them had been sucking down cocktails faster than Sarah could make them.

There were only eight of us, but within the confines of my mother's small kitchen, it felt as if it were crawling with people, overflowing as we moved around the space, but comfortable at the same time.

Now that I was here, I no longer regretted that I wasn't spending the evening with Lizzie and Christian.

They needed their own time together, and I certainly *needed* this—a night to loosen the binds of my wound-up heart, to leave it unguarded, and for once not to feel the need to hold myself in restraint.

With that thought, I graciously accepted the glass of white wine that Sarah offered and pulled a chair from the table.

I curled my legs up under me and allowed

myself to relax. I grinned at the conversations happening around me.

It was no surprise that Natalie and Carrie were the most vocal, forever entertaining. They'd always been close from the time they were small children, and their bond had only grown over the years.

While Natalie and I were like sisters, relying upon each other in day-to-day life, Natalie and Carrie were best of friends. They'd spent years talking about boys, first kisses, first loves, every secret.

Sometimes I was surprised it caused me no jealousy.

When Matthew had come along, Natalie had needed Carrie and had relied on her as someone she could count on who wouldn't judge, who'd only listen. Just because I had given

Matthew and Natalie my blessing didn't mean that it hadn't caused them a great amount of guilt, that there wasn't talk, that everyone in the family had viewed their newfound relationship with approval.

I'd seen the shame Natalie bore, and I was the last person she could talk to during that time. I'd just been thankful Carrie had been there to keep her together while I'd helplessly watched her falling apart.

Mom and Donna dove into their favorite topic—greatly exaggerated stories of our youth.

Each of us added our own memories to them. Laughter rang out, our smiles wide, the volume of our voices increasing with each story told, every glass emptied.

I found I was really enjoying myself, unable to remember feeling so relaxed in a very long time. It wasn't as if I didn't treasure every second with Lizzie. But Mom was right. I needed a break, a night without responsibility.

Natalie and Carrie grew louder, giggling and chatting amongst themselves, but not so wrapped up in each other that they weren't a part of the rest of us.

Sarah finally moved from her post in the kitchen and took a seat beside me at the table. She groaned in pleasure when she propped her feet up at the edge of my chair and sipped one of the drinks she'd been feeding Natalie and Carrie all night. I flashed a meaningful smile in her direction, one that told her she deserved a break too.

As the night progressed, we went around in a circle, each one filling in the rest of us on her life, what had happened since the last time we'd all met.

Some stories were of little significance, others of great importance, our joys and struggles, the everyday, the life changing.

"So, how's my sweet little Lizzie?" Mom asked, turning the attention to me.

Apparently, it was my turn.

"She's doing great," I answered without hesitation. I'm sure the smile on my face was a mile wide as I gushed with mother's pride.

It was so strange that my baby girl was now already in kindergarten, and I told them of how well she'd adjusted from preschool to "big girl" school as Lizzie liked to call it, how she blossomed every day, and how I worried if I closed my eyes for too long, when I opened them, she'd be a woman.

I opened and closed my mouth, unsure how to phrase it.

"Christian's around . . . a lot," I said carefully, hopeful not to upset Mom.

Every time she'd asked, I'd skirted around the subject and never answered her directly. It wasn't that I was trying to be dishonest or hide it from her.

I just knew I wouldn't know how to answer the questions she would have.

Just like now.

She frowned, the natural creases that lined her face deepening. "What does that mean?"

I tried to sound casual. "He just . . . tries to spend a lot of time with Lizzie."

"Pssh . . . spend a lot of time with Lizzie?" Natalie cut in as she waved her hand in a gesture that said my statement was ridiculous.

Shaking her head, she leaned forward as if she

had the juiciest bit of gossip to share. She should have known better, because to the occupants of this house, it was. "That man is at her house every day, and it's *not* just to see Lizzie."

I shot her a look that told her to *shut the hell up.*

"What?" Natalie asked in defense as if I should have no problem with her sharing something so private. "It's not a big deal, Liz. I think it's great . . . so does Matthew," she added with a shrug.

A collective gasp went around the room, and that shock shifted to unease.

A mixture of embarrassment and anger flared on my face and heated my cheeks.

This wasn't how this conversation was supposed to go.

I'd wanted to ease the rest of my family into the idea of Christian being a part of our lives, not have Nat giving them fuel for the assumptions I was sure they were already going to make.

She knew my mother didn't know Christian had become something so *significant.*

To the rest of these women, he was still the "infamous Christian Davison."

"Are you back together with him?" Mom demanded with her brow knitted in what I could only assume was disgust.

I couldn't tell if that disgust was due to the idea of that being a reality or if she was hurt because she thought she'd been kept in the dark about something so important in my life.

"No . . . no . . . of course not," I rambled, shaking my head, unsure of what to say because I had no explanation for what he was. I didn't know myself.

"Well if you don't want him, I'll take him," Carrie piped up, laughing through slurred words as if it were the funniest thing she'd ever said. "That is one gorgeous man."

"Shut up, Carrie," I spat in her direction. She had no right to say something like that, drunk or not.

She laughed, not even fazed that she'd upset me. She'd probably not even noticed.

"I mean, come on, Liz. Have you seen the man? You think he's going stick around? Wait for you forever? Somebody's gonna catch him." She shrugged and smirked. "Might as well be me."

My hands shook and tears pricked at my eyes. Right then, I hated my little sister.

"Shut up," I said through gritted teeth, seething before I stood and slammed my wine glass down on the kitchen table. "Just shut the hell up!"

She sat back, shocked by my reaction, before a horrified expression crossed her face when she realized she'd really hurt me.

"Liz, I'm sorry, you know I was just playing around," she slurred, reaching for me.

I shrugged her hand off and shook my head. I

couldn't listen to her right now.

I stormed from the room to the sound of Sarah's mock applause. "That's really great, Carrie. Real cute."

"I didn't mean—" Carrie said, trying to defend herself, but stopping short when Sarah's voice overtook hers.

"Just shut up, Carrie. You've said enough tonight."

The door closed behind me, leaving me with trembling hands and the sound of muddled, heated words coming from the other room.

I rushed to get my jacket on, shaking as I fumbled with the zipper on my bag and then flung it over my shoulder and onto my back.

The door swung open, and for a moment Aunt Donna's words became clear as she scolded Natalie and Carrie as if they were schoolgirls who'd been caught smoking in the bathroom, rebuking their banter, criticizing for inconsiderate words.

Mom stood in the doorway, her eyes sympathetic and worried. As soon as they landed on my face, I broke.

Tears rolled down my cheeks, hot and angry and hurt.

She crossed the room and took me in her arms. She wiped my tears and whispered that Carrie didn't mean what she'd said.

I shook my head against her shoulder, allowed

myself to fall apart in her comfort. "I don't know what to do," I cried again and again, desperate for Mom to understand, to have an answer.

I didn't know what to do.

She shushed me, pushed the matted hair from my face, and shook her head in empathy.

"Oh, Elizabeth, honey." She tightened her hold and ran her hand through my hair. "I can't tell you what to do, sweetheart. That's something you're going to have to decide for yourself," she murmured against my head, a hopeless consolation.

I cried harder, clung to her, wished for the day when just her touch had eased my every fear, her advice an answer for my every question.

How could I ever decide if I could never know for sure that he wouldn't hurt me or wouldn't leave me once again?

She stepped back and lifted my chin, searching my face. "You still love him?"

I was sure she knew I did, had probably always known, although every word I'd ever spoken of Christian to her had been riddled with scorn.

Closing my eyes, I nodded once against her hand.

She released a heavy breath, and I opened my eyes to her slowly shaking her head. Her eyes were sad and she seemed to struggle with what to say.

After what he'd done, I knew it would take a

very long time for her to forgive Christian for hurting her child so deeply, and I could see in her face that she was scared for me, scared for Lizzie.

But I also knew she'd never ridicule me if I chose to be with him.

She turned up a small, understanding smile and reached out to squeeze my hands, a reiteration. *You have to decide for yourself.*

I squeezed back. "I love you, Mom."

Her smile grew just a fraction. "I love you so much, Liz."

She looked over her shoulder, back to me, and tugged on my hands. "Come on. Let's not let this ruin our night."

Grimacing, I stepped back and wiped my eyes with the back of my hand. "I think I'm going to go home."

There were too many thoughts racing through my head, too much confusion, too many suppressed emotions vying for release.

Mom's face fell. "Liz, honey . . . it's late and you've been drinking."

"I'll call a cab. I just want to be alone." It wasn't really the truth. I just didn't want to be here.

She sighed but offered no further argument and instead, stepped forward to take me in her arms again. She made no false promises, didn't tell me that it would be okay, and didn't tell me that it'd all work out.

She simply smothered me in her warmth, showered me in love and unending support.

Finally, she dropped her arms and told me to call her if I wanted to talk.

"Night, Mom."

"Goodnight."

I stepped out, the cool night biting my flaming cheeks. I tugged my jacket tighter and hugged myself. I was feeling embarrassed, foolish about my overreaction, vulnerable in my thoughts.

Sniffling away the evidence of my tears, I dug in my purse to find my phone and dialed the number I'd seen plastered on the side of taxicabs so many times before.

The night was quiet, the city covered in a heavy sheet of dark gray sky. I breathed in the damp air, lifted my face to it, never felt more alone.

It took only a few minutes before headlights cut through the night and lit the street, and a taxicab came to a stop in front of my mother's house.

I stole one last glance behind me before I climbed into the backseat and gave the driver directions to my home.

Blowing the air from my lungs, I tried to clear my mind. My head lolled against the dingy vinyl seat, and I was unsure if the sick feeling in my stomach stemmed from the excess alcohol in my system or from the confrontation I'd just had with my sister.

My phone buzzed in my lap with a text message, then buzzed again and again with a progressive string of apologies from my little sister begging for forgiveness, promising she was just kidding, that she didn't really mean it, that she loved me.

I knew I really wasn't upset with my sister, but with the truth of what she'd said. Christian wouldn't wait around forever.

Could I handle it when one day he came to *me*, his blue eyes dancing as he told me that he'd met someone, as he confided in his *friend* that he had fallen in love? Would I be able to smile and tell him how happy I was for him? Could I give him encouragement? Offer advice?

I rolled my eyes at myself.

I couldn't even handle my little sister joking about it.

I typed back a quick response, one that would ease her and let her know it was okay, that she was forgiven—a simple *I love you too.*

Fifteen minutes later, the taxi pulled up to the curb in front of my house. The windows were dark and the faint yellow glow of the porch lamp offered the only light.

Alone.

The driver looked over his shoulder, frowning.

Shaking myself out of my daze, I pulled my wallet from my purse and handed him a twenty, mumbling a quiet, "Thank you," as I floundered my way from the backseat of the car.

He waited until I opened the door to the emptiness of my house before he drove away.

I locked the door behind me and dragged myself upstairs. I washed my face and brushed my teeth, couldn't keep the thoughts at bay.

Brittany.

That name had eaten at me over the last couple of months.

Unknown pictures of her had swam through my head as I imagined what she had been like and what had drawn him to her, and I'd often fallen asleep thinking of him falling asleep with her.

The shame had been clear as he'd admitted his past to me, the many faceless women he'd been with, those whose names he'd probably not even known.

It wasn't *those* that had bothered me, though, *those* that haunted me in the night, *those* that evoked an ache in my chest and made it hard to breathe.

What bothered me was that he'd found someone he'd cared enough about to lie beside night after night, someone he cared enough about to share the day-to-day.

How long before he found someone like her again?

It was with those thoughts that I found myself sitting up in bed in the darkness of my room, clutching my phone with my eyes closed, willing myself to stay strong—to ignore the need to hear his voice. It was only after midnight, not so late that he would think it strange that I was calling, asking about Lizzie an easy excuse.

Would he know that it wasn't the true reason I called?

Would he know I was already certain that my daughter was fine, safe and happy and resting easily in the small bedroom that her father had set up just for her?

Would he know that I longed for his warmth, the way his voice would wrap around me just as if it were his arms?

Would he know that I *needed* him?

Once again, I found myself on the edge looking down, wondering when I'd get so close that I'd fall. Or maybe I'd just jump.

I shook my head.

No.

I talked myself back from the ledge, forced myself to place the phone down on my nightstand, and cried myself to sleep.

"Hey, Liz," the deep voice called from behind.

I stood at my kitchen counter, my fingers wet from slicing tomatoes in preparation for our barbecue and glanced over my shoulder at Matthew standing in the archway.

In my humiliation, I turned away and focused on the task in front of me.

"Hey," I mumbled toward the counter.

Matthew approached, stood next to me, and wrapped an arm around my back with a gentle squeeze. "You okay?"

Nodding, I leaned into him a bit and felt myself relax against my friend.

While I was embarrassed, I knew I really had no reason to be. Matthew only cared, and I knew he wouldn't judge or tease, would offer no ridicule for my actions of the evening before.

"Nat and I brought your car back." He smiled as if nothing had happened, case closed, and went to the fridge to grab a bottle of beer and walked out the back door.

I could sense Natalie hovering in the same spot where Matthew had been.

She was fidgeting and feeling as unsure with me as I felt with her.

I wasn't exactly *mad* at her, but I wasn't thrilled with how she'd acted last night either.

She released a soft but audible sigh, as if she needed to make herself known, to warn me of her presence, or maybe even needed reassurance of her welcome.

"Hey, Natalie." It came out low with a hint of disappointment, but it was mostly filled with my need to make things right between us.

It was enough to bring her across the room, her feet light. She rose up on her tiptoes behind me, rested her chin on my shoulder, and wrapped her arms around my middle to hug me to her chest.

"I'm so sorry, Liz." Far from flippant, her apology was solemn and sincere. "We were just messing around. I shouldn't have . . . I know how . . ."

She swallowed, heavy with remorse, and shook her head. "It was rude, Liz. We made light of something that causes you pain, and for that, I'm so sorry."

I tilted my head to hers in a small embrace, and I set the knife I was holding on the cutting board so I could reach down to cover her hands with mine.

"It's okay." I rubbed my thumbs over the back of her hands.

We stood like that for a few moments, looking out the window into the backyard. Matthew and Christian sat at the small patio table, chatting as they nursed their beers, laughing as if they were old friends.

Lizzie was perched on Christian's knee, grinning while she played with the small dolls in front of her. It seemed that without thought Christian would run his fingers through Lizzie's long hair flowing down her back and play with the ends.

"Sweet, isn't it?" Nat murmured, her attention

focused on Lizzie and Christian.

"Mmm hmm," I said from somewhere in the back of my throat, unable to voice how it really made me feel, how it made my heart soar and made me question everything I'd held onto for so long. How it made me want to *believe* he would treat me the same way.

"You don't have to be miserable anymore, Elizabeth," Natalie whispered as she pressed her cheek into mine, a gentle encouragement.

I closed my eyes to block my mind from what I so desperately wanted, shook my head ever so slightly, and disagreed. "I'm not miserable."

She snorted although it sounded like sympathy and hugged me closer, before she walked to the back door, only to pause just before she stepped out. "That's not what it looked like last night."

She slid the door closed behind her, pulled a chair out from the patio table, and sat down with her back to me.

I gazed out at my family, the family that had grown by one, and couldn't imagine it any other way. Christian caught me staring and looked up at me with eyes filled with adoration, need, want, tender affection, and overt desire.

For once, I didn't look away, and I hoped he'd see in my expression that I felt the same, that he'd know that I loved him, even though I'd never allow myself to say the words.

The afternoon stretched on, peaceful and without strain. For once, my nerves were quiet as I rested at the table with those closest to me. We'd eaten, joked, and shared the trivial events of our week.

Matthew and Natalie never mentioned the night before, the incident forgotten. Lizzie played on the grass, soaking in the last few rays of light as the sun hung low in the horizon, each day shorter than the last as October threatened to give way to November.

It was odd to witness the trust that had emerged between Christian and Matthew, their conversation casual and unlabored, genuine.

Years before, when Christian and I had been together, the disdain Matthew had held for Christian had been clear. It had been as if he could foretell the future and he'd known of Christian's betrayal before it had ever been committed.

I couldn't help but wonder what he saw now, what had changed as the two men talked as friends that I now believed they considered themselves to be.

Our conversation continued on, uncomfortable silences unheard of on this perfect Sunday afternoon.

Christian was laughing loud and unhindered

when his phone rang out from within the confines of his jacket pocket.

Still chuckling, he patted his coat, feeling for the phone, pulled it out and said, "Excuse me a second."

We all quieted, lowering our voices so he could take his call.

I tried to focus on what Natalie was saying, but couldn't ignore the way Christian stiffened and his tone hardened when he answered, "Yes, this is Christian Davison."

Natalie stopped mid-sentence. Her eyes darted between Christian and me, her brow creasing with worry as the silence on Christian's end wore on.

I watched as Christian slumped forward and dug his elbows into his thighs. His knuckles were white from the force with which he held his phone, and his other hand jerked incessantly through his hair.

"What?" he finally choked out in anguish. There was another long break, this time his hand fisting in his hair.

When he spoke again, he sounded detached, stunned, his voice so quiet I was sure whoever was on the other line didn't hear him. "Okay, thank you."

I wanted to drop to my knees to draw his face to mine, to comfort him for whatever was causing him this reaction. But I was frozen, the blood sloshing in my ears, making me sick with unease as

I waited.

Christian sat up, his face portraying nothing, void of emotion, pale and unfeeling.

Shocked.

"Christian?" I began but stopped when he glanced in the direction of my voice and then back ahead, unseeing, muttering in disbelief.

"My father is dead." He squeezed his eyes shut, blinked them open, and said again, "My father is dead."

Oh no.

My hand covered my mouth as I tried to suppress the cry that bubbled up, a seemingly inappropriate sound for a man I had only despised but couldn't help but mourn if solely for the fact that he had fathered Christian.

"I have to go," Christian said in words that were barely audible, directed at no one at all.

He stood and moved as if on instinct but without comprehension. The three of us watched in shock as he disappeared inside my house. before my senses finally caught up and I shook off my stupor.

Christian needed me.

I jumped up, knocking my chair over in the process, and raced inside to catch him, only to trip over my feet when I got to the living room.

Christian was on the couch hunched over, his hands clutching his head, balled up in a position so similar to the one he had been in just seconds before.

Faster than I could give myself time to think, I was on my knees in front of him, whispering soothing words. I pried his hands from his hair, held his beautiful face, and ran my thumbs under his eyes.

It was as if he didn't even know I was there.

I'd never seen him act this way. "Christian, *please* say something."

He shook his head and stood as he once again said, "I have to go."

Natalie and Matthew stood in the archway, watching with horrified expressions.

I looked helplessly to them and mouthed, "What should I do?"

Christian was halfway out the front door when the soft sound of Lizzie's voice hit our ears, scared and shaking.

"Daddy?"

With it, Christian halted mid-stride, her voice enough to break through whatever barrier had his heart and mind trapped.

The release of tension was visible as his rigid shoulders went lax, his eyes clear as he turned and drew Lizzie into his arms when she ran across the room to him.

thirteen

CHRISTIAN

I turned the key in the lock, weary, my mind still muddied, trying to make sense of the news I'd received.

Gone.

Just like that, without warning. I guess I'd always viewed my father as unshakable, an indestructible force—immortal until the day he was not.

The door swung closed behind me, and I stood in the dimness of my condo, lost, the sun burning a thin line as it sank and disappeared at the edge of the ocean, the end of my perception.

I stood in the same spot, watching it fall until it

faded and darkness swallowed the room.

It scared me that I didn't feel anything. At the same time, I felt weak, as if I might collapse and not know why.

Excruciating numbness.

With arduous steps, I walked to the end of the hall and into my bedroom. I flipped on the light in my closest, hesitating at the door before I built up enough courage to tug at the small brown chest shoved in the back corner of the top shelf.

It was light, its weight the box itself. The contents shifted as I crossed the room and set it beside me on the bed. The metal latch rattled as I unclasped it and opened the lid to the photos I kept inside.

For a moment, I sat motionless, wondering why I was doing this and what I hoped to find, before I reached in and pulled them out.

The stack was small and contained the few printed memories of my childhood—each formal and posed. It was probably senseless to look for something other than pride from my father, but I felt compelled to search for a glimmer of something more—a sign of warmth, a glimpse of a love he'd never proclaimed.

But in each one, he was there only because I'd done something notable, something that he'd deemed worth his time.

I shook my head with a harsh snort.

He'd lived in arrogance, had died in arrogance.

A stroke had taken him, something that would have been treatable had he not ignored the symptoms, but he'd been too prideful to believe anything could ever take him down.

I'd learned through my father's attorney that he'd started slurring his words at the office during the day, but he'd disregarded everyone's concerns, told them he just had a headache, and had his driver take him home.

Even my father's wife, Kendra, as self-absorbed as I believed her to be, had urged him to seek care.

Instead, he'd said he had work to do and had locked himself in his office upstairs. She'd awoken the next morning to an empty bed.

When they found him, he was in a coma and too much damage had already been done. He was lost apart from the machine that kept him alive.

They'd left him on it for *three* days, and no one had even bothered to tell me until they had removed him from life support and announced his death.

Sitting on my bed, I stared down at the pictures in my hand, my jaw clenched as the first real wave of emotion hit me.

Anger.

Had he thought so little of me, *his own son*, that no one around him had thought it important enough to call me and let me know what was happening with my father? That I might have liked to have known that he was dying?

Had he ever cared at all?

And why *did* I care?

Why on the fringes of the numbness I felt was there pain? Why had the emptiness in my chest begun to ache?

I dropped the photos back into the chest and pushed away the reminders of how little I'd meant to my father.

I lay back on my bed and stared at the ceiling, hating that this was all we'd ever been, all we'd ever be. That to him, I'd been nothing more than a disappointment, and to me, he'd forever be the asshole who didn't care.

My phone buzzed in my pocket and I glanced at the nightstand.

Seven fifteen.

The ache in my chest expanded, but in an entirely different way. Our seven-fifteen calls had become rare, only because I was usually with Lizzie during that time, but I still always called if it happened I wasn't spending the evening with her.

Tonight, she had beaten me to punch. I wondered if it was Lizzie or Elizabeth who had known how badly I'd need to hear their voices.

I pulled the phone from my pocket, rolled to my side as I tucked my pillow under my head, and lifted the phone to my ear.

"Hi, Daddy." Her sweet voice assuaged the weight on my chest and chased the fog from my brain.

She'd been so scared this afternoon, fearing I was leaving her, not understanding what was happening or why I'd reacted in such a way.

It was that voice that had touched me, had *shaken* me—one that I could never ignore.

"Hi, sweetheart. How's my girl?"

She sighed, the sound wrapping me up in her tiny arms. "Just thinking about you, Daddy."

And for the first time tonight, I smiled.

My mother sat in front of me while I stood with my hands resting on her shoulders. Tremors rolled through her body as she tried in vain to hide the tears she shed for a man she had never stopped loving.

I squeezed her and hoped it gave her comfort, a quiet reassurance that I was there.

Though we felt as if we didn't belong, my mother and I blended in with the sea of black—black suits, black dresses, and black umbrellas that protected from the ceaseless drizzle of rain, the air heavy and damp.

A black casket gleamed bright and ominous in the middle of it all. It was covered in what seemed to be thousands of white and yellow flowers and a million raindrops.

My father's last spectacle, his final farewell.

Samuel Clymer, my father's business partner and probably his only true friend, rose to give the eulogy. He moved heavily to the podium, cleared his throat as his eyes flitted over those in attendance.

He looked upon my mother and me for a moment longer. He was a man I'd known all of my life, tall and stocky, his cheeks round and red. From my childhood, I remembered him with a full head of brown, curly hair.

Now he was balding and wore wire-rimmed glasses that he continually pushed up his nose.

His voice cracked as he spoke kind words of my father and told of a man different from the one that I'd known.

When Samuel finished, he moved aside and lifted his glasses to wipe his eyes with a white handkerchief.

The minister began the last prayer, and my father's casket was lowered into the ground.

With the prayer, I bowed my head and willed tears that never came.

Instead, I watched with a hollow ache as my father's widow stood to throw the first handful of dirt into his grave.

She was young, younger than I was, her black-skirted suit perfectly tailored to fit her perfect body—another prize my father had won.

As she threw the dirt, Mom reached up and clutched my hand. She held her breath in grief as the soil scattered and showered through the flowers. She failed to stifle a cry with a tissue against her mouth.

I kneaded her hand in mine as everyone who had gathered to grieve my father went forward to pay their last respects.

Some faces were familiar, distant relatives and old friends, as well as many strangers. Voices were hushed and respectful as they passed by.

We waited until the crowd cleared before Mom stood and together we went forward. Mom whispered at the edge of his grave, indecipherable words that bled together, maybe a prayer, maybe a goodbye.

Then she reached down and tossed a handful of dirt onto the black casket below.

I knelt and dug my hand into the mound of soft dirt, cold and foreign. I fisted it and wished we had ended things differently, that I could mourn my father as a real son should.

I felt sick as I dumped the handful of dirt over his casket and murmured an unheard goodbye.

The limo turned onto the private drive lined with wiry elms and lush oaks. The sun had broken through the clouds, and rays of light glinted down through the branches as we passed by.

Mom and I sat in apprehensive silence as the driver followed the path that curved around the sweeping grounds and came to a stop in the circular driveway in front of the enormous house we had once called home.

It was an imposing three-story colonial, its roof pitched as it stretched for the sky. Evergreens towered over its height, impressive and strong, so much in the way my father had viewed himself to be.

From the backseat of the car, Mom gazed out at the house I had grown up in. Her grief was suffocating, and I found it hard to breathe in the confined area. She looked at me, her face wet and splotchy as she shook her head as her lips trembled.

"I can't believe he's gone."

I had no words to comfort my mother, so I reached out and drew her to me, hugged her while she sobbed against my chest.

She'd told me once that she'd never stopped loving him, but I'd never understood the depths of that love until I'd first seen her in the hotel lobby when I'd arrived, her face ashen—devastated.

"We don't have to stay." I rocked her as I spoke, unsure if my offer was more for her benefit or mine.

She sniffed, pulled away to wipe her eyes and nose with a tissue, and looked back at the house.

"No." She slid her watery eyes to me, swallowing back the emotion. "We should stay."

Even though I didn't want to be here, I knew she was right. In the very least, I owed my father this, a measure of respect in his passing, my presence as his family and friends gathered to say goodbye.

Maybe he wouldn't have wanted me here, but in the end, I was what I was—his son.

With a tight smile, I extended my hand to Mom. "Come on."

She clenched my hand, breathing through her nose in calculated breaths, unsure of her welcome or where she stood.

This wasn't going to be easy for either of us.

The house was almost exactly as I remembered. The furniture in the formal living room off the foyer remained the same—ornate upholstered pieces widely unused, polished antiques.

A staircase wound to the floors above, and artwork hung from the walls, planned and cold.

How I longed for the warmth of Elizabeth's little house, for the clutter and the mess, for the comfort of stepping over toys abandoned on the floor, and for the ability to rest my bare feet on the edge of her worn coffee table.

I took a deep breath and told myself, "*You can do*

this."

Muted voices echoed over the dark hardwood floors. The first level overflowed with people, family and acquaintances, friends and clients. They converged in small groups, some chatting quietly and others hugging each other and wiping away lingering tears.

Mom's gaze caressed the living room, embracing fond memories before finally resting on the piano at the far end of the living room.

My father had played all his life, his mother dedicating him to lessons from the time he was a young boy. I realized suddenly that the only time I'd ever seen him let his guard down was when he'd play.

I'd forgotten how Mom would sit on the chaise lounge by the window and stare outside, engrossed in the strains of his melody, her body swaying to my father's tempo, at one with him.

Or perhaps I hadn't forgotten. Maybe I hadn't been old enough to see it for what it was.

Mom crossed the room to it as if it were a magnet, and I followed a bit behind to give her time. She ran her fingertips along the glossy black wood and sat down at the bench. She reached out her finger and played a solitary key.

Her eyes were closed, lost in the past.

I turned away to give her privacy and parted the sheer curtain covering the huge windows that faced out the back of the house and over the pool.

The view extended out to the salt-water marshes of Lynnhaven River. I could picture myself as a boy running through the high grass, climbing the trees, tossing rocks in the water.

Mom had lolled by the pool, and I'd thought she'd paid me no attention at all, yet she still had an uncanny way of knowing when I'd been up to something I shouldn't be and would call out to be careful just before I did something that was sure to cause me harm.

"You used to play out there for hours."

I was startled from the wanderings of my mind by Mom's soft words and tender touch on my arm. She smiled up at me, her expression wistful as if she were picturing the exact same thing I had been.

A gentle huff came through my nose, an appreciation of those memories that had been buried beneath the pressure that had come from this place.

"I loved it out there," I admitted, taking her hand. "I'd forgotten how much."

"Claire?" We both turned.

Aunt Mary, my father's older sister, stood behind us, wringing her hands in a white handkerchief. She was still tall and slender, her long black hair pulled back in a coif at the base of her neck, her eyes sad.

Mom tensed. Her biggest fear of coming here

had been the reaction of her ex-husband's family, not knowing whether they would condemn her presence or if it would somehow bring them more pain.

Aunt Mary pulled Mom into a hug, cried into her shoulder, and told her how much it meant that she'd come before she turned to me and did the same.

I hugged her close, told her how sorry I was, before I excused myself to allow them the space to reconnect as they made apologies that were not owed, their estrangement a consequence of circumstance.

Standing at the edge of the room, I shifted my feet and dug my hands deeper and deeper into my pants pockets as I accepted the condolences of those who stopped as they passed by.

I chatted with distant cousins who I'd not seen in years, murmured thanks for the apologies of strangers.

It was hard pretending that the strained relationship my father and I had shared hadn't crumbled in the end, that he hadn't disowned me, and that I hadn't walked out of his life.

I wondered how many knew, that as they shook my hand and forced a smile that they weren't questioning what I was doing here and why I had come.

My father's wife wouldn't even look at me, not

that I wanted her recognition.

My father wasn't just a bastard, but a hypocrite.

I couldn't understand his unfounded ridicule of Elizabeth, and then for him to turn around and marry a woman like Kendra.

I tensed when Samuel Clymer caught my eye from across the room and approached with his hand extended. "Christian."

In my discomfort, I averted my gaze, wishing I didn't have to face my father's partner. It had been easy walking from that office in reaction to my father accusations, but in doing so, I'd also walked out on Samuel.

He'd always been kind to me, a mentor who had helped in every aspect when I'd made the transfer to San Diego.

Out of respect, I accepted his hand. "Samuel."

"Can I talk to you a minute?" he asked as he gestured with his head in the direction of the terrace.

For a moment, I hesitated. I really didn't want to have this conversation *here* at my father's funeral. But I relented and followed him out back through the French doors and to the patio.

He was silent as he looked out over the river. I waited behind him, nervous to discover his intentions.

He rubbed the palm of his hand over the top of his balding head, sighing when he turned back to me. He pushed his glasses back up his nose, appearing flustered.

"Listen..." He paused and released a heavy breath, seeming to need to find his words as he took one step forward. "I just wanted to tell you how sorry I am about your father."

Sighing, I roughed a hand through my hair as I nodded and mumbled, "Thanks."

I didn't know how to respond.

Samuel's name was listed right beside my father's on the lawsuit, and as much as I didn't regret making a stand for what was important in my life, I regretted that in the process I'd let Samuel down.

His voice lowered, tight in emphasis. "I mean for *everything*, Christian."

His head dropped into his hand, shaking it against his palm. "Your father was my closest friend."

His words were rough, choppy with emotion. He looked to the sky, struggling. "But what he did to you . . . I never agreed with it . . . and . . . and I *won't* stand by and allow it to happen now."

He lowered his gaze back to me. "The firm is dropping the lawsuit."

I shut my eyes, knowing I should feel relief. Instead, I found myself fighting to control my surging anger.

It was *all* my father—not the firm, not a

decision left up to the board. It had been something my father had led, had spurred.

I backed away, knocking into the wall.

While deep down I'd known, I couldn't help but hope that the lawsuit had been pursued because of my breach of contract or company protocol and not an act of vengeance.

Samuel moved to stand in front of me and exhaled as he placed a sympathetic hand on my shoulder. "I know what you're thinking, Christian. Your father was a complicated man, but he did care about you . . . loved you."

I scoffed, the sound a scornful wound in the back of my throat. "How can you say that?" I looked up to meet Samuel's eyes. "You know as well as I do that my father hated me."

I clenched my fists, and a wave of grief passed through my body when the words passed through my mouth, grief for a relationship that had died long before my father had, maybe had never even existed at all.

Through all the pressures and demands, the obligation and coercion, somewhere inside me I'd always wanted to believe that my father must have loved me in his own way.

But it was clear he had never loved me at all.

The farther I wandered away from the house,

the more distant the voices inside became. I plodded down the graveled path and wended through the opening in the trees. My steps echoed over the wooden planks once I hit the dock walkway and trod above the murky, green waters of Lynnhaven River.

Tossing my jacket aside, I sat down on the edge of the dock, swung my legs, and watched as gulls skimmed inches from the water. I listened to their call and relaxed in the peace.

This had always been my place of escape, and I'd never needed the solitude more than now.

"Hey." The subdued voice came from behind, her footsteps quiet as if she were unsure if she should disturb me.

A smile tugged at the corner of my mouth, and I turned to look at her over my shoulder. Though I was hiding, I didn't mind her company.

The timid expression she wore spread into a small smile, tender and kind. Always kind.

"Hey." I inclined my head to the side, inviting her to take a seat.

She came forward, careful as she took the wooden walkway in heels. She tucked her skirt behind her and climbed down beside me, her apprehension clear.

The last time I'd seen her she'd been in tears, heartbroken, begging me to love her but strong enough to know she wouldn't stay for anything less.

I'd tried so hard. I had really wanted to love Brittany the way she did me, but in the two years we'd lived together, the fondness I felt for her had never blossomed.

"How are you holding up?" she asked as she nudged her shoulder into mine and peered up at me with warm chocolate eyes. Her dark brown hair was pulled back at her neck, wisps falling out and around her face.

Though she wasn't tall, she was all leg, a combination of sweet and sexy.

It had been an immediate physical attraction, the first time I'd seen her here in this very spot.

It had been at one of my father's garish New Year's Eve parties, my presence deemed a responsibility, and just as I'd done so many times as a teenager, I had snuck out back and hidden here by the water when the air became too thick.

Brittany had come with her parents and she confessed later that she'd followed me out.

We'd kissed at midnight, and in that moment, it had felt so right.

I shrugged, glancing at her. "Not well, I guess."

She stared out over the water, fidgeting with the hem of her skirt that was bunched up over her knees.

"I'm really sorry, Christian." She turned her attention to me, her mouth twisting in a grimace.

"I know you two had issues, but I know it must be hard losing him."

Releasing a slow breath, I rested my elbows against my knees, shaking my head. I still didn't know what I felt. "It's just hard to believe he's . . . gone."

Brittany leaned in, caressed my back.

I closed my eyes against the sensation, soothing and so wrong, rebuking myself for again allowing myself comfort at her hand, but I couldn't find it in myself to pull away.

"I heard you reunited with your daughter." She rested her cheek on my shoulder and gazed up at me, her expression filled with joy. She'd known how it had haunted me, had witnessed the sleepless nights, the guilt.

"She looks like me." I leaned my head against the side of Brittany's, grinning at the thought, Lizzie's face never far from my thoughts.

I wished she were here to experience the place where I'd grown up.

I knew I'd never be back.

Brittany laughed, a small, wistful sound. "Mmm . . . beautiful."

In sync, our legs swung and our hands touched.

"Funny . . . I always pictured a little boy," she said softly, her words laced with a hint of sadness as her gaze traveled out over the water

I tilted my head to look down at her. "She's

amazing, Britt. I wish you could meet her. She's the sweetest little girl."

"I'm so happy for you, Christian." She looked back up at me, her brown eyes sincere. She bit her lip, snuggled closer, and clung to my arm. "And her mother?"

I swallowed, the movement jerky, and shook my head. Suddenly, I felt uneasy, our faces too close, her touch too intimate.

"I miss you, Christian."

With her whispered words, she moved closer, brought her hand to my neck, and pressed her lips to the corner of my mouth.

Her kiss was soft, wet, filled with need, lingered as she waited for a response.

On instinct, I turned to her, brought my hands to her cheeks, and held her face, restraining her.

"I can't," I said, my tone strained.

"*Please.*" Her breath spread out over my face as she clung to my arms and pled, "Just tonight."

My body reacted, hungry for release, deprived of it for so long, knowing how good it would feel to lose myself in the familiarity of her touch.

But to me, even considering what Brittany suggested was the most debase form of infidelity.

Even if Elizabeth never again belonged to me, I would forever belong to her.

I edged away just a fraction, but enough to make it clear that I was pulling away, that I was saying no.

"You love her?"

I nodded and held my friend's face while tears gathered in her eyes. The decision I'd made more than six years ago was *still* hurting the people I cared about.

"I'm so sorry, Britt. I *hate* that I hurt you." I held my hands firm against the wetness of her cheeks. "I never wanted to hurt you."

She removed herself from my hold and looked away, embarrassed.

"I guess I always knew." She sniffled, her mouth twisting in a self-conscious sort of smile and her expression sad. "I'd always hoped that it was all about the child, that you punished yourself because of it, and wouldn't allow yourself to move on and love me."

More tears fell down her face, and she looked down in a shame that was really my own. "But when you'd make *love* to me . . . well . . . I knew you weren't. You were always a million miles away. I just didn't want to believe you were with her."

More regret.

I couldn't even bring myself to apologize again, knowing words would never make up for what I'd done.

Instead, I held my palm to her face and wiped away another tear that fell down her cheek.

"You deserve so much more than one night,

Britt."

She deserved so much more than the two years I had stolen from her, so much more than I had ever given her, so much more than I could ever give her.

All I had was for Elizabeth.

Brittany closed her eyes, leaned into my hand, and for a moment, seemed to indulge in my touch, before she stood and, without looking back, walked away.

***

Never had I wanted Elizabeth more.

The need was suffocating as I rode the hotel elevator to the eleventh floor and opened the door to my suite.

Not bothering to switch on the light, I stood in the dark, empty room, the only illumination coming from the glow of the street lamps below.

The aching numbness I had wandered through since Sunday had become a constant throb, pressing, pulsing, and forcing its way out.

Today had been torture, burying my father, facing the pain I'd caused my friend, sitting through the reading of my father's will.

Confusion clouded my heart and mind with uncertainty, too many questions, and too many whys.

I'd wanted nothing that was his, and I still

hadn't come to terms with what he'd wanted me to have.

I was sure he'd have erased me from his will and, in essence, from his life, removing me from what I knew in his mind would be his most valued gift.

To his widow he'd left the house, his cars, and enough money to maintain it all, to afford her to live out the rest of her days comfortably.

But he hadn't left her his vast fortune, the inheritance he'd received from his parents.

A quarter of it had been left to me and the rest he'd given to my mother.

With this announcement had come the first real emotion I'd seen from Kendra, first her look of confusion and then the offense with being denied something she believed she deserved.

Mom had broken down and cried out that she didn't understand. She'd begged for answers to questions that no one knew, why Richard would choose this life over her and then turn around and try to give it to her.

For both of us, it was an exacerbation to our confusion.

When we'd stood to leave my father's study, his attorney had taken me aside and given me a key to the bottom drawer of my father's desk.

The key had been left in a safety deposit box in an envelope with my name on it.

Inside the drawer, there were pictures, all of them of me. Some I could remember, others I could not.

But it was what I had found at the bottom of the drawer that had really shaken me.

It was an envelope, and inside was the picture of Lizzie I'd left him the last time I'd seen him and a crinkled, folded up sheet of paper, the edges frayed and torn as if it had been folded and unfolded a thousand times.

It was a picture that I had no recollection of, but one that had obviously been drawn by my hand, the crude child's work depicting a man and young boy, the worn caption *Daddy Loves Christian* written at the top.

I'd understood immediately what he was trying to say.

It had hit me full force, and for the first time it really hurt that I'd lost my father.

He'd loved me, and he'd never once told me.

I looked around my empty hotel room and tried to hold onto the anger, but it was gone. In its place was only pity.

The clock beside the bed read just after midnight.

For the first time since I'd reunited with my daughter, I had missed our seven-fifteen call.

I kicked off my dress shoes and peeled the jacket from my body. As I unbuttoned the first couple of buttons of my shirt, I felt despair setting in.

My head spun and my stomach twisted in knots.

My father was dead, and I'd never see him again. Gone.

I wanted Elizabeth. I *needed* Elizabeth.

Grabbing my jacket from the chair where I'd tossed it, I fumbled through the pockets, produced my cell phone, and sat down on the side of the bed.

I was desperate to hear her voice.

She answered on the first ring, as if she'd been expecting me, waiting for me, the dulcet sound of her voice my consolation, my breaking point.

"Elizabeth." The tears I'd prayed would come finally broke free, and I was at last able to mourn for my father.

"Oh, Christian." Elizabeth's tone was soft and understanding and held me the same as if I were in her arms—the only place I wanted to be.

"Elizabeth," I cried again. She was my only solace, my first reminder to never become like my father. I'd come so close—had nearly given it all away.

Had he ever felt the regret that I felt? Had there ever been a day when he'd realized he was living the wrong life, that he never should have let my mother walk away?

When he knew he was dying, did he wish he

could have been given one last chance to tell us how he felt about us instead of waiting until he was gone and telling us the only way he knew how— with what he'd left behind?

I choked over the emotion, sobbed against the phone, pleaded with her again. "Elizabeth."

I felt as if I were drowning in my father's mistakes—mistakes that I'd made my own.

I was through wasting my chances. If I died tonight, I'd leave Elizabeth with no questions, nothing to decipher, no reason to wonder.

"Christian?" Elizabeth's worry traveled over the distance and touched my heart.

I cried harder, wept for my father who'd been too proud, and vowed to myself that I would *never* be too proud.

"I love you, Elizabeth," I wheezed out the words, unashamed and laid bare. She had to know. "I love you so much."

From the edge of the bed, I curled in on myself and pressed the phone to my ear, silently begging her to be brave enough to say it back.

Please, Elizabeth, say it back.

I needed to hear her say it back . . . I needed her to take me back.

Her phone rustled, and I heard her shift, felt her movements. I pictured her lying down on her bed, envisioned her long, dark blond locks splayed out over her pillow, saw her in the black tank top and pajama pants she wore to bed—wished I were lying down beside her.

"Christian . . ." she whispered in what sounded adoration.

If I could see her face right now, I knew what I'd find. I'd see what was in the expression she'd worn as she had gazed out at me from her kitchen window on Sunday afternoon, the same thing that I had felt in her touch when she'd knelt before me and begged me to look at her, one I'd recognized but had been unable to respond to.

She swallowed, and in her hesitation, I knew she wasn't ready to say it.

Turning to lie on the cold sheets of my hotel bed, I faced the wall in a way that I was sure would mirror her position, pretended that she held me, felt her ghost her fingers along my jaw, and listened to her breathe.

It calmed me, soothed the sting, caressed the pain.

"Elizabeth," I said again, this time softly, matching the calm her distant presence brought, her name a promise on my tongue—*soon*.

"I miss you, Christian." The words were muffled, slurred against what I could only imagine was her pillow, but still distinct, powerful.

Burying my face in the pillow, I rejoiced and thanked God she was giving me this moment, as innocent as it was intimate.

I gathered myself enough to whisper, "I miss you, too, Elizabeth. More than you know."

We lay together in silence listening to each other breathe. Still wearing my pants and dress shirt, I tugged the sheet and blanket over my body and hugged a pillow to my chest.

I refused myself the fantasies flickering on the outskirts of my consciousness and forced myself to rest satisfied in Elizabeth's peace.

Finally, Elizabeth whispered, "I'm so sorry, Christian."

"I'm sorry too."

fourteen

ELIZABETH

It was usually only Lizzie who waited by the window for her father, but today I couldn't help but join her.

Every few minutes I went to stand beside my daughter who waited perched on her knees, peering out at the street. The blinds were drawn wide, opened in invitation. The glass was smudged and painted by Lizzie's eager hands and dotted by her tiny nose.

Christian had sent a text about twenty minutes before to let us know he'd landed and was on his way.

My heart palpitated, raced in anticipation, sped in fear.

Christian had told me he loved me.

My chest constricted as his words flowed through me again with their tenor, their depth.

His declaration had nearly undone me, had almost unraveled the knot I held so tightly twined around my broken heart.

I'd wanted to say it so badly.

I'd felt it dance on my tongue, longing to admit that I loved him too. Somehow, I'd reined it in, harnessed it, and left it to smolder, knowing it would only grow.

For one more day, I'd kept my heart hidden and protected.

Running my palms over my arms, I attempted to tame my nerves. I forced myself into believing that the moment we'd shared in place of those words hadn't been so much more powerful than had I just said them aloud. I pretended that my heart wasn't the farthest from secure and that I didn't feel more vulnerable today than I had ever in my life.

Movement from the street brought Lizzie to her feet, the tail of Christian's silver car visible as he pulled into our driveway.

"He's here," she all but whispered. Her face looked determined as she set out the front door and ran down the sidewalk to meet him.

She had not been herself all week but quiet and contemplative.

Finally, last night as I'd tucked her into bed, she'd opened up, confessed her fears, and asked, "What if my Daddy dies too?"

It had been one of the hardest things I'd ever discussed with my daughter, the balance of giving her both peace and honesty, the truth that life ultimately ends in death.

She'd only been able to fall asleep once I'd lain down next to her and ran my fingers through her hair. I'd whispered for her not to worry and promised that she'd see her father again.

Pushing a hand through my bangs, I steeled myself for the emotion I knew would come. I hesitated at doorway and listened to their greetings.

Even though they were out of view, I could almost feel Christian's relief when Lizzie was finally in his arms.

When they rounded the corner, Lizzie was attached to her father's hip, clinging to his neck as if she'd never let go.

Christian came to a standstill when he saw me, his breath rushing from his chest as his gaze washed over me. His eyes swam their deepest blue—midnight—warm but so very tired, his body weary, leaden with obvious exhaustion.

Chaotic shocks of black hair stood up in disaccord, salient circles beneath his eyes, his white, printed T-shirt wrinkled—his expression hopeful.

I couldn't refrain from taking a step forward and whispering, "Welcome home."

Slowly he approached, each footfall measured, calculated, and purposed.

Every step that brought him closer escalated my already rapid breaths.

The pieces of my broken heart were at war, tangled and twisted, the smoldering, conflicting emotions threatening to burst.

Inches from me, he stopped and kissed the side of Lizzie's head, before he set her down, never taking his penetrating gaze from me.

Frozen, I waited, unable to look away.

Somewhere inside me, I knew I shouldn't reach out when he reached for me, knew I shouldn't wrap my arms around his waist when he wrapped his arms around my shoulders, knew I shouldn't bury my face in his chest at the moment he buried his in my hair.

I just couldn't stop myself.

Christian tugged me closer, his body heavy and perfect against mine, fatigued and seeking support.

"I missed you so much," he whispered against my ear as he pulled me impossibly closer and breathed me in.

The heat of his breath licked at my skin, his nearness setting it aflame.

He clouded every faculty, interrupted reason, tempted me to *forget*. I closed my eyes against the sensations and tried to block the resurgence of memories, to ignore the familiarity of his touch. I pushed it all aside and focused on what he needed— comfort.

He clung to me as if his life depended on it.

A warning signal flared somewhere deep within my soul.

Dangerous.

For once, I ignored it.

Instead, I crushed my chest to his, allowed the rush of relief to surge through my veins, and savored the heat of his skin and the warmth of his body.

Echoes of our past surfaced in my mind, our happiest moments, the way only he could make me smile, the way only he could make me feel, our most intimate times.

I wanted to hold onto them, but they fluttered and flickered and gave way to vivid images so strong I could almost taste them—sick, cold, alone—and I remembered why I could never give into this.

Even then, I didn't want to let go and allowed myself a few moments more before I placed a hand against his chest and gently pushed him away.

He covered my hand with both of his, pressed it over his heart, and smiled at me in a way that chipped away another piece of my armor.

Averting my eyes, I made the mistake of looking down at Lizzie who gazed up at us with the same expression I'd seen Christian wearing the second before—like she'd just been allowed a small piece of heaven.

What the hell was I doing?

Teasing my daughter?

Giving her false hope, stoking her imagination, painting a picture of things that could never be?

I forced myself to take a step back from Christian, gathered up the emotions that were slowly slipping away, and drew another line.

For Lizzie, I told myself. This was for Lizzie.

I glanced back up at Christian, reminding myself we could only ever be friends—*partners*.

Purging the remnants of my desire from my face, I straightened myself and put back on my mask. I smiled and stood aside. "Go on in. Dinner's almost ready."

Christian inhaled and threw a grin in my direction, lopsided and achingly cute. "You made spaghetti and meatballs?" His voice teemed with appreciation, swam in awareness.

My mask fell, so easily penetrable, evidence of my weakness. I felt my face flush and I ducked my head. I knew how obvious I was in preparing his favorite dinner just as I had prepared his favorite breakfast the morning after Lizzie's fall.

"Yeah, I figured you'd be starved after the long flight," I mumbled toward my bare feet, shrugging to make less of it than we both knew it was.

I looked up in time to see his lopsided smile spread. "You have no idea how good that sounds. I haven't eaten all day."

Turning his attention to Lizzie, he wrapped one of her tiny hands in his and asked, "What about you, princess, are you hungry?"

Overwhelmed, I hung back and tried to convince myself that nothing had changed as he led her inside.

Christian glanced back at me with a lazy grin. "You coming?"

Sighing, I told myself another thousand lies and followed him inside.

"Do you want to talk?"

Pointing the remote at the television, I lowered the volume and let the cartoon Lizzie had wanted to watch play out.

She'd fallen asleep about fifteen minutes before, curled up in Christian's lap. Her sweet breaths came in soft pants against his chest, rhythmic and soothing in the dimness of the room. He played with the strands of her hair, appearing lost in thought and most likely minutes from sleep.

Glancing at me, he grimaced through a heavy

sigh, ran his palm over his weary face, and blinked.

"I . . . don't . . . know." It didn't seem an answer to my question but was more a statement of how he was feeling.

If I were in his place, I wouldn't know what to feel either.

Those unanswered questions formed as lines across his forehead. "I've spent so much of my life resenting my father . . . blaming him for all of my problems . . . for every mistake I've made."

His brow furrowed as he left those mistakes unspoken, though many of them were glaringly obvious.

He snorted through his nose and shook his head. "Do you know he left me a quarter of his inheritance?"

He focused on his fingers weaving through Lizzie's hair while still shaking his head. His words dropped in slow disbelief, maybe even hinting at a newfound respect.

"And the rest of it to my mom."

"What?" I couldn't keep my shocked reaction contained.

Christian cut his eyes to mine. In the muted light of the family room, they were dark and mournful.

His mouth twisted and twitched, and he seemed to be struggling to keep his emotions in check.

Supporting Lizzie, he leaned forward, wrenched

his wallet from his back pocket, and produced a folded-up piece of paper from it. With his head bowed, he passed it over to me.

"He'd kept this in his desk."

Wary of what I'd find inside, I stared at the piece of worn and tattered paper in my palm. I was sure whatever it held had broken a part of Christian's heart.

Gingerly, I unfolded it, smoothed it out on my lap, and gasped at the simple picture.

Christian must have understood my surprise, must have read in the message the same thing I saw now.

"I can't remember drawing it . . . or feeling it. I just wish I could." The words shook as they fell as grief from his trembling mouth.

"Damn it," he suddenly spat, raking his hand through his hair. "He wasted his whole life."

Again, his expression shifted and the fire behind his words dulled and eased into pain, as if he didn't know whether to revile his father's memory or mourn him.

"He knew he was dying, Elizabeth. I know it, and he wanted me to know he cared about me."

The sadness poured through him, a mixture of anger and pity and so much regret. "I just wish he would have had the courage to say it to my face."

Tracing the lettering, I imagined a little black-haired boy drawing it, the concentration he would have had on his face as he worked on the choppy, misspelled letters, the pride he'd have had as he'd given it to his father.

I didn't flinch when Christian reached out to do the same.

I closed my eyes as he pried my fingers from the page and wrapped them in his hand. "I don't want to become like him, Elizabeth." His throat bobbed in unspent emotion. "I don't want to waste my life. I don't want to waste *this*," he stressed as he squeezed my hand.

I laced my fingers through his and blinked back tears. He followed my gaze to Lizzie, and I brought our joined hands to touch the porcelain rosiness of our daughter's cheek, before I turned back to face the intent in his eyes.

"You're not."

A sad smile whispered at the corner of his mouth, and he laid his cheek against her head as a heavy breath fell from his tired lips.

In the stillness, I held his hand, brushed my thumb over his soft skin. I watched as his eyes gradually faded and closed in exhaustion, listened to his deep breaths even out, felt his muscles twitch as he drifted to sleep.

As quietly as I could, I uncurled myself from the couch, lifted Lizzie into my arms, and carried her upstairs to her bed.

I tucked her under her covers and spent a

moment adoring the amazing child Christian and I had created, before I kissed her on the forehead.

Then I went into my room and dragged a blanket and pillow from my bed.

I tiptoed back downstairs to find Christian had slouched and sank deeper into the crevices of the couch. His arms were sprawled out, his body relaxed.

My stomach clenched in both pain and desire.

Why did loving him have to hurt so much?

Putting the linens aside, I crouched to untie his shoes, pulled them from his feet, and lifted is legs to lay them across the couch.

He stretched and groaned incoherently as he shifted, pulling at the twines twisted around my heart.

As gently as I could, I maneuvered the pillow beneath his head, shook out the blanket, and spread it over his body. I hesitated as I leaned down to pull it to his chin.

So beautiful.

His mouth had dropped open, just enough that he expelled soft breaths of air against my face, sweet and distinctly man, his long black lashes casting slight shadows across his face.

I leaned in further and let my fingertips wander over the day old stubble along his jaw, ran them tenderly over his lips—wanted what I couldn't have.

So, like a fool, I stole it and pressed my lips to his, knowing he'd only be mine for a few moments.

They were hot, damp, and perfect; they scorched my skin and brought tears to my eyes.

A tremor rolled through my chest, stuck in my throat, and shook my body.

I took a little more, held his face in my hands and in my desperation, kissed him deeper—tasted my tears and the sweetness of Christian's mouth—flirted with disaster.

Why? I begged him with my thoughts, with my touch as I kissed him again. *Why did you have to ruin us?* My mouth traveled to his jaw, kissed him there against the rough skin, fire against my lips and torment to my soul, where I mouthed out my deepest secret, *"I love you, Christian."*

Sickened and ashamed, I ripped myself away, escaped upstairs, and wept for a man I'd never allow myself to have.

Grabbing my things, I sighed in satisfaction, thankful it was Friday and another long workweek had drawn to an end. I shrugged on my jacket, smiling at Selina. "Goodnight."

She grinned and looked at me awry as she dug through her locker. "Night . . . see you tomorrow." She shook her hips, suggestive and slow.

I giggled and waved over my shoulder as I left her in the break room.

Natalie and her parties.

She'd never let a year go by without planning something outrageous. They were always too much and always *too* fun. She'd invited next to everyone I knew, and I was certain we'd all be paying for it Sunday morning.

Anxious to start my weekend, I rushed across the bank floor as I called goodnight to everyone in the lobby. I came to an abrupt halt two feet from the door when I saw my daughter's face pressed against the glass door, peering inside.

Her huge smile assured me I had no need to worry.

I laughed, returning her excited wave when she noticed me.

Pushing the door open, I poked my head out. She wore a maroon dress with a satin bodice and a skirt of tulle, wrapped at the waist in black ribbon. The outfit had been finished off with white tights, black patent shoes, and a matching maroon bow tied in her hair.

"What are you doing here and all dressed up?" I asked, grinning.

Lizzie grinned back, twirling away from the door as if she were a ballerina, and I stepped the rest of the way out.

Christian's voice hit me from somewhere

behind, smooth and warm—intoxicating. "We're celebrating."

Jerking around, I found him leaning with a shoulder against the bank wall. He wore an almost cocky look on his face, his mouth twisted in casual confidence. He was dressed in a deep-blue collared shirt rolled up to his elbows, the first two buttons undone, and black slacks that looked better than they should.

"I figured since the rest of your family and friends get you tomorrow night on your actual birthday, Lizzie and I get you tonight." A smile pulled at one side of his mouth, and he pushed from the wall and took a step forward.

Lizzie took my hand and danced beside me as she sang, "Surprise!"

My spirit soared.

This was the birthday I wanted.

Kneeling beside my daughter, I hugged her while I looked up at Christian. "Thank you."

He smiled so wide it touched his eyes. "Did you really think we'd let them keep you all to themselves?" He came forward and extended his hand to help me up, once again igniting the flames I futilely fought to squelch. He froze, just for a second, as a palpable quiver traveled up his arm, and I knew he felt it too.

After I'd kissed him last Friday, I'd felt so ashamed. I was sure he could somehow see the guilt on my face—find in it in my eyes.

The next morning, he'd seemed to watch me carefully, attentive to my every move. It was as if he were counting each breath I took and reading every word I spoke.

It had begun then, the timid fingertips across my upper arms as he'd leave the room, gentle brushes of skin, testing, tempting.

In spite of my promise to myself, my promise to Lizzie, I'd done the same, furtive fingers, roaming eyes—played with fire.

Christian tugged on my hand. "Come on. We'll follow you home and you can hop in my car."

Forty minutes later, we walked through the parking lot to the restaurant, swinging Lizzie between us. She squealed and begged us to do it again and again. Christian smiled at me over her head, and I fell in love a little bit more.

All three of us were laughing when we entered the loud, crowded restaurant. Filled with young families with small children, parties and celebrations, it was one of those places people flocked to on a Friday night to unwind, to forget about the week, and to share a meal and drinks.

Christian led us through the throng of people waiting for tables and to the podium, announcing our arrival and name for the reservation. The hostess weaved through the tables to the far corner of the restaurant, seating us at a booth.

I laughed and dropped my mouth in mock offense when Lizzie once again crawled up next to her father.

"How come you never want to sit by Mommy anymore?" I teased.

Lizzie clung to his upper arm, laid her head on his shoulder, squeezed as she giggled, and said, "Cuz Daddy doesn't always get to sleep at my house."

Christian smirked, threw me a mischievous look that said *that would be easy to fix.*

Instead of cringing and cursing my heart, I rolled my eyes and laughed to let him know I knew exactly what he was thinking.

I surprised myself with the action, but I was feeling free, swept away by the atmosphere and the roaring energy of the room.

He grinned as he opened his menu and muttered something under his breath. His smile was evident even as he buried his face in the menu.

My smile matched his, wide and unrestrained.

It was my birthday, and just tonight, I was going to allow myself to enjoy this, to enjoy my family, as unconventional as it was.

Christian ordered me a birthday drink, a huge concoction of rum and chocolate and whipped cream. He didn't hesitate to dip his finger in it to steal a taste.

We ordered burgers and fries, drank and ate as

we talked and teased. We laughed until we cried when a clown stopped by to make us balloon hats.

All of the tension was gone, for a few precious moments our past forgotten.

Sated and appeased, Christian leaned easily against the booth with his arm slung around our daughter's shoulders, his burger polished off.

Happy.

Blue eyes danced with merriment as he announced, "Present time."

Lizzie bounced and clapped her hands. "Ooohhh, Momma, open mine first!"

Christian produced a small box he'd kept hidden from somewhere beneath the table. It was square and shallow, covered in shiny red paper bunched and uneven with a crooked silver bow—*perfect*—wrapped with great care by little hands.

I released a small, surprised giggle of appreciation and wondered when the last time I'd felt so loved.

"When did you have time for all of this?" I held the small gift near my ear and gently shook the tiny box.

Christian shrugged, smiled wide. "I took the afternoon off to take Lizzie shopping and to get ready." He nudged her and they shared a knowing smile, thick as thieves. "I called Natalie last night to let her know I was picking Lizzie up from school today."

I hoped my expression was enough to portray how much this meant to me, that he would take the time to help our daughter do something that was so obviously important to her.

That he took time for me.

"Mommy, open it!" Lizzie prodded.

I smiled, shook it again, and drew the words out as I said, "I *wonder* what this could be?" I figured she must have picked out a piece of jewelry.

Slowly, I pulled away the bow and ribbon and ran my finger under the paper to loosen the tape. I felt my chest flutter when I realized the box was black velvet, its contents real, and I worried that it had cost too much.

Then I lifted the lid to the sweetest gift I'd ever received.

The white-gold charm bracelet was a rod and ball type, simple *and* beautiful, and made me feel incredibly special.

"Do you like it, Momma?"

I glanced up at Lizzie who was on her knees, eager for my reaction, and answered in complete honesty. "I love it."

I traced a finger over it, unhooked its snap from the box, and held it up in the air over the table.

Three silver bead charms slid to the bottom, one with an emerald for Lizzie's birthday, one with a yellow topaz for mine, and another simply engraved with Mother.

Christian leaned over the table and reached out. "May I?"

Smiling, I nodded and passed it to him. I stretched my arm across the table and couldn't ignore the tingles that spread out over my skin as Christian's fingers worked the bracelet around my wrist and screwed the locking clasp in place.

He twisted it, wet his lips in concentration as he did, and then glanced up at me and then back down to finish his work.

He murmured, "You know you can add to this, right?" He ran the tip of his forefinger down the sensitive skin of my wrist.

It sounded nothing like a question but an invitation.

My face reddened, but I refused to look away.

Lizzie gushed as she nearly climbed on top of the table to admire the bracelet now dangling from my wrist.

"Oh, it's so pretty!" My sweet child looked up for my approval, hoping to find I liked it as much as she wanted me to.

Fingering the charms, I smiled back her, told her again how beautiful I thought it was and that I would wear it with pride.

"My turn." Christian produced an envelope, larger than a normal card. It was thick and rectangular and it spiked my nerves with the way it shook in his trembling hand.

"Happy birthday, Elizabeth," he said with the softest of smiles.

I returned an uncertain smile, hesitated as I held the card between us, and realized I didn't want to be scared.

Just for one night, I didn't want to be scared.

So, I ripped it open.

At first, I was confused as I looked at the brochure and reservation slip in my hand, until my mind finally came to recognition.

When I snapped my head up in surprise, I found Christian's eyes burning into mine.

His words came more hopeful than any I'd ever known, impassioned as they passed through his lips, "Come to New York for Christmas with me, just you and Lizzie. I . . . I want her to see the tree . . . to show her where she was born . . . where we met."

In his expectation, I lost all reason and threw all sanity aside because I actually *wanted* to go. I pretended I didn't know what Christian meant when he asked me to go to New York *with* him, lied to myself again, and assured myself anew that nothing had changed.

Because by the look on Christian's face when I released the breath I'd been holding and nodded that I would go, I *knew* everything had changed.

For a few moments, a new heaviness hung in the air, a new fear vying for my attention, imploring with me to pay it heed.

I pushed it aside and laughed through my embarrassment as our server suddenly appeared at the edge of our table and shouted over the clamor of the room, demanding attention as he called out, "We have a birthday in the house!"

Christian's eyes glinted with deep satisfaction as he sang me the birthday song along with the rest of the restaurant. He seemed to make his own wish when I blew out the single candle stuck in a massive piece of chocolate cake.

"So how does it feel to be twenty-nine, Ms. Ayers?" All teasing from earlier aside, Christian's eyes softened as he asked.

Like you missed too many years, I thought much too quickly, before I had the time to dismiss its meaning.

Before I answered, I glanced at Lizzie, my reason for living, and back at the man who had somehow snaked his way back into my life and had become such an important part of my family.

I realized in all honesty that it felt amazing.

For the first time in many years, I was truly happy.

Even if being with him took great restraint, at times tore me apart and turned me inside out, it was worth every second.

I swallowed and answered, "It feels amazing."

Christian grinned and touched the tip of his

shoe to mine under the table, a gentle caress, chaste affection.

I blushed, flicked the bangs from my face, a subconscious tic, and knocked my balloon hat from my head.

Squinting, Christian suddenly leaned forward as he tilted his head to one side. "How'd you get that scar above your eye, anyway?"

He reached across the table to brush my bangs aside, and instinctively, I jerked away. I shook my head and forced out a feeble, "It's nothing."

Christian frowned and slowly withdrew his hand with my reaction.

"Shawn was mean to Mommy."

Christian's head whipped in Lizzie's direction as she spoke the words before fiery eyes darted back to me.

I watched as a storm raced in, violent and destructive.

And just like that, the peace of our evening was gone, leaving in its place a Christian I'd never seen.

A Christian I didn't know.

He put distance between himself and Lizzie, sitting rigid in the booth and saying nothing as he paid the bill.

He wouldn't look my way, not even when I whispered, "Thank you for dinner."

He just stood and ushered Lizzie from the bench, never looked up from the ground as he walked behind us out to the car.

It took only seconds for Lizzie to fall asleep in the backseat of his car. Christian stared ahead and left me alone to suffocate in his seething silence. He said nothing as he rose from the car and collected our slumbering daughter from his backseat.

He stood aside and waited for me to unlock the front door and took her up to her room.

I waited at the bottom of the stairs to give him space.

I understood he was angry, not with me, but with Shawn.

Minutes later, he emerged from Lizzie's room and stared down at me with raging torment.

Something inside him had fractured—ruptured.

"Christian." My tone was quiet, pleading for him not to make a big deal of this.

It was something I'd not wanted to delve into with him. I had no desire to resurrect old ghosts and had been thankful to have dodged the subject when Christian had asked about Shawn at the beach.

What happened with Shawn was long over and done with, something I'd dealt with emotionally, had come to terms with, and had vowed to never repeat.

Unable to escape from the intensity of Christian's gaze as he slowly took the stairs, I knew there was no way to evade it now.

On the last step, he stopped inches from me and clenched his fists. "Shawn *who*?"

I shook my head. "It doesn't matter."

Over.

Done.

Forgotten.

Christian studied his feet, palmed the back of his neck, pushed past me, and paced my living room.

Coming to an abrupt halt, he turned and glared at me.

"It doesn't matter?" His voice rose. "It doesn't fucking matter? Are you *kidding* me, Elizabeth?"

He flung his arm out in a wild gesture at my head.

I didn't cower, didn't flinch. I knew none of the fury flooding from him was directed at me.

This time he begged, wanted me to agree, "That asshole hurt you, and it *doesn't* matter?"

He turned away, buried both hands in his hair, and hid his face as he released his torment toward the floor. "I can't believe I let this happen to you."

Taking a step forward, I placed a cautious hand against his back and pressed my palm into the warmth of his body.

Tremors rolled through his muscles with the contact, and my explanation came in hushed tones and filled the otherwise dark, silent room.

"It doesn't matter because I've healed, Christian.

He means nothing to me, *meant* nothing to me, and he paid the price for what he did. The only part that hurts me now is dealing with the fact that my daughter had to witness it."

Christian's shoulders slumped further, Lizzie's involvement another blow. Defeated, he choked over more guilty words, "I'm so sorry, Elizabeth."

I caressed his back, ran my hand up his spine, and twisted my fingers in the fine hairs at the nape of his neck. "You can't blame yourself for everything that happened while you were away."

He looked at me over his shoulder. His beautiful face was illuminated by the light on the stairs and contorted in what could only be physical pain. "How can I not?"

I turned him and wrapped my arms around his neck.

He exhaled his burden, groaning from somewhere deep within his chest when he wound a single arm around my waist and tugged me flush against his body.

With the other hand, he brushed away my bangs, tucked the heavy lock of hair behind my ear, and ran his thumb over the long-healed scar.

My heart thrashed, protested its chains, loosened its binds.

Dropping his hand from my face, he brought it to my hip and dug in his fingers to draw me closer. He massaged his way up my back and to my neck and buried his hand in my hair.

Held me.

Rocked me.

Loved me.

The clock against the wall chimed midnight.

Christian pressed his heated cheek to mine and whispered, "Happy birthday, Elizabeth."

* * *

Lizzie posed in front of the full-length mirror in my bedroom. She slicked bright red lipstick across her lips, smearing more of it around her mouth and over her teeth than on her lips, and teetered in a pair of four-inch heels three times too big for her tiny feet.

I laughed under my breath from where I watched her out of the corner of my eye and wondered where I'd left my camera.

"Look at me, Mommy. Don't I look pretty?" She spun in place, twirling the old red skirt I'd discarded on the floor as I'd dug through my closet for something to wear.

Crossing the room, I took both of her hands, whirled her around, and dipped her in an old-fashioned, impromptu dance. "You look absolutely gorgeous, darling." Then I tickled her and kissed her solidly on the cheek.

She howled with laughter, her face red from both the lipstick and her surprise. She sobered, reached out, and touched my cheek as she searched my face with observant eyes.

"You look really pretty too, Mommy," she said in quiet assurance, surely having noticed my nerves as I'd hunted through my clothes, tossing aside the modest outfits I typically wore to work for something Natalie and my sisters would find appropriate for the night.

I'd settled on a too short, black tiered skirt, coupled it with a white ruffled blouse that showed just a bit too much cleavage and, of course, a pair of much too high black heels. Even though it made me a bit self-conscious, I didn't even bother to dress in something more conservative.

Natalie would have just marched me straight back upstairs to change.

Before I could thank Lizzie, the doorbell rang, and she wriggled from my arms and bolted out the door and down the stairs.

Christian.

A tremor of apprehension rolled through me, flared and balled in my stomach as I heard his voice drift up from below.

Sleep had evaded me for most of last night. I'd chased it, only to drift to the edges of unconsciousness to find myself back in his arms, surrounded by his presence, begging for his touch. Panic would bring me back, jolting me up in bed, leaving me gasping for air as blood pounded through my veins.

Those immeasurable minutes spent in Christian's arms had felt so good, *so right*, like peace and eternity, made me feel as if I would choose to stay.

When the solace offered in my arms had shifted, we'd both felt it—when it'd become *more*—when the heat of his body had washed over me in waves, hot and hard, nearly drowning me in his desire.

I wouldn't have had the strength to say no.

It had only taken him untangling himself from my hold and forcing himself out my front door for me to slip back into fear, to question what I'd done—what I'd agreed to.

In six weeks, I was supposed to go to New York with Christian, and I had no idea what that meant, what he expected, or what I could give.

I shook my head, smoothed out my shirt, and adjusted my skirt, wishing not everything had to be so complicated. I wished that I didn't have so much hurt buried inside, so many deep-seated fears. I wished I could trust in him and believe that this time he wouldn't let me down.

Most of all, I just wished to give up and give in.

God, I wanted to give in.

I clutched the railing for support at the top of the stairs as I looked down over my living room where Christian gazed up at me, hugging our daughter in his arms.

He was in dark low-slung jeans and a black T-shirt, his hair unruly, his eyes intense. It was as if the moment our eyes connected our bodies picked up right where we'd left off last night.

The energy was dense, swirling with need and dripping with want. It rained down, sucked us in, and urged me forward.

Christian settled Lizzie onto the couch so she was facing the television, not in neglect, but as if this were something she could take no part in, the moment too intimate, not to be shared.

As I edged down the stairs, I watched him as he watched me, didn't shy from the touch of his gaze, but welcomed it as it traveled down, kissed my body and caressed my legs.

His lips parted, tacit desire calling my name.

I stopped a foot away.

He hesitated and swallowed deeply before he finally took a step forward, assailing my senses as he placed a heated palm against my cheek. With the pad of his thumb, he caressed my jaw.

I closed my eyes and leaned into his touch as the sweet of his breath washed over my face. I waited, wanting more than I should.

His movements were tentative as he slanted forward and brushed his nose along the opposite cheek. He ran it to my ear and whispered, "You are so beautiful."

His words sent a thrill rushing over my skin. He

ghosted his lips over the same line and pressed his mouth against my jaw.

I gasped and clutched his shoulders for support, unprepared for the onslaught of emotion—for the ache.

For the first time, I was completely defenseless, subject to Christian's mercy.

Somewhere inside me, I knew he would hurt me. Once again, he'd stolen my heart and held in his hand. He had taken control and I didn't know how to get it back.

I recognized it in the panic I felt when he pulled away, in the way my nails burrowed into the skin of his shoulders and begged him, *Don't let me go.*

Christian dropped his arm completely and stepped away.

A low, "Ahem," made me turn my attention to a red-faced Matthew standing frozen in my doorway. He looked down and cringed over an apology.

Natalie popped up on her tiptoes, peeking over Matthew's shoulder to find what it was that had caused her husband to stumble to a standstill.

fifteen

I didn't want to let go—ever.

Elizabeth's fingers burned into my skin and anchored in my soul.

Did she understand how much I cherished her? As I pressed my mouth to her jaw and held her face, did she know that I was praising the goodness of her heart and her ability to forgive, and that I fell in love with her more and more each day?

It took everything I had to pull away, to step back, but I knew where we were heading, and the last thing I wanted was an audience for the first kiss Elizabeth and I had shared in six years.

Elizabeth was so wrapped up in the moment, I'm sure she hadn't even realized Matthew and Natalie were standing in her doorway with their mouths gaping.

Spreading a frustrated hand through my hair, I looked to the opposite wall, hoping to quiet my thundering heart, to quell the roar screaming through my veins, demanding Elizabeth.

When I looked back, Matthew remained frozen in the doorway and appeared to be studying Elizabeth. Natalie broke through the tension, pushed under her husband's arm, and entered the room to embrace Elizabeth as if she hadn't just walked in on one of the most pivotal moments of our lives.

"Happy birthday, Liz. You ready to go?"

I watched as Elizabeth nodded and returned Natalie's hug, before she gathered her purse and black sweater from the entryway table. She looked back at me warily.

Once again, the two of us were propelled back into the unknown, unsure of where we stood.

I offered her a gentle smile, one that I hoped told her I understood, that I was scared too, but that I was finished wasting time—done wasting nights without those I loved.

I'd boarded the flight from my father's funeral with a newfound resolve, an unvoiced pledge to my daughter and to Elizabeth that I would finally make this right.

It was time to take back my family.

Natalie approached with a knowing smile, wrapped an arm around my waist, and grinned up at me.

Draping an arm around her shoulder, I hugged her to my side and smiled down at the girl who had become my friend, my confidant, the one who seemed to *get* both Elizabeth and me.

I dropped my arm from her shoulder to shake Matthew's hand. His grip was firm but lacked any animosity.

His eyes darted to Elizabeth before they rested on me as he shook my hand.

It was clear he knew exactly what had been taking place between Elizabeth and me when he'd walked through the door. He squeezed once before he dropped my hand and nodded almost imperceptibly, seeming to be giving me both a blessing and a warning—a statement that he wouldn't stand in our way, but it was also clear where his loyalties rested.

His protectiveness didn't bother me because my loyalties were in the very same place. I met his eyes with a nod.

Natalie and Matthew smothered Lizzie in love and goodbyes, made her giggle as they teased her, telling her to make sure she took good care of her daddy while they were away.

Elizabeth took Lizzie in her arms, hugged her close, ran a tender hand through our daughter's hair. "Have a great time with Daddy."

Elizabeth seemed uncertain when she stood and turned to me. Vacillating emotions flickered across her face—need and love and too much fear. I'd recognized it in her touch when I'd stepped away, the fear that was rooted deep and clung to her like a disease.

I'd spend my life driving it out.

Extending my hand, I reached for her, pulled her to my chest, and murmured against her ear, "I'll be waiting."

Reticent, I released her hand with a heavy breath and watched as the three of them filed out the front door. I prayed they'd be safe, counted on Matthew to bring my girl home safely to me, refusing myself the sudden surge of possessiveness I felt when I realized I wouldn't be the one there to witness her on the dance floor with her friends or there to celebrate her birthday.

It was shocking how badly I craved to be the man on her arm. But the last thing I had the right to was jealousy, so I forced those thoughts away and glanced at Lizzie who studied me with an astute curiosity from where she leaned over the back of the couch.

I smiled at my precious daughter. "Guess it's just you and me tonight, Lizzie."

Lizzie trailed me into the kitchen and helped prepare our dinner, a box of pasta, white sauce, and fresh cut broccoli florets.

She grinned at me from across the table as we ate our simple meal. Affection swelled as I shared the evening with my sweet, sweet girl. I listened to her simple words, so honest and pure, and thanked God for grace because I knew there was nothing I'd done to deserve the sublime.

Lizzie asked about New York—what it would be like and what we would see. Then in a quiet voice she asked, "Will you hold my hand on the plane? I'm kinda scared, Daddy. I've never been on a plane before."

I smiled at my daughter, brushed a hand through her bangs, and answered, "Only if you hold mine."

After dinner, I helped her into her sweater and we stepped out into the crisp evening air.

Hand-in-hand, we followed the sidewalk to the small park at the end of the street. I pushed her high on the swings, chased her over the grassy hills, relished in her laughter as I caught her at the bottom of the slide.

My spirit danced as we played, rejoiced in this gift, my heart forever devoted to this precious child.

When Lizzie began to shiver, we returned home and went upstairs where I bathed her in her mother's alcoved bathroom. I filled the tub with bubbles and her small bathtub toys and didn't mind when her rambunctious play soaked my shirt. I let her splash and dunk until her fingers had shriveled and the water had turned cool.

"Come here, sweetheart," I gently prompted, helped her safely from the tub, and wrapped her in a huge, fluffy white towel. I ran it over her damp skin and dried her hair, wondering how I'd become so favored that in less than a year, my life had gone from completely empty to overflowing.

"I love you so much, Daddy," she professed as she peeked up at me through the towel wrapped around her head and body as I carried her to her room.

Leaning down, I kissed her forehead and pressed her to my chest. "I love you more than anything, Lizzie."

Keen eyes probed my face as she whispered, "But you love Mommy, too."

My feet faltered, frozen, amazed at my young daughter's poignant perception, far from oblivious, always aware.

I should have known she would have noticed the change between Elizabeth and me in the last week, the newfound affection, the embraces, our timid touches.

Swallowing the lump in my throat, I nodded and met her hopeful gaze. "Yes, Lizzie . . . I . . . I love your mother very much."

I'd never spoken it aloud to Lizzie before, afraid of getting her hopes up, worried Elizabeth and I would never reconcile, and that we'd go on as partners in Lizzie's parenthood—*friends* as Elizabeth had somehow considered us.

Even if Elizabeth had claimed it, she should have known there was no chance that we could just remain friends.

She was mine, had always been, and I'd always been hers. Despite what I'd done, the wounds I'd inflicted, she had always been mine. When I'd lain with other women and she with other men, our hearts had been tied, our bond one that neither of us could ever escape.

I think I'd known all along that one day we would be together again, and as my mother had said, it would just take time and patience. When Elizabeth had realized it, I wasn't quite sure.

Maybe she'd realized it somewhere along the way as we'd shared our daughter, as she'd taught me how to be a father and what loyalty and commitment really meant.

Maybe she'd felt it when my father died and her heart had bled so freely for me or perhaps in the embrace she'd met me with on my return— certainly by the time she'd kissed me that same night.

It'd taken every ounce of resolve for me to lie

still, to keep from tugging her body against mine, to pretend that I remained asleep, to pretend that the warmth of her fingers hadn't brought me to consciousness, to pretend that I hadn't felt her mouth upon mine.

I'd been strong enough to give her that moment and allow her the space to deal with the emotions that could no longer be contained. I'd listened to her cry in the room above me as I tasted the salt of her tears on my lips, silently promising her again and again that one day I would erase that pain.

I tucked Lizzie into her bed, smoothed her damp hair from her face, and told her again that I loved her.

Yawning, she snuggled down in her covers as I pulled them to her chin and murmured, "Night, Daddy. See you in the morning." The idea of her proclaiming that each night made me dizzy with joy.

"Sleep well, Lizzie."

At her door, I watched as she drifted off to sleep before I flipped off the light. I left her door ajar and walked downstairs. I glanced at the clock on the microwave as I grabbed a bottle of beer from the refrigerator.

Only ten o'clock.

Patience.

I'd waited for months—for years, really—I could wait a few more hours.

I slid the back door open, left it open a crack in case Lizzie woke, and dragged a chair to the edge of the patio. I leaned back to look up at the night sky that was a jaundiced haze with the glow of lights and tipped my beer to my mouth as I listened to the hum of the city—dogs barking at passersby, the whirr of the highway a few miles off, an ambulance blaring in the distance.

I wondered what Elizabeth was doing, hoped she was safe, and wished she were home.

I thought of the scar above her eye, the one that had twisted me in knots last night, made me sick with rage and starved for vengeance before her words from months ago had come to mind.

Nobody has ever hurt me as badly as you hurt me, Christian. No one.

Never had I hated myself more than then, knowing I had scarred her deeper than the disfigured evidence of abuse on her skin.

But somehow, her heart went deeper than that, deeper than my betrayal, and she had *comforted* me.

Breathing in the damp air, I drained my beer, stood, and went inside to get another.

Only eleven.

I dropped onto the couch, turned on the television, flipped through channels, and listened to a newscaster drone on. I sipped from my bottle, letting it ebb at my restlessness and soothe my impatience.

On my third trip to the kitchen, I heard the rattle of keys, the slide of metal, and a rush of laughter as it flooded the room. I popped the cap from the fresh bottle of beer and tossed it aside as I moved to lean with my forearm against the archway to watch Natalie wobble in, giggling with Elizabeth who was close behind. Matthew followed them in, shaking his head in what appeared to be slight amusement, his hands full of gift bags.

I couldn't help but grin.

Matthew glanced in my direction and rolled his eyes when Elizabeth and Natalie fell into another fit of laughter and looked back at them with unquestionable affection.

"I think our girls may have had a bit too much to drink tonight," he said while setting the bags aside.

Natalie held onto the back of the couch and tried to regain her balance in the ridiculously high-heeled boots she wore, laughing as she accused, "You're just mad 'cause you were DD."

Elizabeth wrapped her arms around his waist, kissed his cheek. "No, seriously, thank you for driving, Matt. I had a great time."

She grinned up at him as he kissed her atop her head. "No problem, Liz. Happy birthday."

Natalie laughed for what seemed no reason at all and swayed in the middle of the floor.

"Whoa there." Matthew was immediately behind her, supporting her as he drew her back to his chest. He hugged her and splayed his hands over her stomach as he hooked his chin over her shoulder. "I think I'd better get this one home."

He nuzzled her neck and made her giggle before he motioned with his head in my direction. "You stayin' here tonight?"

I waved my half-empty bottle in the air and nodded. "Yep. I've had a couple of these."

Not that I was going anywhere, anyway.

"Good."

No bitterness, no distrust.

Natalie tottered forward, hugged me, and stepped back to pucker her lips and squeeze my chin before she turned to kiss Elizabeth on her cheek.

I suppressed a chuckle. Matthew was definitely in for it tonight.

I shook his hand and clapped him on the shoulder. "Drive safe."

"Sure thing . . . see you two tomorrow." With a final happy birthday wish to Elizabeth, he wound an arm around Natalie's waist and led her out the door.

In their absence was a charged silence. Elizabeth looked to the ground, fidgeting in trepidation.

I didn't want her to feel this way, pressured or coerced, and I knew right then our reunion couldn't be tonight. Even though we both knew she was mine, that I was hers, it was obvious she still wasn't ready.

Patience.

"Did you have a good time?" I asked to break the tension as I crossed the room and gathered her bags to take them into the kitchen. I gave her a gentle smile.

It's okay, Elizabeth, I already know.

I set the brightly colored bags on the kitchen table and snooped through wads of tissue paper at the bottles of wine, soaps, scented lotions, and lingerie.

Elizabeth spoke from behind me where she lagged at the archway. "Yeah . . . we had a lot of fun." She giggled mostly to herself. "But my feet really hurt. I'm getting too old for this."

Chuckling at her assertion, I poked around some more through her things. I wished I could have been there to see her open her gifts and somehow have been with Lizzie at the same time.

I pulled a bottle of red wine from a gift bag, inspected the label, and turned it toward her as I held it up. "Shall we?"

I knew we probably *shouldn't*, that we'd both had enough to drink, but I didn't yet have it in me to tell her goodnight.

Her mouth twitched at one corner. "You know Scott got that for me?"

I looked between her and the bottle and cocked an eyebrow.

"Well, then we definitely *should*."

For some reason, my teasing seemed to relax her, and I saw the strain drain from her eyes and melt from her muscles.

She shook her head and laughed lightly as she crossed the room and hoisted herself onto the kitchen counter.

I swallowed and tried to orient myself, to maintain control.

She was *so* beautiful. Many times I'd seen her sitting on that counter, chatting with Natalie and laughing, but never dressed like that.

I tried not to stare as I dug through the drawer next to the sink for a corkscrew, though I couldn't help but steal glances.

She leaned forward with her hands holding the edge of the counter, her long, slender legs exposed all the way to her thighs.

She swung them slowly, and the backs of her black heels thudded rhythmically against the cabinet beneath her, the swell of her breasts peeking out the top of her white blouse—a near irresistible temptation.

She wore a shy smile as she watched me opening the wine, her head tilted to face me, blond curls falling to one side. I poured two glasses, handed her one, and whispered, "Happy birthday,

Elizabeth." I clinked my glass to hers.

She sipped while looking up at me. "It's not my birthday anymore."

I closed my eyes, struggled to breathe, and took a step away to put some distance between us.

It was clear what was simmering just under the surface, what hung in the air. I knew I should end this and tell her goodnight.

Instead, I glanced over at her, smiled, and found an excuse to keep her for a few minutes more. "Tell me about tonight?"

I watched the movement of her mouth as she told me about her party, her friends, family, the things that were said, and the things that were done. I watched as she brought the glass to her lips again and again.

Time ticked on, topics changed, drifted to old college stories, the places we'd been, the fun we had shared. We laughed, we teased.

I refilled her glass, refilled mine, opened another bottle, listened as her words began to slur just as my mind became slack.

I was too relaxed, felt too good—loved the sound of her voice. I was drawn, edged closer, wanted more.

I found myself facing her and standing between her legs. I set my wine aside and pressed my palms onto the countertop. My thumbs gently brushed the outside of her thighs, her calves grazing my jeans as they slowly swished back and forth.

Her mouth was seductive, her eyes dark.

Needing to see her, I reached out and pushed away the veil of hair obstructing her beautiful face. She leaned her head into the movement, inviting the contact.

I ran the back of my hand down her cheek and over her lips, breathed her name. "Elizabeth."

She trembled as she hesitantly lifted her fingertips to touch my face and then cupped my jaw.

Our breaths filled the room, heavy and hungry. Her eyes flickered over my face, resting on where she touched me.

Under her touch, my skin burned like fire. She looked back at me almost in awe, as if she'd forgotten the power of our connection—forgotten that together we felt like *this*.

We'd been fools to think it could ever be contained.

"Elizabeth…" I whispered, this time a petition.

Please.

I needed her and was desperate to feel her.

Don't be afraid.

She brought her other hand up to hold my face and wet her lips.

As she leaned in, I inched closer, tilted my head, and gently brushed my lips against hers, kissing my girl for the first time in over six years.

Her lips were soft, just as I remembered, tasted like wine and the potent sweetness of Elizabeth's spirit. My heart leapt and tangled with hers as her fingers tangled in my hair. Our mouths were tentative, cautious, and slow.

I wanted more.

My tongue tested, and I groaned into her mouth as the tip of Elizabeth's tongue brushed across mine.

Yes.

Hit with a wave of lust, I sank my fingers into the bare skin of her thighs and tugged her to the edge of the counter, my mouth aggressive against hers.

Mine. Finally she was mine.

Her hands created the worst kind of desire as they roamed my body, over my shoulders and down my back. She drove me to the edge of sanity as she pressed her palms into my chest and down my stomach, then snaked her hands under my shirt as she wrapped her legs around my waist.

I was gone, losing all control in a fog of alcohol and lust and pent-up desire, my body starved for hers for far too long.

Her flimsy skirt was bunched over her hips and her black lace panties pressed against my jeans as my mouth sought out every exposed inch of her heated skin.

Still, I wanted more.

I yanked at the top of her blouse, exposed the rosy bud of her perfect breast, and took it in my mouth.

More.

My hands rushed up over the silky smoothness of her legs, my thumbs running desperate circles on her inner thighs as my fingers dug into her supple skin.

Elizabeth moaned and tore my shirt over my head.

More.

I panted into her mouth as I slipped two fingers under the edge of her panties and into the warmth of her body.

She gasped, bracing herself on my shoulders. I pulled back just a fraction, searching her face while my fingers searched her body.

Do you want this?

She answered by attacking my belt and rushing through my button fly.

I found enough sensibility to whisper against her mouth, "Not here."

My mouth crashed back to hers as I pulled her from the counter.

She wobbled as I set her feet on the floor.

I held her up, my hands on her hips as I pushed her backward and pressed her against the opposite wall, kissing her hard.

She ground out my name, strung it along, and

sent my heart crashing in my chest. *"Christian . . . please."*

I spun her again. Frantically I kissed her as I backed her through the family room. I fumbled through the buttons of her blouse as we stumbled up the stairs and toppled to her bedroom floor.

Somewhere inside of me, I knew it should be different from this. I knew I shouldn't be pushing her panties down her legs and her skirt up her waist. I knew her blouse shouldn't be left hanging open, her bra stretched beneath just one breast, my jeans shoved down to my thighs.

I knew I shouldn't thrust inside of her, frenzied, moaning at how good she felt.

I should have heard something in her small cries of pleasure, buried somewhere below the surface. Even in the shadows of her darkened room, I should have read it in her face as she came, found it in the horror in her eyes that followed.

I *knew* the beauty of Elizabeth shouldn't be wasted, that she should be savored and cherished.

But I was too distracted, too consumed by her skin, by her softness, by her heat—by everything she finally was giving me—what I could no longer live without.

I drove into her fast and hard, a quick release. I cried out into the darkness of her room and collapsed on top of her, gasping for air.

I kissed her closed mouth and ran my hand

through her knotted hair, wishing I had thought to tell her I loved her long before now.

I murmured it against her mouth.

She silently nodded in return.

sixteen

ELIZABETH

I opened my eyes and squinted against the low rays of early morning light streaming in through the slatted blinds in the otherwise darkened room.

I squeezed my eyes shut and pressed the heel of my hand into my left one in defense of the sharp, stabbing pain that felt as if it were splitting my head in two.

I tried to sit up but the room spun and pinned me back down. Blinking, I tried to orient myself.

Memories of last night flooded in and swept over me in waves of nausea and shame—the kitchen counter, the bedroom floor.

Oh my God came as a cry from deep within my soul.

Heat blistered my skin, his bare chest scorching my back where we touched, his arm slung over my waist. Deep, heavy breaths sounded against my ear and spread out over my face, his pulse a steady thrum.

Oh my God.

I pressed my hand to my mouth to stifle a cry.

I tried to untangle myself from his grip without waking him. I froze when he tightened his hold.

Unintelligible mutterings spilled from his mouth, and I held my breath as I slipped from his grasp and stood from the bed. I held my head in my hands to combat another rush of dizziness.

Christian groaned and mumbled, rolled to his stomach, and buried his head in my pillow. The sheet covered him to his waist, dipping to reveal the edge of his black boxer briefs and exposing the defined contours of his broad shoulders that tapered to his narrow back.

Oh my God.

With weak knees, I steadied myself with my arm against the wall. I looked down at myself in disgust, unable to remember how I'd ended up in a tank top and underwear, unable to remember how I'd made it into my bed.

How could I have allowed this happen, allowed him to treat me this way? I should have known he was just the same and that he would never change.

In my shame, I stumbled to the bathroom, shaking as I wrapped my trembling body in a black robe that covered my legs to my knees. I knotted the belt and then clung to the bathroom doorway as I stared back out at the beautiful man sleeping in my bed.

I felt my heart break again.

Why? Why did he have to ruin everything? I'd seen this coming like a storm churning out in the middle of the sea, only days until landfall.

He'd turned us upside down, smiled with dishonest intentions, pushed until I'd fallen over the edge, waiting to strike until I trusted again.

I'd known all along where that trust would lead, that he'd laugh in my face as he threw it away.

Was it all just a game?

I looked over at the spot where he'd treated me like trash, where he'd fucked me on my bedroom floor. Like garbage to be tossed aside, he'd spilled into me without a second thought.

Just like years before.

We'd been out at a college bar, drank until we'd staggered back to his apartment laughing, kissing, reckless.

We hadn't even thought about what we'd forgotten until it was over.

Christian had shrugged it off as if it was nothing, and I'd pushed it to the back of mind until I could ignore it no longer.

He'd leave me, just like he had before.

And once again, I'd be alone.

I'd trusted him implicitly right up until the moment he'd driven me away, and I knew I could expect nothing different this time.

Forcing myself down the hall, I slid my palm across the wall for support. I closed Lizzie's door with a soft click and felt something splintering inside as old wounds ripped wide open.

I could barely stand under the deluge of memories, the burden I'd carried, every internal injury meted out at Christian's will.

Everything spun as I clutched the railing and slowly took each step downstairs. My head throbbed with the pulsing and pounding of blood in my ears. It turned my stomach and soured my mouth.

I raced across the family room and purged my guilt and hangover into the downstairs toilet as I berated myself for being such a fool to have given in.

I shouldn't have expected anything different or anything better.

On unsteady feet, I stood and held onto the basin as I splashed cold water on my face and rinsed my mouth. I tied my matted, tangled hair back with a band before I hunted through the medicine cabinet for a bottle of ibuprofen.

Shaking, I placed four tablets in my mouth and cupped my hands under the running faucet to chase them down.

Tears stung my eyes as I looked back up into the mirror and wiped my mouth with a towel, unsure if I'd survive this time.

I lumbered out and was met with the remnants of the night before—two empty wine bottles, two glasses left half full, Christian's shirt discarded on the floor.

Bending down, I picked the shirt up and closed my eyes as I pressed it to my mouth, to my nose, inhaling the sweet of the man who would *never stop* breaking my heart.

I stiffened when I *felt* his presence, and then heard the heavy release of air that sounded something like relief from across the room.

His movements were subdued as he moved across the kitchen floor.

I flinched when he wrapped his arms around me from behind, buried his nose in my neck, and whispered, "Good morning."

It felt like a caress on my skin.

I whimpered, my mouth trembling as I made a decision before it was much, much too late, forcing out a barely audible, "Don't touch me."

Old pain was fresh, tormenting my weakness, insulting the mistake I'd made in allowing him into my home and back into my life, mocking how easily I'd handed over my heart.

He stiffened but didn't back away. I felt him shake, swallow, understand. "Please, Elizabeth, *don't* do this."

My hair brushed across his bare chest as I slowly shook my head.

For the briefest moment, my desire confused my resolve, the continuous fire that roiled between us, a reminder of just how badly this was going to hurt.

But I would be strong enough to end *this* now before he completely destroyed Lizzie and me, while Lizzie still had a chance to recover.

In time she would heal, though I knew I would not.

No amount of time could undo the devastation I felt as I turned on him and wrenched myself from his grip, spitting the words as I inched back toward him and slammed his shirt against his chest.

"I want you out of my house . . . out of our lives."

He seemed to sway, to lose his balance. His face contorted in agony as he first looked at the wadded-up shirt fisted in his hand and then back at me.

Is that what I'd looked like when he'd cast me aside? Is that what the shock of heartbreak looked like? Could he *ever* feel the way he had made *me* feel? Could he ever understand?

His expression shifted and set in determination as he clenched his jaw.

"No." He shook his head. "I'm not going anywhere, Elizabeth."

I closed my eyes, refusing to see the commitment on his face as I forced out the words. "Get out."

I opened my eyes, dragging to the forefront the memories of what he had done. I remembered the callused expression on his face when he'd told me to choose him or my daughter. I remembered how it had felt to be alone, sick, and scared. Remembered what it felt like to fight for my child's life.

I'd given up my goals, not because of my daughter, but because he had been too much of a coward to stand up for what was right, because he had refused to take responsibility for his family. I clung to long suppressed secrets of shame.

I'd hidden from my family just how bad off Lizzie and I had gotten.

When I'd already asked my family for far too much, I'd gone hungry because I couldn't afford to feed both of us. The time Lizzie and I had been evicted from our small apartment and I'd driven through the night, feeling too ashamed to tell my mother and Matthew that I'd failed again, and I'd still ended up at Matthew's house at four in the morning.

It was then that Matthew and Natalie had taken us in to live with them.

I held fast to the memories of their sacrifice—a sacrifice Christian hadn't been man enough to make.

I stalked forward, backed him into the next room, and let everything boil over. "Get out!"

This time he pled, reached for me, and attempted to restrain me in his arms. "No, Elizabeth. I won't leave you, not this time. I *love* you . . . oh my God, please don't do this."

I fought against him and twisted out of his grip, refusing to allow him to convince me of anything different than what he'd shown me the night before—remembered the five-minute exchange on my bedroom floor where he'd reminded me just how little I actually meant to him and let that anger bleed free.

"I *hate* you."

He jumped back, releasing me as if he'd been stung.

I didn't stop, but spewed my anger. "How dare you come in here and turn my life upside down . . . lead me on . . . make me believe you'd changed. I *trusted* you, and the *second* I was vulnerable, you took advantage of it!"

His eyes were wide with shock when they flew up to meet the tortured fury in my own.

"What?" he demanded in a low voice as he took two steps forward. "Is that what you think last night was?"

His eyes narrowed, and I cowered as he took another step that had me backed against the wall. "Don't *you* dare stand there and act like you didn't want it every bit as much as I wanted it, Elizabeth . . . pretend that this . . ."—he gestured wildly between us—"wasn't already happening. Yeah, things got a little out of control last night, but it doesn't change *anything.*"

He was right. Nothing had changed. He was just the same. He would promise his heart until it no longer suited him. He would take what he wanted and toss aside what he didn't.

He will never stay.

Defeated, I slid down the wall and buried my head in my hands, unable to stop the rush of emotion.

He will never stay.

I felt myself breaking apart as tears poured unchecked down my face and the reality of my foolishness sank in and became real. I whispered again, "I hate you."

Christian leaned down, his nose nearly touching mine, his voice fire.

"You are a liar."

He glared down at me with heartbroken rage and pointed up toward Lizzie's room. "I love you,

Elizabeth, but you need to know . . . I will fight for her."

Squeezing my eyes shut, I put back up the walls he had torn down, wouldn't listen to what he said. I lost myself in self-pity, in my mistakes, in his betrayal.

In my mind, I saw him as the selfish boy who had ripped me apart.

He will never stay.

My tortured cries did nothing to drown out the echo of Christian's feet as he walked away, taking with him the last piece of my heart.

The front door grated on its hinges as it opened, taunted, *He's leaving you.*

I couldn't have imagined anything could have hurt worse than what had just transpired, that there could be anything more painful than cutting Christian from my life.

But I should have known better, known that it would only compound.

I fought for resolve, for a way to stay strong when Lizzie suddenly appeared on the stairs, panic in the clamor of her feet and in the flood of hysteria from her mouth.

"No! Daddy, don't go!"

Christian turned in the doorway as if in slow motion. All color drained from his face as he dropped to his knees to catch Lizzie in his arms.

She clung to his neck and cried again, barely

coherent as she begged, "Don't leave me, Daddy! Please don't leave me!"

The nausea from before made a resurgence as I lay limply against the wall, disconnected, and watched my daughter fall apart while Christian tried to hold her together.

He rocked her, whispered against her head, and promised, "It'll be okay. It'll be okay."

Pulling back, he faked a smile. "I'll come back, sweetheart. It might take a little while, but I promise I'll come back."

Lizzie held him tighter. "Please, stay with me, Daddy."

He choked over her plea and hugged her to his chest. Over her shoulder, he begged me with his eyes.

I looked away.

He will never stay.

I had to end it now for her sake—and mine.

"I can't right now, princess. Mommy and Daddy just need a little time apart." His eyes flitted over her face as he tucked a piece of hair behind her ear. "Try not to be sad and just remember that, no matter what, Daddy loves you."

Then he stood and walked out the door.

With the click of the latch, a sob erupted from Lizzie, and she rushed to the window. She pressed her face against the glass, her voice small and broken.

"Daddy." It escalated with each breath as she repeatedly called for him, "Daddy . . . Daddy . . . *Daddy!*"

When he backed his car from the driveway, and his tires squealed on the road, she slid to the floor where her cries became muddled and distorted, an echo of my own heartbreak sounding out from my baby girl who rocked herself in a ball on the floor.

For a fleeting moment, I thought I might die, that my heart would falter in my chest, seize as the ultimate punishment for what I had done.

I'd broken the two people I loved the most. I'd destroyed my daughter, destroyed Christian, had ruined what I knew Christian and I could have had—what I knew somewhere beneath the fear that we had already built—broke my own heart.

Christian was right.

I didn't hate him.

I hated myself.

Lizzie stared at the untouched plate of food in front of her. She hadn't said a word the entire day but had lain on the floor for uncountable minutes or hours as I'd done the same, unresponsive from the impact.

Sometime during the day, she'd moved to her room and had shut the door and shut me out. I'd given her space because I'd needed it too. I had called her downstairs when I'd realized the sun had set more than an hour ago, and she hadn't eaten all day.

"Lizzie, baby, you need to eat," I said, my voice cracking from the hoarseness of my voice, and pushed her plate closer to her. *Please.*

My request was met with silence, no reaction, as if I hadn't spoken at all.

I turned away to hide the tears that gathered in my eyes. I blinked and they fell. I wiped them with the back of my hand.

My cell phone rang from inside my purse on the kitchen counter.

I closed my eyes, but not before they had instinctively sought out the clock on the wall.

Seven fifteen.

The night was long and lonely, filled with restlessness—too many thoughts and too much hurt. Christian chased me down in my dreams, haunted, hunted, woke me as he shook me and demanded to know *why.*

I'd left Lizzie's door wide open, hoping she'd call out for me, need me. Instead, the same quiet distress as my own had seeped from her room.

She'd tossed and turned, whimpering through her burdened sleep.

In the early morning, I found her awake, sitting

up in bed glassy-eyed and staring at nothing while she rocked the doll Christian had given her in her arms.

I called in to work, barely able to form a coherent sentence as I told Anita I wasn't feeling well.

She laughed and teased that I must have had too much fun on Saturday night to still be suffering the effects on Monday morning.

I mumbled a weak, "Something like that," before I hung up the phone and hung my head, having no idea how to deal with what I felt inside.

My gut twisted in guilt when I dropped my daughter at school, still mute, her face expressionless—numb.

But I left her anyway because I couldn't stand to stay to face what I'd done.

Our beach was nearly deserted on a Monday morning in November. I sat at the edge of the water with my arms wrapped around my knees.

The wind stung my face as it licked at my tears. I clutched my phone as it buzzed, the wind and waves drowning out the sounds erupting from my throat as I wept when his name lit up the screen again and again.

I pulled up in front of Matthew and Natalie's house at five. The door opened a second later and Matthew stepped out.

Pressure seemed to drain from him when he saw

me before it changed and the corners of his eyes creased in worry masked with anger.

He met me halfway down the walkway, demanding to know what was wrong with Lizzie, why she wouldn't speak, and *why* I hadn't returned their calls all afternoon.

I stared at him and whispered, "Christian's gone."

I felt another piece of myself wedge itself free when I admitted it aloud.

Christian is gone—because of me.

I closed my eyes.

No, Christian did this, I thought, unconsciously clenching a fist as I tried to stand up under the guilt eating me from the inside out.

"What?" Matthew stepped forward and put his hands on my shoulders. He shook me lightly, forcing me to look at him. "What are you talking about, Elizabeth?"

"He's gone," I said again, felt myself sway.

Matthew caught my waist, held me up, and helped me inside.

I sat silently on their couch all evening, huddled under a blanket. I couldn't speak, couldn't explain. Matthew left the house in a whirlwind of indignation and returned two hours later, weary.

He took his ball cap from his head and ran his hand over his face and through his short hair as he looked down upon me in both compassion and disappointment.

I turned away, knew where he'd been.

Natalie took his hand and led him down the hall. From their bedroom came hushed voices as they whispered my secrets.

I hid my head under the blanket and covered my ears like a four-year-old child. I didn't want to hear, to know what he'd said, the excuses he'd made, to listen to the part that I knew was my fault.

Still, Lizzie wouldn't speak, wouldn't eat. She sat at the opposite end of the couch, clinging to the neck of her doll, and cried in her sleep.

———

They say cowards run in the face of danger or pain.

I supposed that's what I was, what I'd become, too fearful to love, too fearful to be loved, too afraid to live—so I ran.

The week passed in a blur of darkness worse than I had ever known. I'd tried to go back to work on Tuesday.

Anita had sent me home. She told me come back when I'd resolved whatever it was I was dealing with.

I spent long days at the beach lost in guilt, anger, and remorse, and I spent the even longer nights torturing myself with his messages.

Like a masochist, I pressed his broken voice to

my ear and listened to him again and again.

Sometimes he begged me to call him and said he didn't understand what he had done, but he was sorry for whatever it was. He told me too many times that he loved me.

As time went on, the messages became filled with anger and accusations, demanding to know how I could do this to him, do this to our daughter. He implored with me that if I wouldn't allow him to speak to Lizzie, then to at least have the decency to tell her how much he loved and missed her, that he was thinking of her every second of every day.

Other messages were filled with silence, though the pain of his presence was thick enough to speak for him.

Each day, I stood aside and watched my little girl suffer, the one person I was supposed to love the most, the one I was to protect and care for.

I told myself that I *was* doing this to protect her, and then had to ask myself when I'd become such a selfish liar.

She had withdrawn inside herself. She still wouldn't speak and could barely eat—didn't cry except in her restless sleep.

Her eyes were sunken, their sweet intensity deadened, her vibrant spirit snuffed out and trampled under. Her teacher had called full of concern, saying Lizzie wasn't acting like herself, and that she was *worried*.

I'd given her some pathetic excuse that we'd just had a hard week and promised that Lizzie would be fine.

Friday, I pulled up to Matthew and Natalie's house at five just as I had every day of the week. Sitting in the car at their curb, I tried to compose myself and pull myself together.

I felt cold, chilled to the bone from the day spent with my feet submerged in the cold autumn water of the Pacific Ocean. I closed my eyes and held the steering wheel, willing away the sickness in my stomach, the ache in my heart, the fog clouding my mind, but there was nothing that could chase them away.

Sensing movement, I looked up to see Matthew had emerged from the house with Lizzie in his arms. Her face was buried in his neck, and he held her protectively while he glared at me from over her shoulder.

He'd attempted to talk to me all week, but each time I had shut him down. I told him I didn't want to talk about it—I already *knew* what he would say.

I rose from the car to meet them, but Matthew pushed by me, gently placed Lizzie into the backseat of my car, and buckled her into her booster seat. He kissed her head and told her he loved her.

She said nothing, stared ahead with vacant eyes.

He paused for a moment and then placed his palm on her forehead as if he were checking for a fever. He mumbled something before he stood and shut her door.

For a moment, he stared at me. His expression told me everything I needed to know. He was furious with me—blamed me.

I straightened my shoulders and lifted my chin defensively.

He shook his head at my reaction and started up his sidewalk without a parting word.

Halfway to his door, he paused and shifted, before he turned around with his eyes narrowed.

"Don't you think you've let this go on long enough, Elizabeth?"

I shook my head and scrunched my brow, pretending I didn't know exactly what he was talking about.

Matthew scrubbed his face, agitated as he forced the air from his lungs. It was as if he had to regain control before he could even look at me.

"You have to put an end to this, Elizabeth." He pointed at Lizzie sitting in the back of the car. "She's miserable." He punctuated both words with an angry jab of his finger, though they sounded sad and desperate.

"You don't even know what happened . . . what he *did* to me."

He laughed in an almost incredulous way.

Coming from Matthew's mouth, it still sounded a lot like sympathy.

"What? You two slept together? Did you really not see it coming, Elizabeth? Because the rest of us sure as hell did."

His voice softened and he took a step forward. "I get it, Liz . . . why you're upset. The timing was wrong, and he should've waited. He knows he should have. But you know as well as I do it was going to happen, and it's not right to make Lizzie pay for it."

I flinched and stepped back against my car, both embarrassed that Christian had told him outright and confused that it hadn't angered Matthew.

My throat constricted as I, once again, used my daughter as a way to justify my fear. "He's just going to end up hurting Lizzie."

Matthew snorted in disbelief and took another step forward, lowering his head to look me in the eye. "I think it's about time you questioned just who you're protecting, because it sure as hell isn't that little girl."

"I thought you were on my side." Tears welled in my eyes, hurt because I'd believed Matthew would always stand by me, but more so because I knew he was right.

He glanced at the ground, then back at me, and took the last step to bring us face-to-face. His words were intense as if he wanted to shake me to make me understand.

"I am on your side. All I've ever wanted was what's best for you and Lizzie, and if you'd stop being so goddamned scared for once in your life, you'd see that it's Christian."

With that, I broke.

Tears flowed free, and I fell into Matthew's arms.

He held me up just as he always had. He rocked me and shushed me as he told me, "It'll be okay, sweetheart." He ran his hand through my tangled hair and whispered again, "It'll be okay."

He stepped back, gripping my upper arms with both hands and squeezed me in reassurance as he pled, "It's time to allow yourself some happiness, Elizabeth. You've loved that man since the day I met you, and running from him now isn't going to change it."

I gasped and tried to catch my breath. "I don't know how."

He kissed me on my forehead and squeezed me again. "Yes, you do."

Then he touched my cheek and left me standing there while he walked back into his house.

Reeling, I sank down into my seat. I wiped at my tears with the back of my hand and glanced at Lizzie through the rearview mirror.

For the first time since her father had walked out our door almost a week before, her expression was something other than numb, and tears stained her precious round face.

In silence, I drove us home. As soon as I pulled into the garage, I hurried to Lizzie's door and gathered her into my arms, desperate to erase the distance I'd placed between us over these last few horrible days.

I felt sick, finally accepting what I'd done, that I'd kept my daughter at arm's length when she needed me most. And I'd done it to shield myself from the blame—and from her pain.

I stood in my garage, holding my child. I breathed her in, nuzzled her with my nose, and kissed her for the first time in a week. I ran my hands through her hair, her father's hair, and apologized again and again, "I'm so sorry, baby girl. Mommy is so sorry."

She dug her fingers into my skin and wept.

I swayed us in an attempt to console the inconsolable little girl in my arms.

She hiccupped, climbed up higher as she wrapped her arms around my neck, and spoke for the first time. "I miss my daddy."

I released a heavy breath and drew her closer.

"I know, baby. I miss him too."

seventeen

Leaving Lizzie that way was the hardest thing I'd ever done.

The door slammed behind me harder than I'd intended, and I'd felt the intensity of Lizzie's stare through the window as she watched me walk away from her.

I couldn't stop the sound of her begging me to stay from persisting in my ears. The muscles in my chest coiled and constricted, and I had to force myself to get in my car and drive away.

At the end of the street, I stopped, buried my face in my hands, and tried to make sense of how everything had fallen apart—how in one hazy night, my near-perfect life had been destroyed.

It was a life that I'd known only for a handful of months, but one that had erased every lonely day I'd had before it began.

How could I have been so stupid? Why did I have to push and take when I knew she wasn't ready?

I'd awakened to an empty bed with the taste of stale alcohol on my tongue and a hint of Elizabeth on my skin.

It had all rushed back, how the night had escalated out of control and had erupted in pent up passion, fast hands, and impulsive reactions.

I was hit with the magnitude of the mistake I'd made.

I hadn't even asked but had come undone inside of her, careless and irresponsible. I should have known where Elizabeth's mind would go, what it would remind her of.

I'd stumbled from her bed and downstairs to seek her out. I'd wanted to reassure her of my love, to show her that no matter how irresponsible our actions were from the night before, I was there to stay. I'd felt a fleeting sense of relief when I'd come upon her holding my shirt to her face.

That relief had been shattered when she'd pushed me away, demanded that I go, accused me of taking advantage of her.

She thought I'd *used* her.

"Damn it, Elizabeth," I said aloud in the confines of my car as I rammed my head back against the seat. I contemplated turning around and going back to her house. Instead, I turned out onto the main road.

While I drove back toward my condo, I tried to convince myself that Elizabeth just needed some time to calm down, and just like so many times before, any measure of progress we made was met with a step back.

Somehow, though, I knew that this time it was different.

I'd touched Elizabeth in a place that never should have been touched, had unleashed something deeper than I'd ever acknowledged existed—something I'd created in her many years before.

There was no other explanation for her reaction. This woman was one of the best mothers I knew. She was a woman who loved our daughter just as deeply as I did.

Something had to have snapped inside of Elizabeth for her to put Lizzie through what she had this morning.

I'd wanted to shake her, to grab her by the shoulders and demand that she wake up and see what she was doing to Lizzie—to open her eyes so she could see the fear in Lizzie's.

Instead, I was left struggling to comfort our daughter the best I could, to promise her that it would be okay even when I really wasn't sure that it would.

Never had my condo felt more desolate than when I stepped through the door this Sunday morning.

My head pounded with the remnants of last night's excess, a reminder of my indiscretions. I crawled under the cold sheets of my bed and forced my lids closed, hoping for escape, a few minutes reprieve.

Behind them I only saw my daughter's face and heard the echo of Elizabeth's words.

I hate you. I want you out of our lives.

And I didn't know who to blame.

I'd messed up, I knew. I should have been more cautious.

Elizabeth was fragile.

She should have been treated with care.

But I knew, even still, even after everything that had been said, that she had wanted me just as badly as I had wanted her.

It had been building for weeks.

For months.

Besides that, no matter what Elizabeth and I had done to each other, regardless of any mistakes we may have made and whatever consequences we had to face, there was absolutely no excuse for making Lizzie suffer because of it.

Eluded by sleep, I sat up and called Mom. I just needed someone to talk to, someone to offer me hope in a time when I felt entirely hopeless. I told her everything with as little detail as possible.

She sighed and muttered, "Oh, Christian." Her disappointment was clear. I could see her shaking her head, sad and worried, as she told me, "Give her some time."

Time. Always more time.

I tried, but it was nearly impossible.

The hours ticked by, second by excruciating second. The sun filled the sky and then dove toward the ocean, all the while I sat static on my couch, waiting.

At seven fifteen, I called, and a new fear gripped me when it went to voicemail.

Seven fifteen wasn't about Elizabeth and me. It was about Lizzie.

Would she really try to keep me from my daughter?

I want you out of our lives.

A stunning pain tore through my chest as I listened to the unbearable silence on the other end, and I finally pled low, "Please, Elizabeth, don't do this."

I prayed she would come to her senses.

I'd almost forgotten what insomnia felt like, the exhaustion coupled with a racing mind and thundering heart.

Only now it was so much worse than ever before. In place of nagging guilt and what-ifs was agonizing loss.

Shadows that had once concealed an unknown child were replaced by the face of my precious daughter, by her glowing spirit and the pinked roundness of her cheeks, by the trust in her smile and the faith in her eyes when I promised her I would never leave her again.

Those images blurred and mixed with thoughts of Elizabeth, the woman with the sweet, insecure smile and wary heart that I'd come to know over the last months, the woman I loved even more now than the girl I'd fallen in love with years before, only because I'd grown to be capable of that kind of love.

And as much as I wanted to run from the memory, I couldn't help but think of the way Elizabeth's skin had burned under my hands the night before and how perfect she had felt. Even though it had been wrong on so many levels, it still had been completely right—because *we* were right.

Groaning, I rolled over in bed and gave up on getting any sleep. I stood and stretched my sore muscles when the first light seeped through my bedroom windows.

I went into the office early and left just as soon as I'd come. I couldn't focus on anything but the relentless throbbing in my chest.

From my car, I called Elizabeth again and again. I knew I shouldn't, that I should give her time, but I begged her to call me. I told her I had never intended to make her feel used, that she and Lizzie meant the world to me, hoped if I told her I loved her enough she would finally believe it.

Matthew showed up at my condo that evening. I buzzed him in and wasn't surprised at all to see the rage set deep in the lines of his face when I opened the door. It drained when he saw me, catching him off guard, before he stepped inside and demanded to know what the hell was going on.

I didn't spare him the details I had spared my mother.

"Goddamn it, Christian. What in the hell were you thinking?"

That was the problem—I wasn't thinking.

I sank onto my couch, buried my head in hands, and looked back up at him. "I love her."

He scratched at the back of his neck in discomfort, softened his demeanor. His commitment would always be with Elizabeth, but I also felt somewhere along the way we'd become friends, and he believed what I'd said.

"That was really stupid, Christian . . . you should have known you needed to take it slow with her . . . she's . . . she's . . ."

He turned away and blew out a long breath.

"You really fucked her up, man." He cut his eyes back to me, and I knew he wasn't just talking about what happened this last weekend.

"I know."

"Give her a couple of days . . . she needs some space. She's not doing so great right now."

I nodded, and I really did try.

But it didn't take long for the guilt I felt over Saturday night to transform and for my anger to grow.

I couldn't believe Elizabeth would allow this to happen to our daughter. I sat outside Lizzie's school on Tuesday afternoon. I expected Natalie to be there, that Elizabeth would have asked her to pick Lizzie up rather than me as I had for so many months, but I needed Lizzie to see me, to understand that I did not intend to *leave* her.

Looking at Lizzie was like looking at ghost. My child was missing, and in her place was a shell with an ashen face, pale and wan. She plodded along dragging her feet, her only lifeline the doll she clutched protectively to her.

From the car, I watched her from across the street. Only when she felt me did her numbness subside, a second's recognition and a flicker of life.

Natalie trailed her gaze to mine and smiled sadly as she nudged Lizzie forward and into her car.

For the first time, my calls to Elizabeth were not filled with apologizes but with accusations.

As much as I loved her, I hated her for placing our daughter in the middle of something that was so obviously about the two of us.

My anger and concern only grew as the next days passed.

Thursday, when every call I'd made had been unreturned, I made a call I had never wanted to make.

A few hours after first speaking with him, my attorney, Lloyd Barrett, called back and laid out what he had found.

I sat at the small table in my kitchen with my elbows grinding into the tabletop, palming the back of my head as I listened to him first read through the record of eviction during the first year of Lizzie's life, just months after Elizabeth had moved to San Diego.

I hadn't known about it and was still trying to digest the information when Lloyd continued. His next words were like daggers that went straight through my chest as he read word for word the police report of the 911 call from a little girl screaming for someone to help her mommy, the beaten woman identified as Elizabeth Ayers, the paramedics, and the arrest of Shawn Trokoe.

With a hint of disappointment, he said, "That's all we have, but it should be enough to at least provoke some doubt in her judgment as a parent."

That was all?

I cursed myself, wanted to curse him and ask him how either of these things didn't reflect upon *me* and *my* judgment.

Lloyd pushed on through my silence, knew me we well enough that he sighed through the phone as he offered advice.

"Listen, Christian, I know this is rough on you, but with your history, you're going to have to use this or you won't have a leg to stand on. You had no contact with this child for five years, and that's not going to sit very well with any judge that I know."

I sat with my phone to my ear, saying nothing, having no idea how to proceed.

The last thing I'd wanted to do was drag Elizabeth's name through the mud, shed her in a negative light, and paint her as a bad mother, because I truly didn't believe that she was.

I just wanted mediation, a legal agreement saying I had some right to see my daughter.

"Chances are we'll settle this thing out of court, and we may not even need to use this, but you have to have somewhere to start."

I knew he meant it as encouragement, but he really didn't understand the consequences of what he was asking of me.

Giving the go ahead on this would seal our fate.

Elizabeth would never forgive me, and I'd never be given another chance to prove to her how much

I really loved her. It destroyed me to think of shutting that door forever, but the truth was, she had broken my heart—had broken my daughter's heart.

I didn't *want* to break the promise I'd made to never put her through a custody battle, but I would *never* break the promise I'd made to Lizzie—that as long as I lived, I would never leave her.

Matthew's and Mom's voices played loudly in my mind.

Give her time . . . give her time.

I just didn't know how much time I had left.

How much longer I could tolerate watching my little girl suffer.

I raked a hand through my hair and slumped further onto the table. "Just . . . give me a couple of days, and I'll let you know what I decide."

Thursday night was fraught with nightmares I wasn't entirely sure were dreamed.

I wrestled with the decision that had to be made. I contended with the part of my heart that said I would wait for Elizabeth forever, the part that loved her so much it caused me physical pain.

I pushed that part aside as I rose from my bed Friday morning so fatigued and drained that I could barely stand.

I went into the office in a haze with no idea how

I would survive this, but knowing for Lizzie, I would let Elizabeth go.

By late afternoon, I felt myself ripping apart, coming unglued. The pain and guilt and anger I'd shouldered all week had become too much.

The last bit of hope I'd held onto withered when I entered the hollow space of my condo. I shed my suit for jeans and a t-shirt, wishing for the Friday before when Lizzie and I had shopped and made plans, how she'd buzzed in excitement as I'd helped her dress for her mother's birthday.

It was the same night Elizabeth had agreed to go to New York with me—the night she held me in her arms at the foot of her staircase.

Instead, I sat on the couch with my phone in my hand, building up the nerve to make the call that would sever Elizabeth from my life forever.

I looked out at the boats bobbing in the bay and pictured Lizzie's face and hands pressed to the window, could hear her sweet voice as she counted them, and knew there was no other choice to make.

The light tapping at my door stopped me mid-dial. It was a tiny sound coming from low on the door—a knock I knew could come from no other person than the one I wanted most.

Crossing the room in two steps, I tore the door open.

For a moment, I froze as I came to the

realization that I wasn't hallucinating.

Lizzie and her mother were actually standing in my hallway.

Lizzie stared up at me. She looked sick, her little body weakened with the wear of the week. Her deadened expression was gone, though, her cheeks pink and chapped and stained with tears. The emptiness had vanished from her eyes. In its place was both hope and despair.

I lowered myself slowly, reached for her, and pulled her into my arms.

She wrapped her sweet arms around my neck and stuttered over the tears that began to fall, "Daddy."

The emotions I'd repressed the entire week in my shocked grief now fell free in an overwhelming surge of relief, and I sobbed into her neck as she sobbed into mine.

I chanted her name, hardly able to believe she was really here.

"Lizzie," I said again as I pulled away just enough to see her and to wipe the tears from her cheeks. I held her face between my hands, probably a little too tight. "I missed you so much, baby girl. Do you understand how much I missed you?"

I stressed the words, desperate for her to understand I'd never wanted this separation.

She nodded and cried as she spoke in her soft

angel's voice, "I missed you too, Daddy."

She scraped the nails of her fingers against my skin, dug in, and hung on.

Exhaling heavy and deep, I brought her against my chest, and she locked herself to my neck. I squeezed her with one arm around her waist and a palm on the back of her head, looking up at Elizabeth over Lizzie's shoulder.

I was almost shocked to see she looked like death, as if she'd been to Hell and taken me with her—the fatigue, worry, and hurt marring her face the perfect partner to mine.

Her jaw quivered and shook from where she stood, shifting her weight from one foot to the other. She swallowed and looked away as tears streamed down her face.

Pushing to stand, I pulled my daughter up with me.

Lizzie latched her legs around my waist just as tightly as she wound her arms around my neck. She whimpered, "Don't let me go."

I shushed her, ran my hand through her hair. "You're not going anywhere. I'm not going anywhere."

I didn't intend to let her out of my sight any time soon.

Turning on my heel, I left the door wide open.

Elizabeth could stay or she could go.

At this point, I couldn't bring myself to care.

The only thing that mattered right then was the shaking little girl in my arms.

I carried Lizzie across the room to the adjoining kitchen and rested her on the counter, the distance of the large room and my back to Elizabeth our only privacy.

I didn't go far, just inched back enough so I could drink in her eyes, read her expression, and understand what she felt.

With her hands in mine, I asked her, "Are you okay, sweetheart?"

Were any of us okay?

Would we ever be?

Lizzie shed a new round of tears, trembled under my hands. "You left me, Daddy. I was so scared you might never come back."

I had no idea how we would ever be all right or if I could ever forgive Elizabeth for what she'd done.

I pressed my lips to her head, smoothed away the matted locks of hair sticking to her cheeks. "I'd never let that happen, princess."

I held her there for the longest time, and while she cried a week's worth of tears out against my shirt, I murmured every reassurance I could find.

"I thought of you every second. No matter what, your mother and I will make sure this never happens again. You are the most important thing to us. I promise, sweet girl."

From behind, I heard Elizabeth's movement, the sound of the door close, and the soft shuffle of her steps over the hardwood floor.

When her weight settled on my leather couch, I knew she had chosen to stay.

Honestly, I had no idea what to do with her as she sat silently in my living room.

Had no idea whether I wanted to scream at her or thank her.

Whether I should tell her to leave or her beg her to stay.

Whether to shout out her that I hated her the way she had done me or tell her how desperately I loved her.

When Lizzie finally settled down, I pulled away and smiled at her, touched her nose in a playful way, desperate for some sort of normalcy with my daughter. "Are you hungry, baby girl?"

She nodded and smiled a real smile.

Nothing but tiny gapped teeth and dimples.

"Come here." I helped her from the counter and led her to the refrigerator.

There was little there, mostly delivery leftovers I'd ordered and hadn't been able to stomach over the last week.

In the microwave, we heated up orange chicken and rice from the Chinese place down the street while we shared small smiles and tender embraces that still bore the sadness of our separation.

I fixed her a plate and set it in front of her. Kissing her on top of her head, I whispered, "There you go, sweetheart."

She grinned up at me. "Thanks, Daddy."

We ate together side-by-side with my arm wrapped possessively over her shoulder. We sat with our backs to Elizabeth because I wasn't ready to face her any more than she was ready to face me.

Between bites, Lizzie and I murmured words of love and encouragement to each other and little things I hoped would restore her confidence.

She'd smile up at me while she chewed, though I could still sense her wariness in the way she clung to the hem of my shirt and watched me as if I might suddenly disappear.

I swallowed down the anger it provoked, reminding myself that I had to accept the fact that part of this had been my fault, too.

Lizzie ate her entire plate and then she squealed an excited, "yes," when I asked, "How about we make sundaes?"

She fed me little bites with her spoon and giggled, and for the first time, I smiled, unrestrained and uninhibited as I leaned in to tickle her tummy.

"I love you so much, Lizzie."

She climbed onto my lap, kissed my cheek. "I love you even more, Daddy."

I laughed with the game she wanted to play, knowing I had already won because there were no bounds to how much I loved my child, but teased and poked her belly anyway.

"Nu-uh, I love you more."

"Well, I love you this much, Daddy." She spread her tiny arms wide.

That was right before I wrapped her in mine.

I flipped off the light switch in the small second bedroom.

When I had bought this place, I could never have imagined it would eventually become Lizzie's room. There was a warm glow resonating through my body, a peace that she finally was here.

I'd lain beside her until I was sure she was in a deep sleep, sure that she felt safe and loved and secure. When the fists curled in my shirt finally loosened and her soft breaths spread out in an even rhythm over my face, I'd slowly risen from the tiny twin bed, pulled the covers up to her chin, and kissed her for what seemed the millionth time that day.

I would have been content to watch her sleep all night, but it was time to confront what was waiting for me in the other room.

At the end of the hall, I stopped and looked out to where Elizabeth sat at one end of the couch in the muted light of my living room. Her back was to me, though I saw her face reflected in the darkened panes of the windows—so sad and forever beautiful.

I swallowed, and she looked up and caught me staring at her in the glass.

So damned, incredibly sad.

I wanted to wipe her sadness away, though now I doubted that I ever could.

I moved to the opposite end of the couch, sat on the edge of the cushion, and slouched over my thighs with my hands dangling between my knees.

There was so much to say, but I had no idea where we'd ever begin, and I feared that this may very well be the end.

Minutes passed by while nothing was said, the room quiet except for the sound of our breathing in the sadness and apprehension that hung stagnant in the air.

"I'm sorry, Christian," Elizabeth suddenly said, her raspy voice cutting through the strained silence. She looked down at her fists clenched in her lap and whispered lower, "I'm so, *so* sorry."

From the side, I appraised her curled up in a tight ball on my couch, appearing so small and defeated, and I wished desperately to believe what she said.

"Are you?" I lashed out, my tongue unexpectedly sharp and severe.

She winced with the words, pressed the pads of her fingertips deep into the hollows beneath her eyes, and wiped at the tears that seemed to have fallen endlessly since she'd walked through my door hours before.

"Yes."

I searched her face for honesty and found no deceit, just a broken girl who was hurting just as badly as I was.

"What did I do wrong, Elizabeth? I . . . I thought we were going to make it."

She pinched her eyes shut, her beautiful face wasted and worn, my offense aged and old. "You *left* me."

I leaned against the back of the couch and dragged both hands through my hair as I blew the air from my lungs toward the ceiling.

Gazing back at her, I gave my surrender through a whispered apology.

"I know I did, Elizabeth, but I *can't* take it back. God knows, I wish I could, but I *abandoned* you, and there's nothing I can ever do to change that now."

As painful as it was, I ignored the part of me that wanted nothing more than to reach out and comfort her. To take away her *sadness*.

The part that loved her so damned much the only thing I wanted to do was beg her to give us a chance.

It was time to give up that piece of my heart and accept that I'd done too much damage, it would never be erased, and I'd never be forgiven.

"I can't do this anymore, Elizabeth. You run every time we get close. I . . . can we just . . ."

I blinked a bunch of times.

"Can we just forget about what happened last weekend? Go back to being friends for the sake of Lizzie? Because I *won't* live without her, and I refuse to allow what happened this last week to ever happen again."

What appeared as grief rocked her body, and she wheezed over broken, strangled words. "Is that really what you want?"

"God, Elizabeth. Of course not."

I looked at her and touched my chest in sincerity. "I'm *in love* with you. Do you still refuse to believe that?"

I shook my head, pushed forward through the anguish of my concession, the devastation that blazed as I let go of the only woman I had ever loved—the only woman I *would* ever love. "But Lizzie's happiness comes first. Before you. Before me."

For a few painful moments, we sat in silence.

Elizabeth's mouth twisted in shame before she finally swallowed, licked her lips, and labored through halting words. "I love you, Christian. So much. And . . . and I don't want to give that up. I don't want to give *us* up."

Her eyes were closed eyes as if shielding herself from my reaction or maybe from her own admission.

My heart stuttered with her confession, both heartbroken and overjoyed.

For so long, I'd wanted to hear those words fall from her lips.

I'd just had no idea that in those words there would be so much sadness, that they would be tainted by years of her sorrow, and that my own thrill in finally hearing her say them aloud would be tarnished by the immense amount of resentment over what she had done.

She opened her eyes, still heavy with tears, and she angled toward me.

Her expression was altogether intense and scared, but for the first time, was completely laid bare.

There was nothing left for either of us to hide.

Her mouth and hands shook as she continued, "What happened on my birthday? I wanted it. I wanted you. But when I woke up next to you, I panicked. Everything I'd gone through after you left me the first time came rushing back. The way it happened . . . the fact that we'd been drinking. It made me feel cheap—dirty, and all I could think was that you'd leave me again. Even when I *knew* that morning you weren't lying when you said you loved me."

Her voice cracked, and she paused, pain etched on her face before she forced herself to continue.

"I *knew* I was wrong the entire week, Christian. *The whole week.* I watched our little girl fade away while I clung to my fears and insecurities and tried to convince myself I was doing it for her. What I put Lizzie through this week . . ."

Elizabeth closed her eyes as if she were protecting herself from the memory.

"I pushed my own child away when she needed me most, and I don't know if I'll ever be able to forgive myself for it, but I can promise that it will never happen again. She's my life, and I'll never again let my issues get in the way of my responsibility to her. My love for her."

Her brow pinched. "But I'm so tired of running, Christian. So tired of running from the only man I've ever wanted. The only man I've ever loved. If you can somehow forgive me . . ."

She wet her rose-colored lips. "I want to find a way to forgive you. I want to let you love me and not be afraid when you do."

Maybe now I really understood why Elizabeth had run from me all of these months.

Why she would never allow herself to believe.

A love as intense as the one we shared, one that had not dimmed through years of betrayal but had only grown, was terrifying. We had the power to destroy, to devastate and ruin, to lay the other to waste.

But I wasn't running.

I reached for her hand and pulled her to my chest. With the connection, the silent tears she'd cried all evening erupted.

She clung to me just as tightly as Lizzie had and wept just as hard. She whispered muddled pleas into my shirt while I ran my hands through her hair. "Don't leave me, Christian . . . please don't ever leave me."

I shushed her, kissed her on top of her head. "I'm not going anywhere, Elizabeth."

I laid us down on the couch on our sides, held her close, and let her cry.

Her body quaked as she sucked in shuddering breaths and buried her face in my chest.

I cradled the girl I had broken, ran my hand up and down her back and through her hair.

She curled up closer, molded herself to me, and I held her tighter. On the cusp of sleep, she whispered, "Don't ever let me go."

I tugged the throw from the back of the couch, draped it over our bodies, and drew her closer still. "Never."

I'd known when I'd woken up the next morning with Elizabeth still wrapped in my arms that things were different.

She didn't push me away when I hugged her and murmured good morning against her forehead.

Instead, she had pressed her lips to my chest and looked up at me with a small, timid smile.

It was then I knew we were going to make it.

That was the last night I'd slept at my condo.

I'd spent the rest sleeping on Elizabeth's couch.

Over the last five weeks, Elizabeth and I had spent every second we could together.

I met her every day for lunch and we actually *talked*.

There was no skirting or softening, just honesty—even when it hurt.

In the beginning, there were constant tears and a lot of anger. But she finally opened up and told me how devastated she had been when I'd abandoned her, everything she'd gone through, and how badly she had needed me.

While it crushed me to hear it, I welcomed it because I knew we could never truly move on until we actually faced our past.

As the weeks went on, those tears began to dry as a firm future came into view—our future.

We spent our evenings together as a family, mom and dad and daughter.

As much as we laughed and played, we devoted a lot of time talking with Lizzie, giving her reassurances and straight answers for what we had done.

For the ordeal we had put her through.

Even then, we had started taking her to a counselor once a week to help us weed out the seed of abandonment that had been planted, just as Elizabeth and I had started to see a counselor as a couple.

We were doing everything we could to make this work.

The nights—the nights were perfect and entirely tortuous. We spent hours on Elizabeth's couch making out like teenagers.

Tangled tongues and wandering hands.

When she'd finally groan and roll off me, I'd chase her upstairs and kiss her senseless against the wall outside her bedroom door.

Weak-kneed, she'd career into her bedroom, giggling and mumbling under her breath, something about me being *dangerous*.

When I'd curl up each night on her worn couch with my senses overwhelmed by Elizabeth, my body throbbing and craving more, I couldn't imagine feeling more satisfied.

Now, movement from upstairs caught my attention, and I looked up.

"Okay, we're out of here." Natalie held Lizzie's hand as they descended the stairs, Matthew following close behind.

Lizzie had her backpack on her shoulders, her

doll tucked under her arm, and the sweetest grin on her face.

I went to her, knelt in front of her, and touched her cheek. "Mommy and Daddy will be at Aunt Natalie's and Uncle Matthew's first thing in the morning to pick you up, okay?"

She nodded and wrapped her arms around my neck. "I know, Daddy. I can't wait!"

I smiled down at her. "I can't wait, either. I love you, princess" I brushed my lips across her forehead and stood.

Natalie popped up on her tiptoes, wrapped her arms around my neck, and whispered against my ear, "I'm so happy for you guys. I love you all, you know?"

She stepped back, looked up at me as if to see if I understood.

I squeezed her hand. "I love you, too, Nat."

Lizzie grinned and swayed from where she waited at our sides.

Matthew shook my hand, his words a touch pensive. "Take care of my girl."

I nodded.

Always.

Matthew drew Lizzie into his arms and ushered Natalie outside.

I watched them until the door closed behind them.

When I *felt* her, I looked up.

She stood at the top of the stairs wearing a fitted blue button-up dress that tied around the waist, flowed over her hips, and flared at her knees. Her hair was curled in soft waves and her face seemed to glow.

She looked both modest and sexy, and she absolutely took my breath away.

I waited at the bottom of the staircase and smiled softly as I watched her every step as she came to meet me downstairs.

She stopped a foot away.

I swallowed deeply and reached for her hand. "You look amazing, Elizabeth."

She blushed. "Thank you."

Her attention wandered down over my maroon button up, black slacks, and back up to my face. "You look amazing, too."

I helped her into her coat and led her out to my car. I kissed her softly before I opened her door and settled her into the front seat.

The ride was quiet, filled with anticipation and thrumming hearts. I held her hand the entire way, kept stealing glances at the most beautiful woman I had ever seen.

I parked and went around and helped her out, popped the trunk to grab the blanket and the picnic basket Lizzie and Natalie had helped me prepare earlier in the day.

With clasped hands, we made our way up the

pathway and over the embankment.

Elizabeth stopped to pull her heels from her feet when we hit the sand. Maybe it had been silly for us to dress for a nighttime trip to the beach, but we'd dressed for a celebration.

Tonight, we would celebrate *us*.

The moon was high and lit up the beach, the waves gentle in their swell and roll, a peaceful calm. The cool San Diego air of December chilled our skin as it rushed over the water and against our faces, and Elizabeth hugged her coat to her body.

She shivered and curled up closer to my side as she walked barefoot over the cool sand.

When we reached the spot where she'd first shared this beach with me, I spread out the blanket and pulled her down beside me.

We laughed as we fought against the wind.

It whipped around us while we shared our meal of fruit and cheese and drank champagne in small plastic cups over timid smiles of expectation.

Neither of us could stop grinning by the time we'd finished.

"Come here." I extended my hand and helped her settle between my legs so she could lean against my chest. I hugged her close as we looked out over the darkened water that rippled and gleamed in the moonlight.

I whispered against the back her head, "I love you so much, Elizabeth."

She nodded against my chest and clasped her hands over mine.

I turned her and pulled her up to her knees before I shifted to bow in front of her on one of mine.

We both knew why we were here, and I already knew what her answer would be.

But that didn't keep my hands from trembling as I fumbled through my coat pocket and drew out the small black box.

I lifted the lid, held out my modest offering, and with it, forever promised my heart.

"Be my wife."

Tears flowed down Elizabeth's face, but this time they were different—filled with joy and hope and a love no longer kept hidden and restrained.

She nodded and whimpered a little as I took the simple platinum solitaire from its box and slid it onto her finger and to its rightful place—six years late and bittersweet—but sweet nonetheless.

We both stared at her hand for a few moments, absorbing the moment, realizing the commitment we had just made.

My smile was one of devoted elation as I looked back up at her.

Hers was soggy and irresistible.

Tugging her to me, I wrapped my arms around her back and kissed her. I held her face in my hands and whispered, "I love you."

She didn't hesitate. "I love you, Christian."

We gathered our things, anxious for home.

As always, the neighborhood was quiet as we pulled onto her street.

Houses sparkled with Christmas lights. Plastic Santa Clauses and reindeer stood glowing in front yards and on roofs, and fake snow that would never fall in San Diego decorated windows.

Tomorrow, Lizzie would see real snow for the first time.

I parked in the driveway and rushed around to help Elizabeth from the car.

We walked hand-in-hand to her door and locked it behind us. It took only a split second for desire to grab hold of us, to swallow us in silence, to leave us staring at each other with quickened pulses and pounding hearts.

Elizabeth said nothing but tugged on my hand and led me upstairs and to her room.

I stopped at the threshold, turned her to look at me, and held her face in my hands. "Are you sure, Elizabeth?"

There would be no more assumptions, and I would take no more of what she wasn't ready to give.

She placed her hand on my chest, ran it up to the back of my neck and into my hair, and pulled me down to her mouth.

Her kiss was slow and maddening, and she

whispered softly against my lips, "I'm yours."

My hands found her hips, and I kissed her gently as I edged her back into the muted light of her room.

Our movements were slow, tender, and adoring.

Standing in the middle of the room, we slowly undressed each other.

Carefully, I picked her up and cradled her in my arms, laid her down on her bed.

Our bed.

My condo had been put on the market a couple of weeks before, and we'd live here until Elizabeth's house sold.

We both wanted something similar, a comfortable home where Lizzie could run and play, but closer to our beach and a couple of rooms larger so we could fill them with a brother or sister or two.

My spirit soared as I thought of an addition to this family, as I thought of watching Elizabeth's belly grow with another child.

Of standing by her side and being there when it was brought into this world.

I could only imagine the doting big sister Lizzie would be, her amazement at a new life, the wonder that would fill her eyes.

That would have to wait, though.

Elizabeth and I would marry this summer, and we needed to take time for the three of us to learn how to be the family we were always supposed to be before we added to it.

I stared down at where I'd laid Elizabeth on our bed, the curves of her naked body fully exposed and entrusted to me.

Her body was thinner than what I had known before, the cut of her legs and shoulders defined, though her stomach was no longer perfectly flat.

Silvered lines were barely visible on her pelvis where Lizzie had permanently left her mark.

Love and devotion pumped through my veins as she so freely bared herself to me.

"You are so beautiful, Elizabeth."

She gazed up at me, her eyes damp and steeped in emotion. She extended her hand and beckoned me to her.

I climbed onto the bed, hovered over her with my hands cradling each side of her head, and dipped down to kiss her deeply.

Her hands were firm and like fire as they moved up my back and down over my sides.

I pulled away to whisper her name, "Elizabeth." I moved to kiss her over her heart and murmured, "Thank you."

Once again, I found her mouth and lowered myself down to her. I wrapped her up in my arms, chest to chest, skin to skin, rested on my elbows so I could hold her precious face between my hands.

I pushed her hair away from her face and let it

billow out over her pillow, stunned again by her beauty.

My eyes bore into hers, seeking understanding, praying that she fully and finally believed. "I love you so much, Elizabeth."

She brought a trembling hand up to my face, ran her fingertips over my lips, her ring shimmering prominent and proud, and whispered, "I know."

Her eyes glistened as I smiled softly down at her and pressed a closed-mouthed kiss against the sweetness of her lips, brought her palm to my face, and kissed her there.

Her heart pounded against my chest as I shifted and settled between her legs. Her breaths came short and rapid, the pulse in her neck drumming under my hands.

Swallowing, I gripped her shoulders and slowly slid into her body—made us one.

Her mouth dropped open in a soundless gasp, her fingers burrowed in the skin of my back.

For a few moments, we remained still, locked to each other.

Body and soul.

Our eyes intense and filled with this desire that had never escaped us, brimming with a love that should have died in its affliction, but had only seemed to grow.

Elizabeth raked her fingers up my back and to my shoulders, setting me aflame and in motion.

I moved in her slow and hard as she rose to meet me with shallow moans and murmurs of love, our bodies speaking of unshakable commitment and eternal faithfulness, a reverent consummation.

Never would I take what I'd been given for granted. I'd never look at her through indifferent eyes, listen to her fears and worries with distant ears, or touch her with impassive hands.

Elizabeth was a gift and Lizzie was my treasure.

I would adore my family until the day I died.

No longer would I live in regret, striving to make up for what I'd done.

I'd live for the day, each one set out and purposed to be the best father and husband I could be.

And no matter what life brought our way, I would never walk away.

The plane sat at the end of the runway, rumbled and whined as its engines wound and roared.

Lizzie sat beside me, her body vibrating with both excitement and anxiety of the unknown. Her eyes were consuming as she looked up at me with trust through her fear.

I extended my hand, palm up, and she placed her tiny hand in mine, one that now bore a delicate gold ring.

While Elizabeth and I had made promises to each other last night, this morning we had made promises to our daughter.

As the plane barreled down the runway, I clasped my hand around Lizzie's and grinned down at her while she smiled anxiously up at me.

Elizabeth rested her head on my shoulder, and her left hand on my chest, watching the vibrant diamond as it danced.

She smiled over at Lizzie and then up at me.

I brushed my lips across her forehead and couldn't contain the smile on my face.

We sped, lifted and dipped, and ascended toward the sky. Lizzie giggled with the sensation, looked back over at us with wide eyes, and said, "Here we go!"

I squeezed my daughter's hand.

Here we go.

Little did I know what was coming our way . . .

the end

Read the conclusion of Christian and Elizabeth's
epic love story in

IF FOREVER *Comes*

Want a bonus scene of Elizabeth, Christian, and
Lizzie in New York City?
Read it here, completely FREE
http://smarturl.it/ttrbonusscene

I invite you to sign up for mobile updates to receive short, but sweet updates on all my latest releases.
Text "aljackson" to 33222
(US Only)
or
Sign up for my newsletter
http://smarturl.it./NewsFromALJackson

Watch for my upcoming series, *Confessions of the Heart*, coming Fall 2018!

Want to know when it's live?
Sign up here: http://smarturl.it/liveonamzn

More From A.L. Jackson

ABOUT THE AUTHOR

A.L. Jackson is the New York Times & USA Today Bestselling author of contemporary romance. She writes emotional, sexy, heart-filled stories about boys who usually like to be a little bit bad.

Her bestselling series include THE REGRET SERIES, CLOSER TO YOU, BLEEDING STARS, as well as the newest FIGHT FOR ME novels.

Watch for her new series, CONFESSIONS OF THE HEART, coming Fall 2018

If she's not writing, you can find her hanging out by the pool with her family, sipping cocktails with her friends, or of course with her nose buried in a book.

Be sure not to miss new releases and sales from A.L. Jackson - Sign up to receive her newsletter http://smarturl.it/NewsFromALJackson or text "aljackson" to 33222 to receive short but sweet updates on all the important news.

Connect with A.L. Jackson online:

Page **http://smarturl.it/ALJacksonPage**
Newsletter **http://smarturl.it/NewsFromALJackson**
Angels **http://smarturl.it/AmysAngelsRock**
Amazon **http://smarturl.it/ALJacksonAmzn**
Book Bub **http://smarturl.it/ALJacksonBookbub**
Text "aljackson" to 33222 to receive short but sweet updates on all the important news.